The Regan McHenry Real Estate Mysteries

The Death Contingency
Backyard Bones
Buying Murder
The Widow's Walk League
The Murder House

Other books by Nancy Lynn Jarvis

Mags and the AARP Gang

Cozy Food: 128 Cozy Mystery Writers Share Their Favorite Recipes

Backyard Bones

A Regan McHenry Real Estate Mystery

Nancy Lynn Jarvis

Good Read Mysteries
A Subsidiary of Good Read Publishers

**Good Read
Mysteries**

Good Read Mysteries © is a registered trademark of Good Read Publishers
301 Azalea Lane, Santa Cruz, California, 95060

Copyright © 2009 by Nancy Kille

Library of Congress Control Number: 2008935354

ISBN: 978-0-9821135-2-3

www.GoodReadMysteries.com

Books are available at special quantity discounts through the website.

To my grandmother, Ruth Perry McHenry, a master storyteller who, when I was still at an impressionable young age, invited me to curl up in her wicker rocking chair and read murder mysteries.

And to all the clients who made my career so interesting and rewarding, and who gave me endless ideas for stories and adventures.

Acknowledgements

A proper acknowledgement always starts with my husband Craig, without whom I couldn't do this. He reads, edits, finds flaws in reasoning, asks why, figures out my computer and the website — even tastes cookies — to make the books work.

A special thanks goes to Morgan Rankin for her copy-editing.

And thanks, too, to John Grason for his suggestions, and to Santa Cruz writers Judy Feinman and Gayle Ortiz, two of the Mysty W. Moonfree authors, and Ivan Comelli who offered helpful tips and ideas.

Backyard Bones

Nancy Lynn Jarvis

Of course, the fictitious disclaimer is true. Murderers, motives, and characters are made up. But I've met most of the people who inspired these characters, and I bet you have too, if you happen to be a Realtor. Oh — one detail isn't made up at all. The story about backing up is one hundred percent true. I couldn't make up something like that.

Regan McHenry

1

Regan's smile was too big for the occasion, but she couldn't help it. As she parked in front of the Whitlaws' tired looking house, she couldn't suppress her little-kid-about-to-open-a-birthday-present grin. Officially she was stopping by to see if her clients needed anything and to bring them a housewarming gift. Unofficially, move-in visits were a favorite part of her job, a part that always energized her and made her smile.

She noted again how much the Whitlaws' house would benefit from a little paint and some new landscaping — TLC in realtor jargon, but its downtrodden state hadn't bothered her clients when she showed them the house. They liked it right away, even though it needed work. The location was good, the house was sound, the price was right, and they thought of home improvement as a hobby.

The front door was open wide to the late warmth of an unusually long Indian summer. Regan decided not to ring the doorbell, which she remembered didn't work anyway, or rap on the door. "Knock, knock," she sang out as she poked her head through the open doorway. "Joan? Rick? Anybody home?"

Joan answered from the kitchen, where she was taking carefully packed glasses out of a box, unwrapping them, and putting them into a nearby cupboard. She responded with a returned shout. "Regan, is that you? Come on in. I'm trying to get the basics organized."

Regan walked into the house gingerly, working her way through stacked boxes and moving toward the sound of Joan's voice. The kitchen was in a similar state of heaped-box disorder, except some of the boxes were open and partly emptied. She surveyed the disarray.

"I don't envy you the next few days," Regan said as she picked her way through the clutter to reach Joan. "But I bet you've already got plans."

"Huge plans, wonderful ideas ... I just have to get through this part first. As our realtor, aren't you supposed to help me with this?" Joan quipped.

"Oh, no-no-no." Regan held her hands up defensively in front of her and shook her head. "I don't do packing, unpacking, or dump runs. I'm absolutely certain those services aren't part of my job description," she laughed. "But I hope this will help a bit." She handed the new homeowner a gift certificate for Café Sparrow.

"Regan, they use tablecloths at Café Sparrow, don't they? A civilized meal ... yum." Joan closed her eyes and pressed the paper against her chest. "Sanity. The only problem is I'm going to need a shower and a complete makeover before they'll let me in the door. Rick is off getting Togo's takeout sandwiches for tonight, but you are a dear for this. Thank you. I'll dream of sitting at a table that isn't covered with boxes as I fall asleep tonight. Maybe tomorrow," she sighed dramatically.

The back kitchen door crashed open as the two little Whitlaw boys rushed in. "It's my turn to be the pegantolaguest. Give me the shovel," Raymond yelped. "You have to be my assistant now." The red-faced six-year-old flew at his brother who, being close to three years older and a few inches taller, managed to hold the shovel over his head and keep it just out of his little brother's reach as he danced through the kitchen. The young would-be paleontologist wailed, "Mommy, make him give me the shovel! Tell him it's my turn."

"Richard, give your brother the shovel." She hastily added, "Gently."

Regan smiled broadly. Her sons were way beyond this stage, both were practically men, but she remembered the rough-housing of little boys, and her sons had almost the same age difference between them as the Whitlaw brothers.

"He's so lame. He doesn't even know how to say paleontologist. I don't think he should ever be the lead paleontologist," Richard complained.

"Richard," Joan said forcefully.

"OK, Mr. pegantolaguest," Richard taunted as he handed his brother the shovel, handle first and gently, as his mother had instructed. Possession of the shovel successfully exchanged, the two brothers dashed out the back kitchen door to the yard as quickly as they had come in.

"And don't run with the shovel," Joan called after them.

"What was that about?" Regan chuckled.

"Do you remember when Mrs. Fargers told us about the

dog?" Joan asked.

It came back to Regan. About a week before the sale was recorded, they had done a walkthrough with the sellers, the Fargers. Everything was in perfect order and the walkthrough quickly became an introduction to the workings of the house. Mr. Fargers and Joan's husband, Rick, headed off to discuss the location of shut-off valves and how to run the sprinklers. Mrs. Fargers offered to show Joan the garden. Since the garden was more interesting to Regan than mechanical things, she joined that tour.

Mrs. Fargers was referring to a hand-drawn map, pointing out each of the fruit trees, most of which were leafless in late October, and explaining where the dormant spring bulbs were in the backyard flower beds, when she suddenly became very flustered.

"Oh, dear," she said. "I believe we've overlooked a disclosure. I hope it's not going to disrupt the sale. Honestly, we weren't trying to hide anything. We just forgot until now. We buried a dog in the backyard just under the peach tree. Roscoe was a large dog, a Great Dane. I wouldn't want the children to accidentally come across him and be frightened."

The Whitlaw boys had been assigned to accompany their mother on the garden part of the tour so they wouldn't interrupt the consequential discussion between their father and Mr. Fargers. The boys hadn't been paying attention to the flora, but they suddenly became very interested when a buried dog was mentioned.

"Where is he?" the oldest boy, Richard, asked.

"Well, let's see now ..." Mrs. Fargers hesitated for a moment. "I believe he should be just about here." She drew an imaginary line above the ground on the left side of a leafless tree. "It's been several years — twelve, fifteen, oh my, more than that. But yes, if this is the peach tree, that seems about right."

The younger boy, Raymond, jumped up and down and eagerly asked, "Can we see him?"

"As you can tell, a buried dog isn't a cause of distress for our family," Joan laughed to Regan and Mrs. Fargers. Then she quietly promised the boys they would talk about the dog later and whispered to Regan, "but not in front of Mrs. Fargers, in case she'd be upset at the idea of her pet being disinterred."

A smile crossed Regan's face as she recalled that whispered end of the conversation with Mrs. Fargers. "Oh yes, the dog buried in the backyard," Regan said.

"I thought the boys might have forgotten about the dog by now, but we hadn't been here twenty minutes," Joan said, "when they demanded a shovel so they could begin digging for that animal. We have more than one shovel but, with all the moving confusion, we've only been able to find one, so they are supposed to take turns being the lead paleontologist and the assistant. We've resorted to a timer, can you believe it, and we have a serious and ever growing hole in the backyard," she smiled and shook her head.

Wild shouts returned to the kitchen. "We found him, we found him," shrieked Raymond as he raced through.

"I told you he was lame. We didn't find the dog; he just thinks we did," Richard brought the women up to date with all the older-brother disparagement he could manage.

Both boys returned to the yard with an earsplitting slap of

5

the back door.

"Regan, my manners are terrible. Would you like some coffee?" Joan offered. "I've succeeded in finding the coffee pot and put our dishes and cups away in the cupboard. We may have to stir in sugar and milk with wooden spoons though — the silverware has eluded me thus far."

"Thanks, but I think I'll get out of your way and let you get back to work."

"I was afraid you were going to say something like that." Joan dropped her head to her chest. "Work," she said with a pretended sob. She took another glass out of its box and began unwrapping it. "As a realtor, I'm sure you've seen homes in this condition many times before. Please promise me I'll get through all this and everything will find a place."

"I can definitely promise you that, and with your sense of organization, I bet it won't take long, either."

The back door opened again with what was becoming routine suddenness. There stood a beaming Raymond, his little hands holding a skull up for his mother's approval. "See Mommy, we found him," he screeched. "He has teeth and everything."

"I told you he was lame," Richard announced. "That's not a dog skull. It doesn't look anything like a dog skull. Where are the big pointy teeth, little brother?"

Joan dropped the glass she was holding. Its loud shattering on the tile floor barely registered with her or with Regan. The skull Raymond so proudly held up for his mother wasn't a dog skull. It was human.

2

Regan took a deep breath before she spoke, hoping to keep her voice calm. "Raymond, why don't you show your mother where the skull came from?"

Joan recovered her equilibrium, or at least a semblance of it, and agreed with Regan. "Yes, Raymond. I'd like to see where you dug up the dog skull. Could we put it back exactly like you found it?"

"No! I want to dig up the rest of him," Raymond shrilled.

"We can do that in a bit, sweetie. I just want to see how your dog looked when you found him."

"Mom," Richard whined. "You're humoring him again. You and dad always do that. Tell him it's not a dog skull."

Raymond's hands were occupied holding the skull or he might have taken a swing at his older brother. He settled for sticking out his tongue and shaking his head at him as his mother maneuvered him back out the kitchen door.

Richard started to follow, intent on continuing the dispute. Regan did her best to end the boys' arguing by trying to entice the elder brother from his plan.

"Richard, why don't you stay with me for a minute? We

both know the skull doesn't look like it's from a dog. I think the skull is a man's, don't you?"

Richard heaved a disgusted sigh at the obvious. "Duh," he said.

"Finding a human skull is a very big deal. I need to call a friend of mine and let him know about your discovery. He's a policeman. He'll probably have questions I won't know the answers to, but I bet you will. Can you stay here and help me answer them, you know, to help the police?"

Richard nodded slowly at first, then vigorously, as a smile spread across his face.

"Great," she said. "Thank you."

Regan pulled her cell phone out of her purse and hit speed dial to her friend Dave. The number was for his private cell phone. She expected to get his answering machine, but knew it would give his work number at the end of his outgoing message. She was surprised when, rather than Dave's easygoing recorded greeting, she heard a very live, clipped, and business-like, "Dave Everett."

"Dave, I'm glad you're there. It's Regan."

"Hmm, calling during business hours. And what sort of mess have you gotten yourself into this time?" he teased.

"It's not a mess," she explained. "It's just something I think you should know about. I'm at a client's new house in La Selva Beach. Her sons were digging in the backyard trying to find a buried dog skeleton and have unearthed a skull that looks human to me — to us," Regan corrected for Richard's benefit.

"Human?" Dave stopped teasing immediately. "How certain are you it's human?"

8

"About ninety-nine point nine percent certain," Regan replied.

"Have you called 9-1-1 yet?"

"No, just you. It's a skull, as in been-in-the-ground for a long time, not a body. For me there's a big difference."

Now that he'd established no one was in imminent danger, Dave returned to the easygoing verbal jousting that defined their relationship: her friend again, rather than the completely professional cop he'd become with the mention of a skull.

"Well, Regan, I'm impressed. Cool head and all that — at least this time. You can get so overwrought," he added, neatly slipping in a reference to a time not long ago when Regan had been anything but cool in trying to defend a realtor friend from police suspicions.

"La Selva, you said? That's county jurisdiction. What's the address? I'm going to get the Coroner over there ASAP. I'll give the Sheriff a heads up, too."

Richard was getting restive.

"Richard, I forget your address here," she fabricated. "Do you remember it?"

"No," he shook his head.

"Could you go out to your mail box and let me know what the numbers are? It's very important. The police need to know."

The boy took off at a run, happy to have an important job to do.

"It's 3244 Alta Mar Vista," Regan said as soon a Richard was out of earshot.

"3244 Alta Mar Vista. Got it. Stay put. I'm coming by, too. This'll probably make the news; I better know what I'm talking about when KSBW and KION point their cameras at me and start asking questions. Oh, and Regan, don't disturb anything. Even if the burial looks old, you could still be at a murder scene," he said before he hung up.

"3244," Richard burst in shouting the number. Regan pretended to relay the numbers to Dave before putting her phone back in her purse.

Joan returned holding an empty-handed Raymond by the elbow. "After what you've been touching, I want you to wash your hands. You too, Richard. Come on." She lined the boys up at the kitchen sink and encouraged them to lather with dishwashing soap.

"We called the cops, Mom," Richard offered excitedly.

"I called a friend," Regan clarified. "He's on his way and is arranging for the Sheriff and the Coroner to come by as well."

"Cool," Richard drew out the word with awe.

"You didn't call 9-1-1?" Joan queried.

"Dave's a cop. Well, kind of a semi-retired cop assigned to desk duty at this point, who's responsible for police public relations in Santa Cruz County. He's connected. He'll know what needs to happen next." Regan didn't add that she and Dave had a long, solid friendship or that he knew firsthand about her recent experience with discovering a body. That was a different story — one she didn't feel like talking about right now — one she was still trying to forget.

Dave arrived moments after Rick Whitlaw returned with Togo's sandwiches but well before the first deputy sheriff appeared. Dave was good with kids. He managed to keep the boys happily out of the backyard by telling them gory details of how he had been wounded in a real shoot-out, and about how he had an artificial eye as a result. He measured his success with the boys by how many "ooh," "icky," and "oh how gross" comments he elicited.

The homes on Alta Mar Vista were set on large lots with scattered mature trees. As a result, each of the houses had a great deal of privacy. The street was a long quiet roadway with virtually no one travelling on it other than local residents. There weren't any obvious signs of neighbors being home or looking out windows. Yet, people began materializing in front of the house as soon as the first sheriff's vehicle pulled up and its driver got out and began to unroll yellow crime scene tape across the front of the house.

The number of onlookers increased dramatically after the white van with the *Santa Cruz County Coroner* logo arrived and, with its backup beepers sounding, carefully maneuvered into the Whitlaws' driveway.

After a time with the backyard bones, the Coroner came back into the kitchen and announced he was certain the skull was human and fairly certain the burial wasn't recent. He lowered his voice and told Dave and the deputy sheriff, "You can never be absolutely sure just by looking, though."

Regan had learned how to seem inattentive during private conversations between husband and wife clients to give them space to discuss private matters. She appreciated that conversations that weren't meant to include her were private, and she would never repeat what she heard, but she often learned useful information by listening, so she made it a point to stay within earshot of Dave and the Coroner as they talked.

"I've seen skeletons get in that condition after just a few

weeks, but that's usually above ground and because of insect and rodent action. And this guy's disarticulated somewhat by tree roots. This looks like an old burial rather than a crime scene. If I had to venture a guess, I'd say he's been in the ground more than a couple hundred years, so I'm going to give our anthro resource a call."

The Coroner contacted Dr. Smithers, an anthropologist at the University of California, Santa Cruz, UCSC to locals, and asked him to come by for a confirming opinion. Soon the group of official vehicles parked out front grew by another white van.

Regan absentmindedly watched through the kitchen window as a tall slim man with curly dark hair got out of the driver's seat of a Volkswagen bus that had seen better days. He walked around to the passenger side, reached in, and pulled out a large open box that he supported with both of his forearms. He pushed the door closed with his hip. It didn't quite latch. Although she couldn't make out what he said, she guessed he shouted an expletive before he bent down awkwardly, put the box on the ground, and tried again.

Once he succeeded in getting the door closed, he scooped up the box, hoisted it to his shoulder, negotiated a route past Rick's Prius and Dave's SUV and rambled hurriedly to the Whitlaws' still open front door, keen happiness written on his face.

"You got something for me?" he greeted the Coroner and the rest of the assembled group with an engaging smile.

The Coroner nodded. "Out back. Looks like it's in your department, not mine," he said.

"Bones out through there?" Dr. Smithers motioned toward

the back kitchen door. Joan nodded and pulled Raymond a little closer. "I can't wait to have a look," he grinned broadly.

"I'll help you," Richard offered.

Rick restrained him with a look. "Leave the man alone to do his job, Richard."

Dave held the door open for the anthropologist, who disappeared with his kit as quickly as he had entered.

"I assume that was Professor Smithers," Rick said. "I can only assume, since no one introduced us. I'm glad someone besides our children finds this situation so enthralling." His sarcasm hung in the room in an almost palpable cloud.

Dr. Smithers returned to the kitchen within fifteen minutes and plunked his box on a clear space of kitchen counter. Its contents clacked and rattled softly.

"Yep, looks aboriginal. Your crew has the whole skeleton exposed. Looks male because of the pelvis. He has an extreme degree of dental wear, and squatting facets on the talus." Professor Smithers' last comment left blank expressions on all the assembled faces except the Coroner's. "It's a bone in the foot," Professor Smithers simplified. "He squatted rather than sitting in a chair like modern people do. You'd expect both those indicators in an indigenous burial. I'd guess Ohlone.

"We're pretty close to the coast here. There was a thriving native population in this whole region," he waved expansively, "before the Spanish came along with their enlightened ways and decimated the local inhabitants with imported diseases and forced labor." Professor Smithers addressed everyone in the room like he was giving a lecture to his students. "Many Ohlone trash sites have been found in the coastal areas of Santa Cruz, Monterey, and San Mateo counties, even some inland in Santa Clara and San Benito counties, and on up the coast past San Francisco and the whole Bay Area region. Several burial sites have been unearthed as well, although this specific location isn't on any archeological maps."

He was enthusiastic. "This is fun stuff. Great timing, too. I've got a bunch of students just itching to do a little dig. This doesn't look like a trash mound. I think we could have a burial site here. It would be unusual for there to be just one burial, although it happened that way in Berkeley once, but usually we find several individuals. How about, after the Coroner does a couple of tests on the skeletal remains to be sure we have an indigenous burial here, you let me and my students have a go at your place?" he asked Rick Whitlaw.

Regan could tell Rick Whitlaw wasn't as thrilled about the prospect of a group of students uprooting his new property as Professor Smithers was. "Do I have a choice?" he asked testily.

"Well, sure, but someone's going to have to investigate the site. The county has a staff anthropologist. Getting an anthropological clearance shouldn't be too expensive," Professor Smithers smirked, "but we're not backed up several months, we work for free, and we can provide you with a nice county-approved clearance when we finish."

He rummaged through his box until he found a slightly crumpled and dirty paper and a pen. He handed them to Rick. "You're the owner, right? If you'll just sign this authorization, we can get started as soon as the Coroner gives us the all clear," he winked.

"Regan, as our agent, shouldn't you have warned us about this being an anthropological site?" Rick Whitlaw was smiling, but it wasn't a friendly smile. "I wonder how good a job you did representing us here?" he laughed acerbically.

"Rick, please. How would Regan know what was buried in the backyard?" Joan put her hand on her husband's arm. "He doesn't really mean that," she said to Regan. Then, frowning with uncertainty, she turned back to her husband, "You don't, do you?"

"I guess I … no … I guess I don't," he stammered. "It's just the stress of moving, and now this. This is all going to be very inconvenient."

Regan noted he had reason to be upset. She also noted he didn't apologize for the misplaced blame he directed at her. *Let it go*, she told herself. After several months of working with the Whitlaws, Regan was no longer surprised by Rick's manner, even if she was still a bit vexed by it.

"We should be in and out in a couple of weeks, a month at most," the professor said to Rick. "Your boys can learn a lot by observing. You might learn something, too." He shot a conspiratorial glance at Regan and raised one eyebrow.

"Your boys look pretty big and strong." He winked again, this time at the children. "You think maybe you guys can help us dig?"

Richard smiled shyly, but he was clearly excited by the prospect of helping.

"I don't want to help. I want to dig up the dog," Raymond said.

Raymond's persistence proved to be a tension breaker. Regan and Joan laughed; even Rick managed a bit of a chuckle.

"With everything that's happened today, I completely forgot about the dog," Joan said.

Regan smiled to herself. *He sure is a focused little guy.* "You don't forget anything do you, Raymond?"

"Unh-unh, 'specially not good stuff like that ole dog."

3

"I know you'd rather be in Scotts Valley to shorten your commute, Kirby, but this property in La Selva Beach is perfect in every other way." Regan wished she could make her case in person, but had to settle for a phoned-in plea. "You're a flex-time commuter most days. I timed it out: if you don't try to get to work between seven and eight-thirty in the morning or home between five and six-thirty at night, La Selva should only add nine minutes to your commute. How about at least taking a look?"

Regan felt like a pushy realtor. She usually didn't try to sell clients a property that didn't meet all their requirements, and Mithrell and Kirby had been very specific about shortening Kirby's daily commute, but the property she wanted them to see was unique and spectacular. So she pushed.

"The house is gorgeous. It's older, but beautifully maintained. It has character: lots of angles, a steeply pitched roof with matching interior ceilings, several bay windows, and cozy reading nooks. The kitchen is huge, updated, and has enough work stations that both of you could easily work at the same time," she promised the ardent cooks. "The house even has a real library," she enticed. Mithrell and Kirby were avid book collectors who dreamt of a house with a library but hadn't been hopeful of finding one.

"A real library?" Kirby asked. "Define real, please."

"One with cherry paneling around a fireplace, and built-in floor to ceiling bookshelves on three walls, and ..." Regan said before Kirby interrupted.

"Works for me," he said.

"There's more. It has a permitted guesthouse, single-level I might add, for your parents." Kirby had explained that his mom and dad were getting older and were now willing to move from their beloved Chicago, with its bone-chilling winters, to Santa Cruz. Having a private space for his parents was a requirement for Kirby and Mithrell. Having a separate guesthouse was even better.

But Regan knew that for Mithrell and Kirby the land and trees were the most important part of any property, and this site was truly enchanting. It was mostly forested with Monterey pines, a variety of firs and oaks, and some non-native eucalyptus in a pleasing mix. But at its center, at its very heart, was a stand of Sequoia Sempervirens, coastal redwoods, the world's tallest trees — as splendid a mini-forest as Regan had ever seen outside of some place like Henry Cowell State Park.

The redwoods were an ancient species. Their fossilized ancestors had been found in geological strata dating back to the Jurassic Period, the era of dinosaurs like stegosaurs, brachiosaurs, and allosaurs. The property was situated within the southern portion of the 470-mile-long growing range where the trees still survived.

Cool summer temperatures and coastal fog provided the right environment for the trees to thrive. The property was near enough to the ocean that it got many summer days of swirling fog. The magnificent trees loved it; they had evolved an elaborate system for concentrating moisture from the fog and dropping it like rainfall for their roots to absorb. That was how they lived with the lack of summer rain in golden-dry California.

Redwood trees could live for hundreds, even thousands, of years and could propagate, not only conventionally from seeds, but also by means of "fairy rings" where offspring arose around a dead or downed parent tree, and by "burls" where new trees arose from knobby wart-like growths on mature trees.

And to Wiccans like Mithrell and Kirby, redwoods, like all of nature, were very nearly holy. Wiccans — some people called them pagans — often conducted religious services in forests. Trees formed their cathedrals.

"I'm keeping the best for last," Regan added. "The land is magnificent. You'll become stewards of a very special place."

"OK. You've convinced me we need to at least take a look." Regan could hear the implied sigh in Kirby's voice as he thought about his potentially longer commute. "I'm doing an early day tomorrow. We could meet you at the property around four-thirty. That means we should beat rush-hour traffic. I can test your commute theory at the same time."

"Perfect," Regan smiled. Kirby couldn't see her, of course, but he could no doubt hear her zeal. "If it's all right with you, could we meet at 3244 Alta Mar Vista? I sold the owners their house a few months ago. The first day they moved in their kids found some Ohlone remains in the backyard — long story, I'll fill you in as we look at your property — but I want to say 'Hi' to them and see how they're doing. And just in case you think the property is as perfect for you as I do," she gave a little chuckle, "well, a corner of it touches the Whitlaws', so I might be able to introduce you to some of your new neighbors, and introduce your son to the Whitlaw boys, who are on either side of Arthur in age."

"Ready-made playmates," Kirby laughed. "Regan, you think of everything. Fine. I've entered the address into my BlackBerry's GPS. We'll meet you there at four-thirty tomorrow."

Regan knocked on the Whitlaws' front door fifteen minutes before her scheduled meeting with Mithrell and Kirby. If the mailbox with their address hadn't been in front of the Whitlaws' house, she might have driven by without recognizing it. The house was freshly painted. The trim was done in two contrasting colors which smartly brought out architectural details even Regan's trained eyes overlooked the last time she was there. Several large bushes, scraggly when the Whitlaws purchased the house, had been cut back severely; others had been replaced with appropriately sized plants which all looked healthy and thriving; and gone were the two past-their-prime palm trees that had grown so unpleasantly tall they were nothing but bare trunks until twenty feet above the roofline.

Rick Whitlaw answered the door.

"Wow, Rick. You and Joan have done marvelous things to your house."

He greeted her with a polite smile but one that didn't communicate any real warmth or keenness to see her, and he ignored her compliment.

"Well, Regan, what are you doing here? Would you like to come in for a few minutes?" he asked without moving from his position at the doorway. "It will have to be just a few, though. Joan isn't here; she's on one of her trips, this time advising about fundraising for an art museum in Spokane, and I have to get the boys to an overnight at some friends of theirs."

He paused for a few seconds, seemingly debating whether or not to add any details. "Actually, their friends are doing me a favor having them over. I've got a meeting tonight with a political action committee, in point of fact, my political action committee." He smiled broadly and genuinely this time, proud of his declaration. "I believe I told you I was interested in public office. I've already served in several local capacities; now I'm exploring whether the time is right for a run for State Assembly."

"Congratulations, Rick. I'm excited for you. I won't keep you," Regan added, still unsure of whether or not she was expected to go inside. "I'm going to show some clients the property kitty-corner to your backyard. They're going to meet me here in a few minutes to see it. It's a big parcel with an easily-missed entrance. I thought it would be simpler for them to find your place than the way in, so I asked them to meet me here."

She grinned. "And I confess," she put a hand over her heart, "I'm also using that meeting as a way to stop by, say 'Hi', and see how you're doing."

"Checking up on us, are you?" He chuckled as he said it, but Regan could feel the moment of friendly intimacy they shared over Rick's news was fading.

"Just seeing how your family is doing," she corrected. "Have you all settled in? Are you enjoying the neighborhood?"

"Not finding any more burials?" Rick added.

"That, too."

"At least you're candid." His smile did a poor job of masking his disdain.

He looked past her toward the street. "Are those your clients?" Rick nodded in the direction of the white Honda Odyssey disgorging its three occupants in front of his house.

Regan turned from the stand-offish coolness at the door that was Rick Whitlaw toward the unabashed warmth radiating from Kirby and Mithrell Paisley and their son, Arthur, who were standing at the curb. "They are," she said.

"If they may become neighbors, I'd better meet them. Boys," he yelled into the house, "get your gear into the car. I'll be there in exactly three minutes."

He turned back to Regan, "Introduce me, will you?" He strode forward, hand extended, smiling earnestly at the Paisley family.

Kirby immediately returned the smile and the outstretched hand as he headed up the Whitlaws' walkway. The men, both about six feet tall, had a similar stride. They met one another at the halfway point between the curb and front door, with Regan close behind, able to keep up because of her own long legs.

"Rick," Regan made a quick decision to give him the superior position for introductions since they were taking place on his property, "I'd like you to meet Kirby Paisley, his wife Mithrell, and their son, Arthur. Mithrell, Kirby, and Arthur: this is Rick Whitlaw."

It had taken Mithrell a bit more time to reach the halfway point because her stride was considerably shorter than her husband's. She stood less than five-feet-two-inches tall, although if she thought her height was being considered and decided she could get away with it unnoticed, she might cheat a bit by going up on her toes ever so slightly. But even though she was short, no one would ever call her petite. She had ample breasts, and was probably three feet around at her waist and considerably farther around at her hips — her figure reminiscent of a carved feminine fertility symbol revered in prehistoric societies. She was dark, with a Mediterranean heritage that likely portended a bit of a mustache somewhere in her aged future.

Even so, she was a sexy woman — not the conventional willowy glamorous kind of Hollywood sexy — but she had something. Regan thought it was her eyes: beautiful turquoise-colored eyes that she used masterfully to cast sideways, come-hither looks — eyes that conveyed a kind of intelligence that a thinking man could find fascinating. Mithrell also had an ease with her sexuality that seemed to tell men "I know what your deepest secret desire is. I'm an adventurous woman. I'll be unlike anyone you've been with before, unforgettable. Your fantasy excites me, too."

Regan noticed Rick making eye contact with Mithrell as he shook her hand. Was that a hint of color in his cheeks? Possibly. Probably.

"Mithrell," he said, "what a charming name. And Arthur. Hello, young man."

Arthur was dressed in a long flowing cape of forest-green velvet and carried a plastic sword with gaudy fake jewels covering its hilt. He held it up as if ready for a duel, but instead of acting aggressively, he bowed deeply. "My liege," he said.

Rick Whitlaw laughed. "Regan says we're going to be neighbors. Our children will certainly get along well. Mine tend to live in their own realms too, especially my youngest. I'd like you to meet them, but we're running late today, so we'll have to do that some other time."

"That's assuming we become neighbors. Regan, you did tell Mr. Whitlaw we haven't even seen the property yet, didn't you?" Kirby asked with a genial grin.

"She did," Rick answered for her, "but she's good at talking people into buying houses. I imagine she's pretty confident about you."

Regan smiled an awkward little smile. She didn't know how to respond. Rick's comment was almost offered as a compliment, but she was certain it was intended as a slam. Still, it was presented in such an innocuous way, it left her off-balance.

"I've really got to go. Sorry to rush off. Good meeting you all," Rick added as he turned and headed toward his garage.

He pressed a code into the garage-opener pad next to the door and turned to offer a cheery little wave as the door rolled up, revealing Raymond and Richard already in the back seat of their father's Prius, seat-belted and ready for their trip. The boys eyed Arthur as Rick slowly backed the car down their driveway toward the street. Raymond held up his hand and did a little curved finger wave. Arthur bowed again, slightly this time, and offered a salute with his sword.

"What a curious man," Mithrell offered, "He's very tightly wound, isn't he? There's no room for spontaneity in his life, no deep joy, just a careful, controlled way of being."

"Try not to form any negative opinions about him, Mithrell. He's still upset because of all the disruption he had to go through right after moving here, as if moving isn't enough disruption of a family's routine," Regan explained.

"The people who owned the house before him said they buried a dog in the backyard and his kids wanted to find it. The day they moved in, his sons started digging. They unearthed a Native American burial. He had an anthropologist and a bunch of college students crawling all around his property, disrupting his landscaping, and ... well ... just being there. I think he found it all very disturbing.

"He was annoyed with me, too, for not disclosing the burial site, but I didn't know it was there, and I assume the sellers didn't either. I thought he'd be over it by now, but I guess he isn't. I don't know what I could have done differently, but apparently he's still upset with me."

"It's nice to know that mean little exchange was about misdirected upset. Here I was thinking he was just an everyday pain-in-the-you-know-what," Kirby said jovially.

25

"My opinions of him aren't good or bad," Mithrell said. "I just observed how he struggles. He's not good at getting over things or of seeing from a fitting perspective. That's probably why he has to be so careful. He's carrying a lot of anger for perceived injustices and failings, his own as well as other people's. I think he's afraid of what he might do if he ever loses control."

Regan was startled at Mithrell's insight. She had always been good at sizing up people and her job as a realtor had honed her skill. Still, it had taken her a long while to grasp that about Rick Whitlaw.

There was one time when they were looking at a house when Richard took off running through the front yard. She had seen children get out of control and didn't like having to be the one to try to rein them in, but Richard's antics weren't anywhere near problematic. Rick over-reacted wildly at his son's behavior. His temper exploded; he raged almost to the point of fury. When he realized how he must appear to her, he quickly toned down his outburst and got control of himself again.

She liked Joan and the kids, so she wanted to like him, too. But she saw his behavior as objectionable, and she had to make excuses for him in order to do that.

Mithrell saw the same behavior she did, but observed without making any value judgments. It gave her an edge.

"His life could be easier if he let it be," Mithrell shrugged. "But, let's move on. Let's go see the house you're going to manipulate us into buying," she teased.

"By the way, you were wrong about the commute. I'd add eight minutes, not nine like you thought. Please try to be precise about details, Regan," Kirby said, putting his tongue in his cheek literally and figuratively.

Regan's face instantly showed how much she enjoyed working with Mithrell and Kirby. Like Rick Whitlaw, they were careful; Kirby especially was very exacting. But they were also open. Yes, she thought, that was the correct word: open. Open to new experiences, to joy and sadness, to living. Rather than trying to control what life threw at them, they embraced life's adventures.

Regan couldn't refrain from making value judgments. Mithrell and Kirby were charming; she enjoyed working with them. Rick, on the other hand, could be a challenge.

Regan was in the home office she shared with her husband Tom, busily working on her computer when he got home. She was engrossed in her task. The sun had set and daylight was almost gone, but she hadn't noticed enough to turn on an overhead light.

"Pizza night?" he asked.

She held up her left hand in a give-me-a-minute gesture and pressed SEND. "Umm," Regan seemed surprised at the low level of light, now that her eyes were off the screen. "What time is it?" She looked at the time display on her screen and answered her own question, "It's almost eight o'clock. I guess so. I got involved."

"What's up?"

"I showed Mithrell and Kirby that property in La Selva Beach, the one we saw on broker tour, and they loved it. I was just putting together an offer for them — just finished and emailed it for their signatures."

"So, pizza and champagne then? It sounds like it was a good day."

"It was a strange day," Regan said. "We met at the house I

sold to Joan and Rick Whitlaw."

"The Ohlone house?" Tom queried.

"Not you, too; but yes, the Ohlone house. Rick's still hostile about that, by the way. Anyway, we left their van at the Whitlaws' house and took my car to the property. Mithrell and Kirby pronounced it perfect except for one tiny thing: it doesn't have a turnaround space. That's an easy fix," Regan interjected, "Mithrell immediately figured out how to create a dramatic circular drive, maybe even add a porte-cochere, which would look great with the house.

"Today, though, I had to back down the long driveway in front of a three-person audience, with Mithrell and Kirby terrified that I would hit one of the oak or apple trees along the drive. They consider oaks and apples sacred trees.

"Once I knew that, my car seemed to become possessed. It seemed to have its own separate controls that wrenched it from my guidance and aimed it at each tree I passed."

"We both know long backups are a challenge for you," he laughed, "but in a possessed car ... I'm sorry I missed that show."

"Yes, I'm sure you are," Regan joined in with her own laughter. "But that's not the strange part of my day. On the way home I stopped for mail. You know how, if you stop in front of our box, you have to back up a bit to make the turn down our road?"

"Uh-huh," Tom said slowly.

"My car wouldn't back up. I couldn't put it into reverse. I managed to make the turn going forward — I almost took the street sign and a neighbor's tree with me, but I did it.

"When I got home, my phone was ringing. It was Kirby.

He said he hoped I hadn't had any trouble getting home. I said, 'no trouble,' but told him what happened at the mailbox. He apologized. He said he and Mithrell had been talking about the driveway and my backing up, and he thought he might have inadvertently put a spell on my car."

"Put a spell on your car?" Tom roared with laughter.

"They are Wiccans. They're both witches, you know ... white witches, but still witches."

Tom rolled his eyes, "Listen to yourself, sweetheart. You don't really believe that stuff, do you? It was just a coincidence."

"The point is *they* thought they might have done something to harm me, so they called to make sure they hadn't. I thought that was very nice of them. And you have to admit the timing of my car's problem was pretty strange."

"A strange coincidence," he said, "to those of us who view the world and its happenings from a rational perspective. Remember, I was a programmer — a logical, sensible person, before I joined you in this wildly unempirical business and became a loony real estate broker. It's just a coincidence, nothing more."

"Kirby's a software engineer. He's very logical and methodical, just like you are. He's also a witch."

🏠🏠🏠🏠🏠🏠🏠🏠🏠🏠

First thing next morning, after reassuring Tom he didn't need to follow her, Regan drove to her mechanic's shop. It was easy to do because no backing up was involved.

Her mechanic only took a second to confirm her car wouldn't go into reverse. "Feels like the transmission is a little off. Let's have a look," he said, as he raised her car on the rack. He walked under the car and a second later whistled, "How about that? Here's your problem. I don't know if you can see it from where you're standing, and I can't invite you under here with me — got all kinds of regulations against that — but there's a small part here that should have a bolt to hold it flush to the bottom. Your car's missing its bolt and that lets this piece here drop down and keeps you from sliding into reverse." He pointed to a place on her car's undercarriage, but Regan couldn't see what he was talking about.

"It's a two-minute job to repair with a four-dollar part. I'll have you all fixed up in a jiffy. I've seen this before, maybe three times in all the years and with all the cars I've repaired."

"What would cause the bolt to come off?" Regan asked.

"Beats me. Like I said, it's a rare thing."

Regan's face lit up with a smile so obviously mischievous that her mechanic noticed and asked her, "What 'cha grinning about? Are you planning on telling your old man this repair cost a couple of hundred so you can buy a dress with the difference," he asked.

"No, no, nothing like that," Regan laughed. "I'm just looking forward to telling my very rational husband what you told me about the bolt."

Strange coincidence, all right.

31

Within the first three months of their ownership, Mithrell and Kirby changed the driveway and built the porte-cochere. Even the new landscaping was complete and ready for the "let's get acquainted" party they threw on May 24th. They invited all their neighbors within a two-block radius. They also invited members of a Morris Dancers group they belonged to, an assortment of other friends and acquaintances, and Regan and Tom.

For the uninitiated, Kirby explained that Morris Dancing was a form of English folk dance that may have originated during the time of Celtic rule, possibly as part of a pagan fertility ritual. The dancers wore special dress with bells that jingled as they danced to precisely choreographed movements. The dancing was supposed to bring luck and ward off evil, the perfect way, he said, to inaugurate their new home and introduce them to their new neighbors. Although it wasn't a participatory style of dancing, it was colorful and fun to watch. Their guests enjoyed it.

The Paisleys had set up a maypole for the children to scamper around, braiding colorful ribbons down the pole as they went. A few children managed to get braided into the maypole in the confusion, but when it happened, it seemed to be deliberate, and added to their fun.

The Morris Dancers provided their own music, with lyrical melodies that Regan imagined must have been heard at medieval fairs — at least they sounded like the melodies used in movies when Maid Marian was waiting at a fair for a disguised Robin Hood to save her from the clutches of the corrupt Sheriff of Nottingham.

The whole party felt like a medieval festival to her. It seemed like a perfect sort of event to celebrate the Paisley's new house and property. The gathering was unlike anything most of the neighbors had been to before, but it was a celebration that encouraged people to mix easily, get to know one another, and laugh freely. People were in high spirits, having a great time.

That made it all the more startling when one of the partygoers grabbed her arm so roughly that she spilled some of her soda.

"You're the one who sold these people this house, aren't you?" he challenged.

"Yes, I'm Regan McHenry, Mithrell and Kirby's real estate agent." Regan smiled as she freed her arm, assuming the man had drunk a little too much ale. Perhaps he had lost his balance, or at least his sense of propriety, and that was why he had been so rough with her.

But he remained an intimidating presence, much more so than his stature would suggest. He wasn't as tall as Regan, but even though he had to look up at her, his eyes conveyed menacing anger, "What have you put in our midst?"

"John, however you feel, this is hardly the place to express yourself." Regan was as surprised by her defender as she had been by her assailant. Rick Whitlaw stood beside her, facing the irate man. "Why did you even come here today? You shouldn't have done that, John."

"I wanted to see for myself. But you're right. Now I've had my look around, I shouldn't be here," he said as he turned and abruptly tramped away.

"Thank you, Rick," Regan said. "Do you know what that was all about?"

"Sort of. He's a neighbor and a local minister. He leads a Pentecostal church a couple of blocks away and lives near here, too, about half way between the church and my house. He thinks the Paisleys are...well," he shrugged, "too different for his taste. Too bad he can't enjoy a great party." He held his glass of ale aloft in toasting-mode before taking a sip.

"It seems best wishes are in order, Rick. I think the last time I saw you, you were just thinking about entering statewide politics. Now I've read in the newspaper that you have your party's nomination and an excellent chance of being elected to the State Assembly. May I tell people I knew you when?" she laughed.

"Sure. You can even say you helped me buy and sell my house."

"Sell?"

"It's handy running into you here. I was going to call you next week. We'll be in need of your services soon. Joan and I have decided we want a different house, one that doesn't need so much work."

Regan was surprised by Rick's announcement. "I thought

your plans were to remodel the house, maybe add a second story eventually, and that you both enjoyed working on houses?"

"Those were our plans, but after the whole Ohlone thing," he heaved a loud sigh, "plans change. Professor Smithers and his students didn't find more remains so our backyard wasn't declared a burial ground, thank goodness, but the more I thought about it, well, there could be complications with permits, that sort of thing. Our options could be too limited, even if we get through the likely permit nightmare those old bones created.

"And of course, I don't want to offend any constituent's sensibilities either, you know, seem disrespectful in any way." He quickly shifted his tone. "I decided it would just be simpler to move."

"Rick, are you certain you want to do this right now? There could be some very negative financial implications for you if you sell so soon after buying. You've just spent money in closing costs and there will be expenses on the way out as well. How does Joan feel about moving again?"

Rick ignored her question about Joan's feelings. "Surely you'll work for a reduced commission," he presumed, "since you got money going into this, and you'll get money going out?

"We're planning to take a family vacation the last two weeks of June. Joan's family is having a big reunion in Atlanta, where she grew up. We're driving back for it. I'd like you to come by when we get back, take a look at the things we've done, and give us some tips on what else we need to do to get market-ready. Why don't you call us at the start of July to work out the details?"

Before Regan had a chance to reply, he spotted someone he wanted to talk to, deemed their conversation over, excused himself abruptly, and left her standing alone.

"You like him or think he's a real tight-ass like I do?" a beaming man with dark curly hair asked her.

His face was familiar. She knew him, but didn't come up with who he was immediately.

"Jerry Smithers, the anthro-guy," he offered, realizing her dilemma.

"Professor Smithers. Of course. I never forget a floor plan or a voice, but I'm embarrassed to say I didn't recognize you," Regan confessed.

"Don't be too hard on yourself. Without a skull or two around, I'm out of context," he laughed. "No, wait. It's probably because of my very expensive Gucci sunglasses." His smile grew even bigger. He started to reach for the glasses with his right hand, realized he was holding a roasted chicken leg, and quickly switched to his free left hand to lift them up. "You probably wouldn't expect to see such hip toys on a geeky college professor," he winked, "but I just hit the big four-oh and I'm trying very hard not to act my age. I'm stylin' — that's what my undergrads call it — with designer shades and tighter jeans.

"Just a minute," he frowned. "I didn't get new jeans or have my old ones taken in. You don't think ... nah ... I'm still maintaining my boyish rear end." He laughed uproariously.

"Why, I'm even contemplating a shiny new toy. Don't you think a big black SUV would suit me? Forty-year-olds shouldn't still be driving the same thing they drove in grad school, now should they?"

"I think you're due," Regan smiled at him.

"Yep. Rumor has it my name is on the short list for promotion from assistant professor to associate professor. The second that happens, I'm out there, with my excellent credit rating and my promise of enhanced salary to cover the monthly bills, buying something that uses an obscene amount of fossil fuel. I'm even going to spring for vanity plates that say 'anthro guy,' or if that's too long then 'bone guy.'"

"The environment can hardly wait for your contribution to global warming," Regan laughed. "Have you finished digging at the Whitlaws? No more remains?"

"None. That's really unusual, too. When they were putting in a stadium at UC Berkeley back in the 1920s, a single individual may have been found. Reports from the time were pretty vague. Of course, the anthropologic commitment to preserving sacred ground wasn't very strong then, especially not when weighed against building a football stadium," he grinned, "but burial areas usually have more individuals in them.

"I suspect we'd find more remains if I could expand our search grid. I keep trying to convince Mithrell and Kirby to let me and my undergrads extend our messing around to their land, but even with one of my students who knows them vouching for me, and with my sincere promise to keep my crew out of Mithrell's garden, they keep declining my generous offer. I got an invitation for today out of my attempts, though. Fun party. Great eats," he said as he enthusiastically attacked the chicken leg.

Regan gave the Whitlaws until July 2nd to be home from their vacation before calling to set an appointment. Joan answered when she called.

"I've never been to a family reunion," Regan said. "How was it?"

"It was terrific fun, as it turned out. The boys had so many cousins to play with. We were all out in the country at one family member's estate. We let the kids free-range. The adults organized into shifts and took turns guarding the exits so the mob of kids couldn't escape," she laughed, "so most of the time we were free to catch up on family gossip or go shopping.

"Rick even did well," she giggled. "He took a day off for a local seminar about campaign organization, which no doubt helped, but I think he enjoyed the reunion — not that he wouldn't," she added quickly, "but it was my family. Reunions are never as enjoyable if you don't share old growing-up memories.

"But now we're back. I guess it's time to think of other things."

Her high spirits damped down as she spoke. "Rick won't be available for a couple of days, but he's very anxious to start preparations for the sale. He said he didn't want to wait for his schedule to loosen up before we got together. I'm willing to take notes. Later today works for me, if that's OK, and you're available."

"How about two o'clock?" Regan suggested.

"That works very well. Two o'clock then."

The meeting was officially the beginning of a listing appointment. Normally Regan wanted both owners present to discuss plans for selling their house, but since she already knew the sellers and knew she would get the listing, she was willing to change her usual routine. Besides, Joan always seemed guarded and had to try so hard to make the boys be quiet and still when Rick was around; meeting without him there was bound to be more enjoyable.

When the Whitlaws bought their house, it would have been considered in need of some TLC, tender loving care, realtor-code for not-quite-rough-enough to be a fixer-upper that needed major repairs or a complete remodel, but a home that would benefit in both appearance and value from some work: things like fresh landscaping and paint, fresh carpets or flooring, and maybe a realigning or opening up of some doorways to make the house feel open and bright.

The Whitlaws had already improved the landscaping and had painted the house's exterior, which was a good start. They probably had other enhancements in mind, too, especially since they labeled themselves hands-on-homeowners. But now that they had abandoned their plans, Regan assumed they would like her to suggest some modest changes that would improve their chances for a quick sale. She also hoped she could help them offset some of the moving expenses they were going to incur by moving out so soon after moving in.

She arrived equipped with a briefcase full of articles and tips on preparing a house for sale. She had all the latest color trends and home staging ideas she could find, coupons realtors got from home improvement centers offering discounts for their clients, and contact information for good contractors and handymen who worked in a variety of specialties.

When she pulled up in front of the house that afternoon, Regan noticed the landscaping redo the Whitlaws had started was completed. Nice job, she thought. Between the fresh new paint and the thoughtful and now complete re-landscaping, they had really improved the curb appeal of the house. She mentally checked "making a good first impression" off her discussion list.

Regan collected her briefcase and took her digital camera out of her car console. She paused to click a curb-side shot of the house. She looked at it, took another shot from a few feet closer, decided the second shot was much better, and deemed it good enough to put on her website under "coming soon." Yes, very nice landscaping she thought as she walked up the path to the front door.

The main entry was offset from the path, at right angles to the curb, not parallel as most front doors are. When she got close to it, she noticed the front door was open, just like it was the first time she came by after the Whitlaws bought the house.

Regan shook off the tiny bit of déjà vu she felt.

She was compulsive about arriving for appointments on time. Joan knew that. It was a trait they shared and had joked about, and since she was expected and it was a nice sunny summer day, Joan had probably opened the door anticipating her arrival. "Knock, Knock," Regan called through the open door. The feeling returned — déjà vu.

"Regan, I'm in the kitchen. Come on in." The sensation became overwhelming with Joan's reply.

Regan stood very still at the doorway, momentarily unable to will herself over the threshold. Finally, she took a deep breath and shook her head. *Don't be silly, Regan,* she said to herself and went inside.

She was immediately taken with the changes the Whitlaws had made during their short ownership. They had painted the tired-looking but still functional wooden kitchen cabinets a soft ecru and replaced the dated cabinet handles with stylish new ones in a brushed nickel finish. The cabinets looked totally renewed. The lower cabinets had been topped off with dark granite counters and backsplashes. New stainless steel appliances replaced worn old models.

The door to the backyard remained untouched, but they had removed the door to the dining room, opened up the remaining wall considerably, and then taken down the wall separating the living and dining rooms to create a great-room effect.

"Wow!" Regan exclaimed. "What an amazing difference. I noticed the new landscaping, too."

"There's more," Joan added. "Let me take you on the official tour." Joan showed Regan their other modifications to

41

the inside of the house. Most of the rooms had fresh paint in tasteful and very current colors. Worn carpeting had been replaced with bamboo flooring.

"We are very conscious of doing our part for the environment. We decided to use bamboo because it grows quickly and traps carbon better than most other timber. We feel it's just generally a better choice for the environment than other woods or carpeting," she said proudly.

"It looks terrific, too." Regan said.

"We were going to put in French doors that would open to the backyard from the great-room and from our bedroom. Those were going to be some of our summer projects," Joan sounded wistful. "But then Rick suddenly decided he didn't want to live here any longer," she said, as they looped back through the kitchen to get to the backyard.

"I'd already bought the doors. I thought we should still install them ... but once he makes up his mind ... we're not going to bother now. Fortunately, the store let me return them.

"Of course, I understand," she added defensively, "and I do agree with him. He's going to be so busy with the campaign and all. We really won't have the time to work on the house."

"You've already done so much," Regan said. "Couldn't you just take a time out for now and finish renovating later? Are you anxious to move, as well?"

"I'm not, really. We're so close to the beach here. We've really enjoyed walking there with the boys," she added softly. "The boys love it here, too. They've made friends. They have settled into their new school very well. That's going to be the hardest part of this move, watching them have to do that all over again.

"Besides, I liked this house the minute you showed it to us. I could see its potential and began designing improvements immediately in my head. Oh, well," she sighed. "I don't want to complain. Rick really does have so much on his plate right now. We'll find another house. I guess I'll start planning new projects there, too, but small projects."

Joan and Regan reached the backyard and were ready for the outdoor part of their tour. Like the front yard, the backyard was completely re-landscaped except for where the boys — three this time, because Arthur Paisley had joined them — had dug up some new annuals that had been planted under what was the clearly recognizable peach tree, and were busily digging a long deepening hole.

Joan cried, "What are you doing? Those plants where you're digging were struggling. They were just finally taking hold."

"If you're gonna make us move, we're gonna find that ole dog before we go," Raymond fired back. "We know he's still here 'cause the diggers didn't find him."

Regan started to laugh. Joan did too, although she tried to be stern as she said, "Your father is going to be angry with you. At least be careful not to damage any of the drip irrigation lines. You know how long it took to take out those wasteful sprinklers and replace them with drip irrigation."

"I can't be too upset with them," she said to Regan softly. "Rick says I'm too indulgent of them. He's right, of course, but sometimes he expects so much of them; they're only children." Joan became momentarily serious as she confided in Regan, but she quickly shook off that tenor and replaced it with a giggle.

"They're convinced they'll find the dog now that they know where to look. It seems the former owners were confused about which tree was which, but now that the trees have leafed in and have fruit on them, they've been eager to try digging under what really is the peach tree.

"That's silly of course, because Professor Smithers and his students dug up everything to a depth of several feet. The dog bones, if they ever were here, must have dissolved. If you ask me, though, I think what really happened was the former owners were confused about which house they were living in when they buried their dog. But just try convincing some very determined young men of that," Joan chuckled.

"I mean it about the irrigation lines," she raised her voice again in a final attempt at authority as she and Regan headed back toward the kitchen. "Let's have some coffee while we talk about this sale."

Joan had just poured freshly brewed coffee into two cups and had sat down opposite Regan when the back door opened with a characteristic Whitlaw-boy-slap.

"We found another Indian," Richard announced happily. "Professor Smithers told us we shouldn't dig anymore whenever we found anything. He said it was important to call an anthropologist right away, because if we kept digging, we would mess up the site. Mom, could you call him right now? Arthur and Raymond are guarding her, but you know how little brother is. I don't think he can wait very long to start digging again. I know he's going to mess her up.

"She's much better than the last Indian. We washed her off with the hose. She has hair and skin and everything."

Joan and Regan stared at one another as Richard told them about the new discovery, first with disbelief that this was happening again, and then with growing horror, as he described what they had found.

"Oh, my God," Joan whispered.

Regan could feel shivers down her spine. She didn't know why exactly, but she felt she should be the one to go see the scene Richard was describing. She reluctantly volunteered.

"I'll go get your brother and Arthur so they won't be tempted to dig anymore while you and your mother call Dave. You remember him, don't you?" she asked.

Richard shook his head, yes. "Shouldn't we call Professor Smithers?" he asked.

"I don't have his number, but Dave can call him for us." Regan tried to sound casual. "Here's my phone," she said as she took it out of her briefcase and handed it to Joan. "Dave's listed on speed dial under his name. Richard, when your mom reaches him, could you tell him what you told us?

"Maybe you'll need to call 9-1-1 this time, if Dave doesn't answer his phone," she added to Joan, who nodded wordlessly.

Regan questioned her decision as soon as she left the kitchen. Why hadn't she stayed inside to call Dave and let Joan go outside to get the younger children? She didn't share the boys' enthusiasm for dead beings. If she'd stayed in the kitchen, she could have avoided any potential contact with the body.

But Raymond could be a handful, she reminded herself, and since he didn't know her very well, should it come to that, she might represent more authority with him than his mother would and have more control over him.

She turned the corner outside the kitchen and saw Arthur and Raymond on patrol. They were marching like toy soldiers, stiff-legged and with ramrod straight backs, around and around a small area of ground. "Boys, could you come here a minute?" she called. They stopped marching.

Arthur started toward her, but Raymond yelled, "No, no, we're guarding her. We can't leave."

"Please, boys. Richard is helping call Dave the policeman and Professor Smithers. She'll be OK until they get here. Come on, now," she waved them toward the house. Arthur obeyed, but Raymond still refused to move. "Do as I say, Raymond," she demanded sternly.

"No!" he said defiantly, as he resumed his marching.

Changing Raymond's behavior was going to take more than just being an authoritative adult that he didn't know well, Regan realized. She decided she would have to grab him and forcefully take him indoors. She would have to get closer to the body — but she would keep her eyes on Raymond, keep them diverted, just like she so carefully did at car accidents. Even if traffic had slowed so she had to inch by an accident, she never allowed her eyes to wander toward the wreckage. Never. She was afraid of what she might see: something she could never erase from her memory, something that would snap into full view in the middle of the night or that would force its way into her dreams.

That was her plan, but her timing was off. Raymond was

behind the grave when she approached, and he stopped his patrol with the opening in the ground between them. She couldn't risk getting any closer to the edge of the grave without watching where she placed her feet. That meant looking down.

Her only alternative was to wait until he resumed his marching and came around to her side of the grave again.

She stopped and waited for him, inflexibly determined to stare straight ahead. An unmistakable smell emanating from the ground invaded her senses; it was an acrid odor, not overwhelming or gagging, but inescapable. It was more than wet soil mixed with rotting organic matter; it was the smell of animal decomposition … just beginning. She was compelled to look down.

The girl's skin was a sienna brown color, stained by death and the grave. Her tongue was swollen enough to force its way out of her mouth. Her long dark hair was wet and muddy, matted from the hosing she had just received.

Only her shoulders and the very top of her chest were exposed. They were bare. Regan fought the urge to take off her jacket and cover the girl's shoulders with it, warm her and comfort her with the garment, like a mother might tuck a blanket around her child; the girl seemed so alone and cold in her shallow grave. Poor child.

Though death bloated and wrinkled her face and made it seem older, she was just a girl after all; and mercifully for Regan's memory, which would come back in vivid photographic flashes, the girl's eyes were closed. She couldn't have borne it if she had seen the girl's eyes open in their full ocean-blue intensity.

Regan knew those eyes. She knew this face. Even though death had marred her, she recognized the girl. Lydia.

By the time Regan returned to the kitchen with a wriggling and kicking Raymond carried unceremoniously under her arm, Joan had the other two boys in the master bedroom watching TV. With the promise he could join them as soon as he regained a semblance of self-control, Raymond soon calmed down. Within moments he was placidly curled up on his parent's bed beside the other two boys.

"We usually don't allow daytime TV, and especially not action movies like the one I found on cable. I hope Mithrell won't mind me letting Arthur watch it, but this is such an abnormal situation ..." her voice trailed off.

"I'm sure she won't mind," Regan said.

"I did get your friend Dave. He said he'd arrange for the proper authorities to come. Should I call Professor Smithers? I still have his number."

"They only call him if a burial appears to be ancient. I don't think he's going to be involved," Regan took a deep breath, "this time."

Three deputy sheriffs arrived within the next ten minutes. One of them deployed yellow crime scene tape. Again.

Joan had called her husband, too. Rick Whitlaw pulled his car into the driveway and rushed into the house. He grabbed his wife in a crushing embrace, "Joan, are you and the kids OK?"

She replied with a barely audible, "Yes, I'm fine." She remained in his arms and nuzzled against his chest, "and the boys seem completely nonplussed." She looked up into his eyes, "Isn't that remarkable? Raymond thinks it's all a game."

Dave aimed a tight-lipped lopsided grin at Regan as he came into the kitchen. She read his expression: I'm a professional, but your friend, too. She was grateful he thought to come. After what she had just seen, she could use a little moral support.

The Coroner's van backed into the Whitlaws' driveway once again, and as before, the quiet street filled with gawking neighbors, speculating about what might be happening this time.

Rick grew more agitated with each arrival. He turned to Regan, "I suppose we'll have to disclose this, too. This is going to affect our property value, isn't it? How long do we have to wait before we don't have to disclose today's events?"

Regan was speechless for several seconds. Finally, she managed, "You are required to disclose if a death took place in the house in the last three years." Lydia's ravaged face flashed before her — she found herself biting her lip to fight back tears. "But a murder? This has to be a murder, doesn't it?" Her anguish made Regan pause, "Rick, I don't know."

"Murder. You're right. Damn, this will make the papers. Can't you just see the headlines: 'Body found in nominee's backyard,'" he complained.

That wasn't what Regan saw at all. She tried to blot out her image of the girl in the backyard and replace it with Lydia as she wished to remember her: as a child ready to start her journey toward young womanhood, but who was, for the moment at least, still a giggly girl with a crush on her son and most of the other boys in his band.

The law enforcement squad divided up their duties. The murder investigation, which would begin with interviews of the Whitlaw family and Regan, would fall to the Sheriff's Department. Dave volunteered that he had some rapport with the Whitlaw boys. Since they already knew him and felt comfortable with him, the Sheriff thought his presence would make the boys feel more at ease during their questioning. Dave agreed to sit in with the deputy assigned to them. Sheriff Spencer would interview the Whitlaws, and Deputy Sheriff Burke was assigned to question Regan.

Deputy Sheriff Burke took Regan's arm and led her to the dining area, still within view of the kitchen, but out of earshot of the Whitlaw interview. He pulled out a dining room chair for Regan, one that faced her away from the kitchen. Once she was seated, he moved around the end of the table and sat down at right angles to her.

He took off his hat, revealing a bald head with a wisp of gray-blond hair combed over it. He absentmindedly ran his hand over the strands of hair to confirm their position and then put his hat on the dining room table. As he sat down, his stomach, softened and grown by years of inactive time confined in a patrol car, pressed against his bomber-style leather jacket. He unzipped his jacket and let his belly comfortably spill over his belt.

"OK," he sighed, signaling both his comfort and the beginning of their interview. "Why don't you tell me about how you found the body?"

"I didn't. The boys did. The oldest boy, Richard Whitlaw, came into the kitchen where his mother and I were having coffee and told us they'd found another Indian. But from what he told us we knew this wasn't like last time."

"Like last time?" Deputy Burke narrowed his eyes, "Is this the house where they found Ohlone remains some months back?"

Regan nodded.

"I missed that one; it was my day off. Humph," he expelled a burst of breath. "This place sure seems to have a lot of bones in the backyard."

She managed the weakest of ironic smiles.

"Tell me exactly what happened after the boy came into the kitchen."

Regan sat up straight, folded her hands on the table, and very formally began her recitation. "Well, as soon as Richard, the oldest Whitlaw brother, told us the boys had unearthed a body, I gave my cell phone to Joan Whitlaw and told her to call my friend Dave ... Officer Everett," she inclined her head in the direction of the bedroom where Dave and another deputy sheriff were talking to the boys. "Then I went outside to bring the other boys in ... so they wouldn't disturb the scene any more than they already had.

"Arthur Paisley came in when I asked him to, but Raymond Whitlaw, the youngest boy, wouldn't. I decided the only way to get him away from the ... burial ... was to pick him up and carry him inside. I never intended to look into the grave ... but he stayed so close to it ... I did."

Her eyes burned with tears. She blinked rapidly to keep them in check. "Deputy Sheriff Burke, I think I recognized the girl in the backyard. I think I know ... knew her. Her first name is Lydia. I can't think of her last name ... I'm not good with last names. She's been to my house. She used to hang around when my son's band practiced.

"Alex, my son, would know her last name. I've called him to ask. He's on tour with his band right now, so I can't guarantee when he'll call back. It may not be immediately; it will depend on where he is, and when they play tonight. I'll let you know as soon as I hear back from him."

Regan dropped her head and her voice became little more than a whisper, "She can't be more than sixteen or seventeen years old."

Deputy Sheriff Burke stopped taking notes and put down his paper and pen. He reached a large paw-of-a-hand across the table and patted her clasped hands. She was pretty sure that wasn't part of his standard interview procedure.

"My youngest is sixteen," he said. "What a waste. I want to get whoever did this. I want to get them real bad."

Alex called home just as Regan was reaching to switch off the reading light by her bed. It was 11:25. She glanced at the band tour schedule she kept on her nightstand as she picked up her phone. July 2nd. That would put them in Philadelphia. Regan figured it was almost two-thirty in the morning for him. She resisted the urge to tell him to take better care of himself. He was twenty and a rock star. Well, not quite, but the band had toured in Europe and this was its third summer tour in the States. She'd try to get plenty of good food into him and get him into a more normal routine before summer was over and he went back to college.

"Ma," he greeted her full of energy, no doubt feeding off the electricity of a live performance with its screaming, squirming, dancing fans. "What's goin' on? You said something about needing to know stuff about Lydia. Lydia Harder or Lydia Feeney?"

Feeney. That was her last name. Regan remembered now. "Lydia Feeney, the little girl with the dazzling blue eyes who used to watch you guys practice. She was younger than all of you by a few years, right?"

"Was, Ma? Is she OK?"

"I don't think so, Alex. There was a murder. I think the victim may have been Lydia. That's why I needed her last name, to help the Sheriff identify her."

"Murder? Oh, man!" he exclaimed.

Regan told him what had happened at the Whitlaws. "She was such a sweet little thing, really smart, too, as I recall."

"She was smart all right. She dropped out of high school classes because she thought they were too boring. She enrolled in junior college, at Cabrillo College, and started aceing courses. She even sat in on a class or two at UCSC. But Ma, she was anything but the sweet little girl you remember."

"What do you mean?"

"It wasn't her fault that she got so messed up, not when you think about what her life was like. Her dad took off when she was three or four; she never saw him after that. Her mom drank. Lydia pretty much had to take care of herself. Her mom got married again about the time Lydia started hanging around the band. She said her stepfather — well, let's just say it wasn't a good scene.

"You know I've told you groupies are real, Ma?" There was a callous tone to his voice that made him sound much older and harsher than he should have, given his years and his outlook on life. "She was into that big time; her goal was to sleep with the whole band. But even with our raging hormones, the guys avoided her. She was way too much trouble."

"A groupie? Are you sure? I thought she had a major crush on Matt."

"Yeah, she did on and off for a long time, maybe because he *really* wasn't interested," Alex replied. "But she was still letting Matt know she was available, at least until a few months ago. And Ma, I'm sure about the groupie thing, too. You can be awfully naïve for a woman of your age," he kidded.

"I know Lydia left home more than a year ago. She may have done the emancipated minor thing, but I'm not sure she was old enough to. I think she just moved out, and her mom didn't care. She learned to forge her mom's signature early on, much better than I ever learned to forge yours," he paused for a couple of seconds to see if she'd take the bait, "so she always had parental permission for whatever she wanted to do."

"Where was she living?"

"That I don't know. She couch-surfed for a while, you know, stayed with people, friends, and caught meals where she could. But after a while she seemed to have a place to stay.

"She got into the whole Goth thing for a while. The only guy in the band who liked that look was James," he chuckled, "the one guy in the band she wasn't into because she thought he was too sweet. Then she turned up the last time we played the Catalyst, which was like early February, and man, I almost didn't recognize her — but in a good way. She was all cleaned up. No more black anything: hair, clothes, lipstick, or eyeliner. She looked pretty — and happy.

"She told Matt he'd missed his chance. She said she'd hooked up with some old guy and was in love. Maybe she was living with him."

"Do you know how old she would have been?"

"Yeah. Her birthday and Matt's were the same date, but she was three years younger. She turned seventeen on June twenty-first."

Regan called Deputy Sheriff Burke early the next morning to relay Lydia's last name. He had been so kind to her during her interview that she felt she could ask, "Would you keep me in the loop?"

"Well, ma'am, it's not like I'll be calling you with daily updates," he hesitated, "but I might need to contact you occasionally for additional information."

Three days later, Regan's first update came not from Deputy Burke but from the *Santa Cruz Sentinel*.

"Have you seen this?" Tom asked, handing her the newspaper left-handed as he took another sip of morning coffee.

"What is it?" Regan looked at the article Tom indicated. The story was on the front page below the fold, important news, if not as significant as the headline story about local fireworks and beach scuffles that always commanded priority placement the day after July 4th. She quickly scanned the article: victim identified as Lydia Jane Feeney, age 17 ... from the Santa Cruz area, current address unknown ... last seen June 21st ... clothing found buried nearby ... possible ritual killing ... Kirby Paisley being questioned as a person of interest.

"Kirby?" she yelped. "That's just not possible! Mithrell must be unglued. And Arthur. Oh ... and Kirby's parents. What must they be going through?" Regan tossed the paper back to Tom and hurried to their office to look up the Paisley's phone number.

The Paisley's answering machine picked up with a cheery greeting in which each family member personally offered his or her name before the message beeped to an end. In keeping with her own upset, Regan began leaving a fairly disjointed message.

"Mithrell, it's Regan. I just read. Are you OK? What can I do to help? I don't believe ..."

"Regan?" Mithrell interrupted. Her voice sounded thick and very tired. "We've been screening calls. You can't believe the things some of the callers have said. I've sent Arthur to stay with friends. I don't want him hearing ... to be subjected to ..." her words ended in what Regan thought was a soft sob.

"May I come over ... I don't know ... give you a hug ... something?"

"Yes. Please."

Regan went back to the kitchen, opened the freezer and took out one of the packages of chocolate chip cookie dough they kept for baking at open houses. "Comfort food," she said to Tom. "I'm going over to the Paisleys. Understandably, Mithrell is very distressed; this is the only homemade thing I can think of to bring on short notice."

"Can't hurt," Tom sympathized. "I'll bake while you get

ready."

When Regan reached the newly created roundabout-driveway in front of the Paisleys, she could barely find a stopping place. Cars were scattered in every direction in a disorderly array, as if people had too much on their minds to organize parking. The front door was ajar, the house was filled with people, and the dining room table and kitchen counters were laden with food. She added her cookies to the abundance.

She recognized many of the faces from the house warming party, but the mood in the house today held none of the festive aura that day had. Regan's Irish McHenry roots kicked in. Today felt more like a wake, she noted, although even wakes were usually less somber.

Kirby emerged from the library, surrounded by several friends. One by one, they patted him on the back or embraced him. Then each one solemnly nodded to him before rejoining the rest of the mourners, as Regan had dubbed them.

After a while, the group began thinning out. Regan had found a chance to offer her support to Mithrell and was moving toward the front door to leave when Kirby caught her eye. "Stay," he mouthed silently. She nodded and returned to the congregation.

A few minutes later, Kirby came up behind her and took her elbow. She hadn't seen him coming; his move surprised her enough that she flinched slightly.

"Boogey man's got you," Kirby said with uncharacteristic harshness.

"No, Kirby," she protested. "I didn't see you. You startled me."

"Of course, Regan. I'm sorry. I'm taking things the wrong way at the moment. That's what happens when the Sheriff questions you and asks you if this is the first time you've murdered someone. It leaves you feeling a little overly sensitive."

"Kirby, I'm so sorry."

"Arthur said you were there when the boys found Lydia. Could we talk for a few minutes? Privately?"

He escorted her to the library. Kirby and Mithrell had filled every bookshelf available; no knick-knack room remained. He closed the door behind them and motioned her toward one of the two cushy chairs nestled into the window alcove, a perfect spot for reading, or like today, for having a private conversation.

"Kirby, you called the murdered girl Lydia. Did you know her?" Regan asked.

"Yes. Lydia did some gardening for us, well mostly for Mithrell — she's the family gardener. But I knew her, too, because of that. She said she attended Cabrillo College and had to work around her classes. Seventeen. She was so young. She seemed older," he searched for the precise word he wanted, couldn't find it and settled for, "she seemed wiser than seventeen." He shook his head, his eyes downcast.

Kirby straightened up suddenly and stared into Regan's eyes. He began asking questions in rapid succession. "Did you see her? Did you see her body? The Sheriff said she was naked and there was a pentagram," he winced as he said it. "Did you see any of that? Do you think they're just making that up? Would they do something like that?"

"I ... ah ... I ... I saw her face and her shoulders," Regan stammered. "I was trying hard not to look at her."

"Please," Kirby implored. "Try to remember. I know you can. I know how you can remember houses in fantastic detail. It must work like that for you with other — with other things. Please, try to remember what you saw."

Regan looked away from him. If only he knew how hard she had to work to keep from doing just that. Her visual memories always came back to her in complete, vivid snapshots. She could remember Lydia in her grave only too clearly, only too easily. It was a scene she didn't want to revisit.

"Please" he asked again, "I need to know."

Regan nodded silently. She closed her eyes and took a deep breath. She allowed herself to be in the Whitlaws' backyard again — and she allowed herself to look into the grave once more. The image of Lydia flooded back in such complete detail, it was as if she was truly reliving the horror of seeing the girl's body for the first time.

Her skin was discolored and blistery, wrinkled, and in the beginning stages of growing too big for Lydia's shrinking mass. At the hollow of the girl's neck, Regan could see the apex of a triangle. The sides of the triangle diverged symmetrically downward until they were covered by the dirt of her shallow grave. An arched line topped the point and curved outward and downward on each side of Lydia's body, until it too, was obscured by dirt.

Regan quickly shook her head and took a quavering sharp breath. The need to escape from Lydia's grave and return to July 5th and the solace of Kirby's library was overwhelming.

"What does a pentagram look like?" Regan was sure she

61

knew, but hoped she was mistaken.

Kirby produced paper and a pen and drew a five-sided star enclosed by a circle. He handed it to Regan.

"Could I have your pen?"

She took the pen and drew a slightly waved line across the pentagram, bisecting it unevenly so one point of the star and part of the circle was on one side of the line. Then she scribbled over the rest of the figure. She turned the paper so the star tip and smaller portion of the circle were at the top of the page from Kirby's perspective, and handed it back to him.

"The part above the line is what I saw." Regan touched her throat, felt the indentation at the base of her own neck and moved her finger down slightly. "The lines converged here," she said. "What I saw could have been the top of a star enclosed by a circle." She hesitated, watching him closely. "I'd guess she was cut, Kirby. I think the lines I saw were cut into her skin."

"A pentagram — one of our most sacred symbols," he almost moaned as he said it, "Such a horrible sacrilege. The Sheriff said she had a pentagram cut — carved was the word he used — into her torso, and that they found her clothing buried on our property. He said a neighbor saw a tall man wearing a cape lurking around the Whitlaws' house on the night of June twenty-first, which coincidentally, was the last day anyone seems to have seen Lydia.

"Well, isn't it as obvious to you as it seems to be to the Sheriff? I must have killed her in our backyard, stripped her dead body, carved a pentagram on her, put on my cape, buried her under the peach tree in the Whitlaws' backyard, and then buried her clothing in our yard as a keepsake. I'm a witch; a warlock is what they called me. Everyone knows that's what we do in our spare time," he ranted sarcastically. "Oh, and don't forget they think I did this on June twenty-first, the Summer Solstice, our witches' Sabbat." His voice rose to an almost hysterical pitch.

His emotional outburst passed, and he resumed softly, "We did have a celebration in the woods at our house. When it was over, I made love to my wife. That's really what witches do on Litha, our Sabbat."

"Surely your friends can confirm that, and Mithrell will …"

"If they believe we aren't all conspiring liars," Kirby interrupted.

Regan arranged to meet Dave for coffee and a quick afternoon snack at Rosie McCann's, a walkup pub on Pacific Avenue, the main shopping street in downtown Santa Cruz. As far as Regan was concerned, the venue's ceilings were too high and the layout too open to qualify as a real pub. But it was a short walk from Dave's base at the police station on Center Street, and since he often said he needed an infusion of Rosie McCann's cheddar-cheese potato skins at least twice a week, she suggested the pub as a meeting place to ask him some questions about Lydia's murder investigation.

Regan decided she could overlook the pub's lack of authenticity if she made her coffee Irish. She was giving it a little stir when Dave arrived. He simultaneously hailed her and caught the attention of the bartender with a little two-finger wave of his right hand, followed by a quick nod of his head and a raising of his eyebrows. To her it was the greeting of a familiar friend, to the bartender the signal of a regular placing his customary order.

Dave greeted Regan with, "Why aren't you asking Deputy Sheriff Burke your nosey little questions? He's in charge of the investigation, you know. You think you can buy me with some cheesy potato skins? Huh?"

"Hopefully."

"Sometimes I don't think you value me highly enough, Regan." His tone was cynical and just a bit offended, but their friendship was a long one and usually involved teasing banter. She recognized the setup and responded in kind.

"I value you; it's just that you owe me. I'm the one who got you involved in this whole thing. If I hadn't called you, you'd be stuck at the police station making nice with some lady with a missing cat. Admit it, you find this a lot more interesting, don't you?"

Dave's answer was a smirk.

Regan leaned forward, her lowered voice indicating she was serious now. "I knew the murder victim, Dave. She was a little girl who used to come by to listen to Alex's band. And your fellow law enforcement officers are hassling a client of mine — a nice man, incidentally, and I'm sure an innocent man — just because of some flimsy coincidences. I know you, Dave. I don't know how you manage to do it, but you seem to have a handle on pretty much everything related to crime in Santa Cruz County. I'm guessing your information-gathering tentacles reach into the Sheriff's Office, too. This one's personal. Tell me what's going on."

Dave's potato skins arrived, delivered as wordlessly as they had been ordered, and acknowledged similarly, with the raising of eyebrows.

"You mean Kirby Paisley, I assume?"

"Uh-huh. See, I told you you're resourceful."

"You've talked to him. What does he say we're doing to

65

ruin his life, especially since we haven't charged him with anything, at least not yet?" Dave had already fallen into a speech pattern Regan recognized well: he made himself a member of the investigating team, liberally sprinkling his conversation with "we" and "us".

"No, you haven't charged him with anything, as you said, *yet*, but he's had to consult an attorney and he's feeling beleaguered by the type of questions he's being asked. He said the Sheriff's Department decided since he was a Wiccan, he must be capable of ritualistic murder. They seem to put his religion under the same heading as satanic cults. And how did you know I talked to him? Is the Sheriff watching him?"

"Of course he's being observed — he's a person of interest — but I know you, Regan, and I know you're gonna stick your nose into this. Did your pal happen to mention why he was being questioned by the Sheriff? Did he tell you he was seen in the woods near where the body was found on the night of June twenty-first, the night we think the murder took place, and that the Vic's clothes were found buried in his backyard?"

"Yes, he said he was in the woods on June twenty-first. He has every right to be, you know; he owns those woods. He and his wife hosted a religious ceremony that night that took place in those woods. And he's got a three-acre unfenced backyard. If someone wanted to bury Lydia's clothing on his property, it's not like it would have been difficult to gain access to it.

"He has a dozen witnesses who will tell the Sheriff he spent most of the night with them, and his wife will vouch for him for the rest of the night."

"He has twelve people who say he was with them most of the night, all right. His coven."

"Do you hear how you sound?" Regan's voice went up a notch. "He's a white witch; he doesn't do evil things. A lot of Wiccans are pacifists. I know Kirby is. He's just not capable of murder; it would go against everything he believes in. If Lydia was killed by a satanic cult like you seem to think, Kirby wasn't involved."

"You finished sputtering yet?" Dave asked jovially, popping another potato skin into his mouth. "We didn't question him because of his beliefs. I know it may be hard for you to accept, but we can tell the difference between Wicca and devil worship as well as anyone else can. We don't think your friend's part of a satanic cult." Dave couldn't resist teasing, "Well, at least some of us don't," he grinned. "All that satanic ritual murder stuff is just a media thing anyway. There's never been a proven case of any murder being done by a satanic cult, but you'd never know that from reading those tabloids that pass for newspapers at the grocery store checkout, now would you? No, we wanted to talk to him for some other reasons."

"What kind of other reasons?"

"For starters, because he was seen alone in his car with the Vic, not just once and not just by one witness. Did he happen to mention he knew her?"

"Lydia helped his wife in her garden, so yes, he did say he knew her."

"Did he say if it was in the biblical sense?"

"What do you mean?"

"She was pregnant, Regan, just over three months worth.

We think that probably had more to do with her murder than the pentagram on her chest. We asked real nice, but your buddy didn't feel good about giving us a DNA sample, which could have ruled him out as the daddy after some testing. He wouldn't even let us figure out his blood type, which might have ruled him out even quicker. Instead of being cooperative, he threatened to lawyer up. Made us feel real bad, that did. Made us feel suspicious, too, like he might be trying to hide something.

"See, now I can tell from your expression, not to mention your very unusual silence, your pal, good old Kirby, didn't mention that part to you."

Dave rocked back in his chair and dropped the last potato skin into his mouth, satisfied from a gastronomic perspective and also for the unrest he had created in her mind. "My work here is done," he smiled.

Regan was caught by Dave's phrase: *Good old Kirby.* Good *old* Kirby. "Dave, I forgot to mention something to Deputy Sheriff Burke that Alex told me about Lydia. Alex said she told his friend Matt, the boy she'd had a crush on for years, that he'd missed his chance, that she'd met some old guy and was in love. How old do you think you'd have to be, to be considered old by a sixteen year old?"

"Everyone's old when you're sixteen. We'd probably seem old to a kid that age. But I'd guess probably over forty," Dave said. "How old's your pal, Kirby?"

"I think he's forty-two."

Dave didn't say a word. He just raised his eyebrows and nodded slightly. That said volumes.

10

"How do you feel about homemade biscotti with your coffee?" was how Mithrell began her phone call to Regan.

"Um, pretty good. Your biscotti?"

"That's right."

"Make that very good."

"Could you come by today, say between one and three?"

Regan checked her day-timer, even though she was certain her afternoon was free. Compulsive behavior, she told herself.

Tom was still trying to convince her to use a BlackBerry like he did, or get an iPhone, but she preferred the feel of a nice little book in a soft leather jacket to keep track of where she was supposed to be each day. There was something very satisfying about opening the book each morning, moving the attached little blue ribbon to a new date, and seeing what life might hold for her that day.

Today was Wednesday, usually a good day for spontaneity. Mondays and Tuesdays were frequently filled with handling details left over from weekend open houses and property showings. Offers were often presented and negotiated on those days. Potential clients she had met at open houses needed follow-up contact. Tuesdays also meant an office meeting and a tour to see the company's new listings.

Thursdays were Broker Tour days, when real estate agents drove around the county looking at properties other agents had for sale. She usually had to hold an open house for other realtors to come by her listings, or go from house to house to keep current on what else was on the market. Broker Tour was the way she kept track of pricing trends, potential properties to show buyer-clients, and what the competition was doing.

Fridays, Saturdays, and Sundays were prime showing and open house days. But Wednesdays were down days, day-off days, homemade biscotti days. Nevertheless, she checked.

"How about one-thirty?"

"I'm getting out my mixing bowl and turning on the oven. I shall expect you at one-thirty," Mithrell said.

🏠🏠🏠🏠🏠🏠🏠🏠🏠🏠🏠

Regan arrived at the Paisleys' home in the midst of one of the dense swirling fog days that July in La Selva Beach was noted for. The mist was advection fog, caused when moist ocean air was pulled over the cooler coastal waters. The fog coincided with days when temperatures in the inland valleys reached uncomfortable levels in the summer. During the day, the heat made the valley air expand. At night, the air cooled and contracted, pulling air from the coast and creating onshore breezes. That was what was happening today.

Inland temperatures were over one hundred degrees. If those temperatures held, the weekend would see an exodus of residents from Stockton, Lodi, and other sweltering areas escaping to cool coastal retreats. Some would come to Pajaro Dunes, an upscale gated community at the southernmost reach of Santa Cruz County, or for those escapees who chose to forgo gates, to Manressa Beach, La Selva Beach, Seascape, Rio Del Mar, and Seacliff.

The trees on the Paisley's property were luxuriating in the fog. Green lichens and mosses on the tan oak trees were plumped up to the consistency of thick green fur. The feathered branches of the coastal redwoods bobbed up and down to individual rhythms as they condensed moisture from the mist, and when the accumulated water became too heavy, cathartically released it to the ground.

As she drove up the Paisley's driveway, Regan noticed it felt different from the last time she'd been there. The apples were closer to being ready for eating. They were starting to turn from green to shades of red or yellow as they got ever closer to ripening and reaching their full sweetness and color, but the trees themselves didn't look very different from the last time she came up the driveway, hurrying to bring cookies and support to the Paisleys.

What was it? What was different? If anything, the apples' increasing plumpness and cheery coloration added warmth to the driveway — yet it felt unpleasantly cold and barren, even less alive and inviting than it had been the first time she showed them the property in February, when all the apple trees were devoid of leaves.

Today it seemed there were rough, disagreeable open spaces along the driveway — bald spots where other trees had stood. She parked, got out of her car, and hesitated, her back to the house, to look down the driveway. Yes, trees were definitely missing.

"You see four of our oaks are gone ... our sacred oaks." Mithrell had opened the front door so quietly, Regan hadn't heard her. Her voice and expression, usually somewhere between mischievous and seductive, was somber.

"We had to take them down because they were desecrated. Someone carved pentagrams and the word 'murderer' on them."

"Oh, Mithrell," Regan frowned, "that's awful. I'm so sorry. Who would do such a thing?"

"We don't know. Most of our neighbors have become kind, supportive friends. It's troublesome to think of one of them holding such hatred in secret, and yet, I find it even more troubling to think of a nefarious stranger on our property this near to our home."

Mithrell waved her hand in front of her face, as if deliberately trying to cast off her sad aura. She smiled at Regan, "Come in, come in." Her manner and words were light and affable, but Mithrell's voice betrayed her; it remained cheerless.

"I'm so glad you could come by on such short notice. I wanted to talk to you alone. It's related to the trees. Please promise me this conversation will be just between us — Kirby and Arthur are not to know about it, at least not yet. Kirby's at work, of course, and Arthur's playing at the Whitlaws. Joan has been absolutely wonderful about helping keep him insulated from," she faltered, "grownup troubles."

Mithrell's request seemed unusual for her. Regan would never have labeled Mithrell secretive; clandestine conversations were not part of her routine. She spoke her mind openly and decisively. But her change from forthrightness to imposed confidentiality might give Regan a perfect opportunity to ask Mithrell about Kirby's relationship with Lydia, something she had been trying to figure out how to do ever since Dave told her what Kirby hadn't.

Regan nodded, "If that's what you want, then I promise."

A faint aroma of anise and cinnamon hung in the kitchen where they settled in over coffee and still-warm biscotti. Both women had swirled a cookie in their coffee before Mithrell rose abruptly and hurried to the freezer. "I almost forgot the ice cream."

"Oh, no thank you. These are wonderful," Regan said, holding her partially eaten biscotti up so the missing bite was obvious. "I don't need ice cream, too."

"Need it or not, we have to finish it before Kirby comes home, or I'll be caught, and then he'll want some."

Regan's face held a puzzled look.

"He's a diabetic. I guess that never came up when we were looking for houses. He has to be very careful about his diet. Ice cream isn't a recommended indulgence, but it's one of the things he loves most in life," Mithrell said wistfully. "Before he was diagnosed, we each used to eat a big scoop of ice cream almost every night. Now he can't, and I don't. It would be cruel to eat ice cream in front of him."

Mithrell produced bowls and spoons, put the container on the table between them, and started to spoon out peach-colored ice cream, being careful to apportion the treat equally. "For the sake of his blood sugar, I promised to forgo ice cream when he does. But when he cheats, I cheat."

"So, is this payback-for-cheating ice cream?" Regan asked, before putting a spoonful in her mouth.

"It is." Mithrell closed her eyes in delight as she took her first bite. "I think he cheated on his way home from work two nights ago, although it's harder to be certain, now that Lydia doesn't keep me informed," she sighed.

"Lydia was his ice cream mistress. She used to tell me about their escapades while we worked in the garden. I don't know how she found out how he felt about ice cream, or that he wasn't supposed to have it, but she did. She said their first time was unplanned, just a sudden burst of uncontrolled passion, but after that they developed quite an elaborate cover for their ice cream trysts.

"Lydia would suggest we needed a plant or some particular garden implement, and Kirby would volunteer to drive her to the garden center to get it. They'd invariably come back empty-handed, saying the store didn't have what they were looking for, or the quality of the store's merchandise wasn't good. I knew better, of course.

"They hadn't gone within a mile of any garden store. Oh no," she laughed a hearty, mirthful laugh. "They'd drive all the way to Ocean Street in Santa Cruz, to Marianne's, and get lovely handmade ice cream instead.

"Some of the neighbors," Mithrell leaned forward conspiratorially, "*confided* in me that he must be having an affair with her. After all, they said, they'd seen them together, and both had giggled and scrunched down in the car to hide, and then acted very embarrassed about being caught." Her laugh was boisterous.

"Lydia and I had a signal, a wink made at the same time as a downturned mouth," Mithrell demonstrated. "I'd adjust dinner to compensate for his ice cream calories, but I never spoiled his fun. Secret indulgences every once in a while are what make life worthwhile, don't you think? Besides, I wanted that girl to eat. Good wholesome dairy cream is excellent for pregnant women, especially such young thin ones."

"Lydia was pregnant?" Regan asked guilelessly. She hoped to give Mithrell the impression she didn't know about Lydia's pregnancy. But with Mithrell, anything less than absolute forthrightness was useless; she had an uncanny knack for recognizing subterfuge.

Mithrell's answer to Regan's disingenuous question began as a pointed and knowing "Mmm," softened into a forgiving and joyous "Umm-yum" as Mithrell savored another spoonful of ice cream, and finally ended as a simple, "Umm-hum. I could tell the first time I met her, right after we moved here. She didn't even realize it herself until I got one of those pregnancy kits and made her take the test. I almost wished I hadn't forced her, because it disrupted her life so much — knowing, I mean.

"She'd been living at the church shelter near here, at John and Libby Simon's church. You may have seen him; he came to our housewarming party. He didn't like us at that point. I think he came to spy on us," she wrinkled her nose and chuckled. "I think he found the chance to see firsthand what wicked witches do at parties quite irresistible. Or he may have come to look for Lydia. She said he wasn't very happy when he found out she was working here. She said he ordered her not to have any further contact with us — one of his many orders, she said.

"Lydia disobeyed him. She continued helping me in the garden and slipping off with Kirby. We invited her to the party so she could receive compliments for the new garden; she had worked so hard she deserved part of the accolade. I think she may have lied to Reverend Simon and told him she had stopped coming here, because she hid when she saw him at the party. He only stayed a few minutes so you probably didn't meet him."

Regan remembered she not only met him, but that he left quite a vivid impression in her memory.

"Of course, he's changed his mind about us since then. We're almost friends now. He's quite a nice man, actually. He and his wife are very kind to runaways and kids having a hard time at home. Their church has a shelter on the property; he pretty much runs it himself. I don't know how he finds the time, given all his other responsibilities to his congregation.

"Lydia had been staying there, but they have very rigid house rules about personal conduct which they enforce rigorously. He's sometimes abrupt and unbending with the children who stay there, like he was with Lydia, but I don't believe it's because of a lack of compassion. Many of them need structure in their lives almost as much as they need love.

"Anyway, getting pregnant was definitely against the rules. He made her leave when they found out about her pregnancy.

"We offered to let her stay here, but she didn't want to.

She only stayed a couple of days. I gave her some money. I called it an advance on her salary so she wouldn't feel like she was accepting charity. I had her continue to help me in the garden, although after our party there wasn't much to do, and I made sure she was eating right and continuing to see her doctor."

"You're a good person, Mithrell."

"Someone needed to help her," she dismissed the compliment.

"What about the father of the baby? Why didn't he help her?"

"I'm not sure he even knew about her baby. At first I assumed the father was one of the boys at the church shelter who wasn't any more secure financially than she was, but she denied that. She said the father was older and established. When I asked her what he thought about his impending fatherhood, she didn't answer directly; she just said it was complicated. I read that as he was married. I can't even say for sure that she told him she was pregnant."

"Did she tell you who the father was?"

"No. She called him her teacher. She said he instructed her in the mysteries of life. He must have been someone she thought of as her guru or a spiritual guide," Mithrell shrugged. "That's all she said."

"I knew her — I knew Lydia, too," Regan said. "When she was younger, she used to follow my youngest son and his friends around like a little stray puppy dog. She was such a sweet, innocent little girl."

"Oh, Regan, I doubt you really knew her at all. Chronologically she may have been a girl, but she was hardly innocent. She had a very old soul. A very troubled old soul."

Regan and Mithrell finished their ice cream in silence, each thinking their own thoughts. Finally Mithrell spoke. "I asked you to come by today because we may need to sell our house. I wanted your opinion. I haven't discussed it with Kirby yet, or said anything to Arthur. I know neither of them will want to move — I don't either — but the trees. I'm frightened that the Sheriff won't find Lydia's killer and that Kirby ... we ... will always be suspect. If that happens, we can't stay here with someone despoiling our trees. That kind of hateful behavior could escalate. I feel our family could be in danger."

Regan wanted to reassure Mithrell, but couldn't. The same thought had occurred to her when Mithrell told her why they had taken down the oaks along the drive. "Before you make a decision like that, why don't you give the authorities a little more time? It may not look like they're doing much, but I know they are investigating. I have a friend with law enforcement connections who assures me they are. Let me tell him what you told me today, maybe ..."

"I've already told the Sheriff everything about Lydia that I told you today," Mithrell stopped her.

"Let me call my friend and be really annoying, so much so that he'll call someone else on the investigating team and annoy them," Regan jested. "If they didn't hear what you said before, they will when I finish with them. I promise.

"But if you really want to put this behind you, the best thing you can do is cooperate fully with the authorities. Jump through any hoops they hold out for you. If you don't like the questions they're asking, answer them anyway. Do whatever they ask," she alluded to the DNA test Kirby had refused. "If the Sheriff thinks Kirby is innocent, he'll direct the investigation to move along to other suspects; word will get out."

"The Sheriff has asked for a DNA sample. We don't see the need for one. We already know Kirby wasn't the father."

"We do," Regan added herself to the Paisley family opinion, "but Deputy Sheriff Burke doesn't. I know it's not supposed to work that way, but he and some of the other officers might think Kirby's refusing the DNA test implies guilt. Try to convince Kirby to consent to a test. It won't solve Lydia's murder, but it will rule him out as the father. I bet the results of that one test could go a long way toward refocusing the Sheriff's investigation, especially if they believe whoever murdered Lydia was the father of her child.

"Remember, Lydia was only sixteen when she got pregnant. Forget the question of the father being married — she was underage. If the father was more than about eighteen, he would be in big trouble and not just with his wife."

"I'll talk to him, but giving a DNA sample goes against our sense of privacy. I don't think he'll do it."

Mithrell pressed her fingertips together and touched them to her chin, considering. "Our religion demands that we do not lie and we do not kill. Kirby has given his word that he wasn't involved in Lydia's death. That should be enough for the authorities. I support his decision. I don't think he should give them a DNA sample, either."

Mithrell's obstinacy caused a momentary reaction in Regan not unlike the one it must have caused in Deputy Sheriff Burke. Would the Paisleys really be willing to give up their home and live in the shadow cast by suspicion if a simple DNA test could prove Kirby's innocence?

She knew they were highly principled people; that became apparent to her when she was working with them. But their attachment to the principle of privacy seemed overblown to her.

Could she be mistaken about them? Could the Paisleys have something to hide? Absolutely not, Regan decided. She was sure they had nothing to hide — well, almost sure.

Regan wanted to give Mithrell hope; that was why she suggested she could influence the investigation. And when she was explaining how she might do so, she believed her own words. But once she was alone in her car, she began to question whether she really could help the Paisleys. She was a persuasive negotiator and good at keeping all parties engaged, but having any effect in this situation was going to take much more than that.

Regan's expectation was that Mithrell would have new information which, when she relayed it to Deputy Sheriff Burke, would get him thinking outside the Kirby-did-it box. But it sounded like he had already been told the whole story. So much for that plan. No, a different way of looking at the facts they already had was what was going to be needed, a different logic.

That meant Tom. There was no one better at thinking logically or asking questions that she didn't think of — questions that could send her mind searching for overlooked details to weave together into new insights and interpretations. She smiled as she thought about how well they worked together. That wasn't the whole picture of course — after ten years of marriage, she found herself smiling when she thought of him for many other reasons as well.

Her mood brightened as she left the swirling fog of La Selva Beach behind. There was no summer fog in Bonny Doon, not at their house anyway. Tom enjoyed telling people they lived above the fog in a house very much like Hearst Castle in San Simeon. Both were at the same elevation, the same distance from the coast, and had commanding ocean views. The only real difference, he'd laugh, was about 250,000 acres, 27 fireplaces, 57,000 square feet of house, the furniture, the landscaping and hardscaping, the art, and unless their cats, Cinco and Harry, and a lonely wild turkey who had turned up recently counted, the zoo.

Living above the fog meant the air temperature was in the low-nineties in July and that she would be looking for cool already-cooked ingredients to use for dinner. She smiled in anticipation. The cold leftover chicken in the fridge would be delicious in one of her favorites: a cucumber and cilantro-laden chicken salad dressed in a Chinese style with sesame oil, rice vinegar, a dash of soy sauce, and chopped ginger and garlic.

Tom was working at his computer when Regan got home. "Is it time for happy hour yet?" she asked as she poked her head into the office.

"Absolutely. Red or white?"

"White."

He wandered into the kitchen a few minutes later with a bottle of chilled Christie Vineyard Chardonnay from Storrs, their favorite local winery. Regan had olive tapenade and crostini ready to accompany it. Tonight's dinner was going to be a breakneck flight from Italy to China.

"Fill your glass extra full," she said as Tom pulled the cork out of the bottle. "I need to pick your deft brain, and I don't want you to lose concentration while you're getting a refill."

"Sounds kind of painful," he frowned. "Am I going to survive this encounter without losing any of my brilliance?" His grimace was replaced by a grin.

Regan made the chicken salad and filled Tom in on the details of her conversation with Mithrell. "She said she told the Sheriff everything she told me. The sense I got from Dave, even with his teasing, is that the authorities really don't think Lydia's murder was ritualistic or satanic. They think she was murdered to keep her quiet about the identity of her baby's father, quite probably by the father himself. So, with that information, how do we figure out who really killed her?"

"Solving this mystery, this murder, is our responsibility because?" Tom left his question dangling.

"Because I'd like some justice for Lydia, and because as long as the crime remains unsolved, some nutcase can keep believing Kirby is responsible for her death. I agree with Mithrell: the Paisley's are at risk if some misguided vigilante feels the need to punish them for what he thinks they did to Lydia."

"You didn't exactly answer my question, so back to my point: why do we need to work on resolving this? Don't we let the Sheriff and his posse, whose day jobs are solving crimes, ride off and catch the bad guy?"

"In the Wild West, posses didn't figure out which man to chase; they went after whoever left the biggest cloud of dust. They chased their man, and when they caught him, sometimes they'd string him up on the spot without so much as a trial. I'm concerned if they believe Kirby is the murderer, the Sheriff's posse will spend more time trying to lynch him than they'll spend looking for another suspect," Regan said.

"I'd just like to be helpful, that's all. If we came up with some new theories I could mention to Dave, he might pass them along to Deputy Sheriff Burke and get him interested in looking at some other dust clouds."

Tom put his wine glass on the counter and formed an inclosing parenthesis around it with his hands. "OK. Let's see if this sounds right. If the Sheriff is suspicious of Kirby, it's not because he thinks Lydia was killed during some gruesome ceremony. He thinks Kirby is a suspect because he was seen alone with her. If that's correct, ice cream mistress aside, the first thing you have to do, if you really want to help his cause, is get Kirby to give up a DNA sample so he can be ruled out as the father."

"I've told Mithrell that. She's no more open to the idea than he is. She says it's a right-to-privacy issue."

"No wonder the Sheriff is still looking at him. I understand the whole idea of right to privacy and people being concerned about their DNA profile somehow getting into the hands of nefarious employers or insurance companies, but the Sheriff probably reads Kirby's reticence in the same way he might think about the accused citing his Fifth Amendment right at trial. It's his right, but it makes him look guilty. The Sheriff probably thinks Kirby is unwilling to be tested because the test results would incriminate him."

"That seems exactly right," Regan agreed. "Dave certainly implied that's how the authorities felt when Kirby refused the test, and I have to admit, the Paisley's insistence on noncooperation gives me the tiniest bit of pause."

Tom spooned tapenade onto a piece of crostini. "I've got another angle for you to consider, then. Do you think it's possible that Mithrell's setting you up? Maybe she thinks, even knows, Kirby was involved in Lydia's murder, and cooked up everything she told you today, expecting if she did it well enough that you'd believe her and plant a counter story in the law enforcement community via Dave."

"How would she know I could do that? She had her story ready before I mentioned my connections."

"That's easy. Don't you think Joan," he raised the pitch of his voice to imitate Mithrell, "'her absolutely wonderful friend,' has mentioned that the first law enforcement official on the scene, the person you told her to contact using the speed dial on your phone, was your friend Dave?" Tom asked rhetorically.

"I don't think Mithrell would ..." she didn't finish the sentence.

"But you can't rule it out, can you? She swore you to secrecy, too — always a good ploy when you don't want someone asking too many questions or asking them too directly. You've told me Mithrell is highly intelligent. She also may be pretty desperate right about now. She could lose her husband and her house — motivation for lying, I'd say.

"But if she's not lying, then I agree; she's probably not

overstating the danger to her family. If you think what Mithrell is telling you is true, I think you have to break your promise to her, go to Kirby, tell him what she told you, and get him to take that DNA test. You could let him know you think Mithrell's frightened. If he's innocent and loves his family, I bet he'll put his aversion to loss-of-privacy aside. The stakes are too high and the threat is too immediate to be that principled about an abstract fear."

Regan nodded her reluctant agreement. "I can do that I guess, even though I really don't want to break my promise. But what happens if Kirby is so stubborn he still refuses to give the DNA sample?"

Tom shrugged. "Then you back off," he said as he prepared another crostini. "You will have tried your best to help them. That's really all you can do." The savory went into his mouth.

Regan suggested they have dinner on the patio. They carried their plates, silverware, and wine glasses outside. By the time Regan returned with the salad, Tom had formulated another plan of attack.

"Something else occurred to me," he said. "Let's assume Mithrell is telling you the absolute truth without any manipulative embellishment. Her tale about Kirby sneaking out for ice cream makes him sound like a big goofy kid, doesn't it?" he snickered.

"That fits much better with the Kirby I've seen than Kirby as a murderer does."

"How does Kirby as a philanderer fit? Do you see him cheating?" He held up his hand indicating a stop. "Back up a bit. You told me he is very rational. Do you see him as a cheater who would be willing to break his marriage vows impulsively, quickly, without giving it much thought, without considering the possible consequences of his actions, maybe without even struggling to resist being tempted?"

"I don't see him cheating on Mithrell under any circumstances. They have an amazing relationship — kind of like us," she smiled.

"If that's the case, even if Kirby was susceptible to seduction, don't you think it would have taken him some time to give in to temptation?"

"I assume you're not speaking from experience here?" she raised her eyebrows, teasing.

He kidded back, "Dozens of women throw themselves at me every day. You know that, sweetheart." He closed his eyes and sighed. "My heart is yours alone; I resist them all."

"Excellent plan. See that you keep doing so."

Tom chuckled. "Back to considering a cheating Kirby here. If you had to choose, how would you classify him: impulsive player if asked, or devoted husband who might eventually give in to a relentless pursuer?"

"If he got involved with Lydia, I think it would have taken him a while."

"Then, as the Rolling Stones so eloquently put it, *Time, It's on My Side*, well, on his side. The timeline is wrong. Lydia must have gotten pregnant very close to when she first met Kirby."

"That's right," Regan perked up, "Mithrell said she knew Lydia was pregnant the first time she met her."

"So, Lydia was probably pregnant by the time she met Kirby Paisley. And even if Mithrell is taking too much credit for her perceptive observations, it sounds like the latest that Lydia got pregnant was right after meeting him. That's seems too fast for Kirby to be the father. He and Lydia would have needed to act on love, or at least lust, almost at first sight, for her to get pregnant by him so quickly. Is he that impulsive?"

"I'd say yes to passionate, but not a chance to impulsive. In fact, the way I'd describe Kirby's personality style would be kind of like his ice cream outings: impassioned, but carefully planned and executed."

"Then, if you don't want to tell Kirby about your conversation with Mithrell and her worries about their family's safety, or if Kirby refuses the DNA test, maybe you could start by trying to convince Deputy Sheriff Burke that Kirby wouldn't have become a player essentially overnight."

"That sounds pretty impossible. Don't most guys have fantasies about young women throwing themselves at them? Wouldn't most men believe Kirby would jump at the chance if Lydia offered herself to him?"

"Most men might have fantasies all right, but most guys, deep down, know what they'd do if a sixteen-year-old came on to them."

"What would they do?"

"Be flattered, maybe very flattered, and as soon as they got over being shocked and feeling a little guilty without knowing why, run like crazy," he laughed. "Talk to Dave. Ask him some questions. My bet is he'll agree it's more likely the father is someone Lydia knew for a while, not Kirby. Ask if the Sheriff is considering other men that Lydia spent time with — men who were in her life before Kirby met her."

"Would that include men like the Reverend Mr. Simon?" Regan asked. "She spent time with him. He fits, doesn't he? Lydia supposedly described her baby's father as her teacher of what mattered in life, or in the mysteries of life, I don't remember exactly, but Mithrell read that as a guru or spiritual advisor. Couldn't that description have included her minister, too?"

"Maybe." Tom rolled the idea around for a few seconds. "Yes, I could see him as a possible suspect. He's older and established. Married. The pentagram thing seems like a potential tie-in as well."

"How do you figure that?"

"Let's assume the killer hoped Lydia's body wouldn't be found any time soon, given where he buried her, you know, in ground that had been so recently and thoroughly sifted for bones. But if I was the killer, I'd like the idea of some added insurance, just in case she was found before becoming only skeletal remains.

"What better way, I might think, to misdirect suspicion than to bury her clothing in a Wiccan's backyard and carve a symbol like that on her, especially if I wasn't too concerned about the vast difference between the Wicca religion and devil worship?"

"And who might be less likely to appreciate the difference than someone who showed up at Mithrell and Kirby's housewarming party, spitting venom at me for introducing *them* into the neighborhood?" Regan asked. "Is that one of the questions you think I should ask Dave?"

"It seems like a good question to ask, doesn't it?" Tom replied.

"You know what else I'd do if I was the murderer and wanted to keep interest pointed elsewhere?" Regan asked rhetorically. "I'd walk over to the Paisleys and carve 'murderer' and that same pentagram symbol I left on Lydia's body on a few of their trees. Since I lived in the neighborhood, I could say I was out for a nice summer evening stroll if I happened to run into anyone I knew."

Tom considered and nodded. "You could run that idea by Dave, too," he said. "Then the last thing you could do to help prompt him is find out what kind of relationship the preacher had with Lydia. All anyone has to work with right now is some very secondhand information from Mithrell, who could hardly be considered a neutral observer. Unfortunately, I don't have a suggestion for how you could do that. It's not like you can just ask Reverend Simon."

Regan smiled a very knowing little smile. "Not directly or in so many words maybe, but I might be able to find out a lot by asking in a roundabout way." She skewered a piece of chicken with her fork. "You know how, when you're looking for listings, you send out letters to homeowners?"

"Yes," he nodded.

"You know how you get better results by asking people if they know of anyone interested in selling, rather than by asking them directly if they want to sell?"

"I know the theory," he said.

"It's not a theory. It's a proven fact." She pointed the impaled chicken at Tom to emphasize her statement. "Sometimes you get straighter answers when you ask a question indirectly, or when you ask someone else the question. I've got a plan, a nice little plan that might work in the same way." She smiled a satisfied smile and then put the forkful of chicken into her mouth.

Regan became a stalker. She drove down Alta Mar Vista until she found John and Libby Simon's church, parked her car nearby, and shadowed kids as they got off the school bus and walked the rest of the way home from summer school. After two days of observing, she had narrowed her field of interest to two girls and one boy who looked like they were about the same age as Lydia and who walked to the shelter every day when they got off the bus.

She printed a dozen flyers with a large picture of Alex's band in one of their most recognizable publicity poses, one that had the band member's names under each of them. The shot had been in local papers from the mainstream *Santa Cruz Sentinel, Scotts Valley Banner,* and *Mid-County Post* to the entertainment weeklies like *Good Times* and *Metro Santa Cruz*. Regan counted on her son being well known enough locally in the under-twenty demographic to entice her game.

The next day she parked her car near a telephone pole which the teenagers would pass on their way from the bus to the shelter behind the church. As soon as she spotted her quarry, she got out of her car with flyers in hand, opened her trunk, and rummaged through her tool box for a small hammer and some nails, went to the telephone pole, and began tacking up one of the posters. She overacted enough through all of this to be confident they would notice her.

"What did you lose? Your dog?" It was the boy who

asked.

Regan did her best startled impression and dropped the flyers she was holding. Her three targets quickly chased down the errant papers and brought them to her.

"Thanks so much. My son Alex says I'm such a klutz," she laughed.

One of the girls was studying her captured flyer. "You're Alex Martin's mother?" Her tone fell somewhere between excited and reverential.

"I am," Regan beamed and offered her hand to the girl. "Regan McHenry," she said.

The girl looked slightly confused.

"I kept my own name; Martin is Alex's dad's name."

The girl's confusion disappeared. "Oh yeah, my friend Seth's mom did that, too. He's Ambert but she's Mrs. Hobart."

The boy looked at one of his retrieved posters. "Dude, I saw them at the Catalyst. They're awesome. They want to do a concert for Lydia?"

Stalked and captured.

"Lydia was a longtime friend of the band. They want to do a memorial concert for her when they get back from tour. They asked me to try to find a good venue around here since ... well ... near where ..." Regan let the impressed girl finish for her.

"Near where they found her body," she murmured. "That's a good idea."

"Did you know Lydia?" Regan asked without aiming her question at any one of them in particular.

"Yeah, she lived where we do for a while. She moved out

a few months ago, though.'"

"We were BFF," the girl who had been quiet until then said in a soft voice, and after a quick glance at Regan added, "best friends forever."

"Living with friends — that sounds awesome," Regan said, attempting to phrase her response in acceptable teenage vernacular. "But you said she left? Why'd she do that?"

"I don't know," the boy said. "I think she just wanted a change of scene."

The BFF dropped her head to intently stare at her feet. It didn't take Regan's trained eye to interpret her body language. The girl knew Lydia hadn't moved on for a change of scene.

"I told you I'm Regan, but I didn't catch your name."

"Shiloh," the girl said in an even softer voice.

"Shiloh, the guys in the band knew Lydia, and I'm sure they will have some personal things to say about her, but you probably knew her much better than they did, since you two were such good friends. I bet you have some really special stories about her you could tell. It would help make the concert for Lydia so much better if you were willing to do that."

"I'd like to help, but I wouldn't want to get up in front of people."

"No, that's not what I meant. Maybe we could talk about Lydia for a bit, and I could tell the band what you'd want them to share at the concert. Suppose we go to Palapas Restaurant? It's close by. We can have snacks and I can take some notes."

"Great, I could use a snack," the boy said.

"Umm, I had in mind just Shiloh and me, this time. It might be easier to remember special times … just one on one."

Shiloh smiled shyly and nodded her head. "I think you're right."

In another minute, the girl was in the car alone with Regan. Shiloh seemed like a child who wasn't used to much attention. Regan marveled at how easy it would be for an adult predator to manipulate the teenager just by making her feel singular and special. Her maternal instincts overwhelmed her.

"It's OK this time, Shiloh, but you really shouldn't go off with strangers like you just did with me," she said as they pulled away from the curb.

"You're not a cop are you? Reverend Simon didn't send you to test me, did he?" The girl seemed genuinely panicked by either possibility.

"Nope. I'm who I said I was: Alex's mom. I knew Lydia. She used to come to our house to hang out while the band practiced. I liked her," Regan explained.

The girl took in a deep breath, and then sighed an enormous sigh, clearly relieved.

"Would Reverend Simon be upset if you talked to the police?"

"He probably would be. He's been upset about *everything* I do since what happened to Lydia. He won't even let me babysit anymore, not even for people who live nearby like the Whitlaws or the Forellis. The fathers always drive me home after dark, too, so it's not like I'm alone outside at night."

"How often did Lydia go out alone at night?" Regan tried

to keep her question open-ended and casual, but it didn't work. Shiloh's eyes darted around anxiously and she said nothing. They pulled into the restaurant parking lot and stopped near the sign that said "Palapas Restaurant y Cantina." *Too fast,* Regan chided herself. *Don't push her or you won't get anything.* She backed off.

"I'm hungrier than I thought. No little snack for me. They make great fish tacos here; that's what I'm going to get. How about you?"

Regan didn't ask any more questions as they ate and Shiloh reminisced about herself and her friendship with Lydia. They had known one another for a couple of years, a lifetime to two sixteen-year-olds. Shiloh lost both her parents and an older brother in a car accident when she was fourteen. Her family had attended Reverend Simon's church. He and his wife had come forward after the accident and offered to be foster parents for her when they discovered she didn't have any close surviving relatives like grandparents, aunts, or uncles. She had spent the last two-and-a-half years under Reverend and Mrs. Simon's official care.

The Simons began caring for other teens soon after Shiloh became their ward, and eventually got their congregation to sponsor a shelter to handle more kids. She was the one who told Lydia about the shelter. Lydia was a voluntary resident, a sheltered runaway, not a ward of the court like Shiloh. Shiloh officially lived in the Simons' house, not the shelter, even though she spent most of the day at the shelter after school.

Shiloh was expected to stay with the Simons. Lydia's tenure was much more open — she might move on at any time, even go back to the streets if she chose to do so.

"But she stayed, you said, for more than eight months, right?" Regan asked.

"She liked it there."

"Because she had friends like you?"

Shiloh chewed slowly, considering. "Yeah ... that's part of it."

"What other reasons did she have for staying?" Regan asked casually.

"She liked Reverend Simon. My dad's dead. I can't ever have him back, and that makes me really sad, but Lydia ... well, Lydia never had a dad. Not really. Do you know what I mean? I think the main reason she stayed is because Reverend Simon was kind of like a dad to her. I mean he tries to be like that to all of us, he's really nice and everything, but he was extra nice to Lydia. He was always hugging her and saying she was smart, and good, and could do anything she wanted if she tried. He spent extra time with her after the rest of us finished our homework. Stuff like that."

Shiloh grew pensive, drank some Coke, put the glass down, picked it up again, and took another sip, put it down again.

Regan almost said, "But Lydia wasn't living at the shelter before she was murdered." She caught herself in time. That statement would have been a giveaway that she knew more than she should have. "Then what happened, Shiloh?"

"Lydia was a really good person. I want people to know that. She was so happy about ... ah ... about everything. She'd want people to know someone loved her, you know, like adult love, not just like friends love each other or parents love their kids, but I can't think how to say it that it doesn't come out wrong."

"Why don't you tell me about it, and then we can figure out the right way to say it together?"

"OK." The girl looked directly at Regan with a big smile on her face — a first.

"Lydia was in love. She said he was wonderful. She said he was gorgeous. And ... I think she said he was important or established, something like that, but I can't remember exactly — it was so long ago," she shrugged.

"But she definitely said he was gorgeous. I remember that 'cause she laughed about it. She said he was kind of old, but that he was tall and dark and gorgeous."

Shiloh paused to lick a bit of dribbled sauce off her lips and looked around. Satisfied that they had privacy, even in such a public place, she lowered her voice and went on. "She got pregnant. She was really excited about it, really happy."

"Was her gorgeous boyfriend excited, too?"

"Ah, I don't know. I know she didn't tell him right away. I think she wanted to be sure she really was pregnant — sometimes women lose babies, don't they?"

"You mean have a miscarriage?"

"Yeah, probably. Or the other thing, you know, they have to get rid of them. I think she wanted to be sure that didn't happen. But she was getting ready to tell him. She said he'd want to marry her. She started reading *Modern Bride*," Shiloh scoffed. "I told her I thought that was so funny since she'd been so Goth just a few months before, and now she was going all traditional. She told me her boyfriend didn't like her looking Goth; that's why she gave it up, and she said she'd have to look right once they were married because of his career, so she might as well start by picking out a proper wedding dress. I think she wanted to look sophisticated or something."

Shiloh smiled broadly. "Lydia said she wanted a big wedding and that she wanted me to be her maid of honor. I started helping her plan her wedding. My dress was going to be midnight blue, almost black, with a band of really soft white bunny fur at the top." Shiloh drew her hand across her neck from shoulder to shoulder, indicating an off-shoulder design for her gown.

"That sounds very elegant," Regan smiled. "It sounds like a winter dress. Was Lydia planning a winter wedding?" Regan asked.

"Yeah. She said they'd probably wait until after the baby was born to get married so she could wear any kind of dress she wanted. They couldn't do it right away, anyway, because people couldn't know they were together yet."

"Did Lydia say why that was?"

"No. She just said some things would have to be taken care of before they could get married."

Shiloh's tone turned darker, "Then Reverend Simon found out about the baby. I don't know how he knew, but he was really angry. He told her to get out. He didn't tell the rest of us why he made her leave, but I knew. He said we couldn't see her or talk to her anymore. I didn't disobey. I just heard she was at the witches' place for a while.

"Then no one saw her anymore. I figured that was good. I figured she told her boyfriend about the baby and they got married and she went off to live with him."

"Happily ever after?"

"Kind of ... yeah. But I guess someone killed her before she could be happy."

Regan reached across the table and put her hand on the girl's hand. "That's the part about Lydia the band will want to talk about at her concert."

Shiloh nodded silently.

"Her boyfriend must have loved her very much. He'll want to come to the memorial concert, don't you think? Do you have any idea how I could contact him? Did she tell you her boyfriend's name or what he did for a living?" Regan asked.

"No. She almost did a couple of times, but she always said she'd better not yet. And I think she liked being mysterious."

"How did she see him? Did he ever come by to pick her up, anything like that?"

"She must have worked for him or she saw him at school. I think that's how they hooked up. I'm not sure. She snuck out a few times, too. She slipped out and he picked her up."

"Did you see his car?"

"I'm not very good at cars," the corners of her mouth turned up slightly, "unless they're Mini Coopers. I like those cars a lot. It wasn't a car anyway. It was something big like an SUV or a van, something like that."

"Do you remember what color it was?"

"I couldn't tell; it was always dark when she met him. But it must have been a light color because it was easy to see at night."

Regan's last question was a wild guess. "Kind of like the van Reverend and Mrs. Simon drive?" she asked.

"Yeah, kind of like that," Shiloh said.

"Dave, you have to get the Sheriff to look into the relationship between Lydia and Reverend Simon." Regan had been so eager to tell him what she'd discovered, she hadn't even bothered with "Hello Dave" when she burst into his small cubbyhole-of-an-office at the Police Department.

"You've been playing detective again, haven't you? Remember the trouble you got into last time you tried that?" he warned with a groan. "Sit." Dave motioned to the one other chair in the room.

Regan pulled the chair closer to his desk as she sat down. She leaned forward eagerly, "Come on, Dave, this is good stuff."

"OK. What about their relationship?"

"I talked to Lydia's best friend, a girl named Shiloh, who lived at the shelter. She said the Reverend Simon had a special soft spot for Lydia. He gave her lots of hugs and even private lessons to encourage her."

"How'd you get the girl to talk to you? Deputy Sheriff Burke tried, but all the kids at the shelter were pretty tight-lipped with him."

"Inside connections with a hot rock band and fish tacos. Works every time. Oh, but Deputy Sheriff Burke shouldn't take the kids' reticence personally. Reverend Simon has them scared of the authorities. Seems he runs a very tight operation there.

"Let me tell you what else she said. Lydia was in love with Mr. Gorgeous, a tall, dark, older guy; an important older guy is what she told Shiloh."

"Is Mr. Gorgeous your name for him?"

"No. That's what Shiloh said Lydia called him. Well, gorgeous anyway. The mister is my invention.

"Shiloh said Lydia cleaned up her act, changed the way she dressed, and lost the Goth look she liked, all to better fit into Mr. Gorgeous' idea of what a wife should be. I don't think Kirby would have been bothered by her style. Mithrell wears some unusual outfits and I've never heard him complain.

"More importantly, Shiloh said Lydia met Mr. Gorgeous months ago. That makes it too long ago for Kirby to be the father. Lydia didn't even meet the Paisleys until right about the time she got pregnant."

"Point for Mr. Paisley," Dave said.

"Point against Mr. Paisley," Regan corrected, "as the father, I mean. There's more. Shiloh knew Lydia was pregnant, but the father didn't. She told Shiloh some story about waiting to be sure the pregnancy took before she talked to the father. Shiloh also seemed to imply that sometimes pregnancies got terminated for reasons other than miscarriage. What I wondered was if she was waiting past her first trimester to let him know she was pregnant. That way, if he wasn't as excited about her pregnancy as Shiloh says Lydia was, there'd be less of a chance he could pressure her to get an abortion.

"According to Shiloh, Lydia was just about to share the good news when the Reverend Mr. Simon found out about the pregnancy and threw her out. I think she may have told him he was about to be a daddy and that's why he made her leave. Evidently he booted her before any of the kids were aware of Lydia's pregnancy, except Shiloh, of course.

"He may have thought Lydia would leave the area, but she didn't. Mithrell tried to take her in, gave her money, and helped her out. In any case, he told all the kids they were not to have any contact with Lydia from that point on. What I wonder is, was he afraid Lydia would tell the other kids she was pregnant by their benefactor?

"Here's what I think is the best part. Shiloh never saw Mr. Gorgeous, but she said Lydia snuck out a couple of times to meet him. He picked her up in a big light-colored vehicle like the van Reverend Simon drives.

"That's at least two points against Kirby and, let's see, one, two, three, four points for Reverend Simon." Regan was triumphant.

"How do you figure that?"

"Don't you see, Dave?" Regan asked, wildly frustrated with him. She ran through her high points again, assuming he must have misunderstood something. "Lydia thought she was preparing for the role of a conservative wife, like a minister's maybe. She probably did get around to telling Reverend Simon she was pregnant; that's how he found out she was. But rather than being thrilled to discover he had impregnated a minor, some might say a child, without his wife's approval, and was about to be outed as an adulterer, he booted Lydia and tried to stop her from telling anyone else she was pregnant. Then when she didn't leave the area, he probably decided it was still too risky to leave her alone.

"He may have thought he'd broken so many Commandments already, breaking one more wouldn't make his place in hell any worse, so he decided to kill her to keep her quiet. He made her body look like she had been killed during a satanic ritual in case she was found. That way, he could completely cover his tracks, implicate someone else, and potentially even get the Paisleys, people he didn't approve of, in trouble. Throw in a few vandalized oak trees for good measure and it all works perfectly, doesn't it?"

"No," Dave said incredulously, "it doesn't. Would you call John Simon tall or gorgeous? We got that tall, dark, and gorgeous phrase from your little witch friend, too, so I'm thinking it's likely that the Vic did describe her boyfriend that way. Tall, dark, and gorgeous? Come on, Regan, open your big brown eyes," Dave rebuked.

Regan had a flash of memory. John Simon's angrily contorted face looked up at her at Kirby and Mithrell's housewarming party. He was beet red and she could see his dark hair combed over from the side of his head to camouflage a receding hairline. Dave was right. Reverend Simon hardly fit her definition of tall or gorgeous.

"Maybe Lydia saw him differently. My eyes are hazel, by the way, not brown, and good looks are subjective," she said. "I remember having a huge crush on my high school history teacher, Mr. Dunning, when I was sixteen. I thought he was terribly handsome. It wasn't until he announced his engagement to Miss Hall, the civics teacher, and I felt personally betrayed, that I took another long and more realistic look at him."

"And?"

"He came up to my eyebrows, had thinning blond hair on an overly large head, and had, not the intense blue eyes I hoped to gaze into during a long meaningful relationship, but pale, watery blue eyes with no remarkable fire in them."

"I rest my case," Dave smirked.

"You'd be wrong to do that," she giggled. "While I no longer considered him handsome in a classic sense, I still found him to be charismatic, romantic, and sensitive. He was still an attractive enough man, as far as I was concerned, that I was left heartbroken by his engagement. My point is that the cliché about beauty being in the eye of the beholder might have been in play with Lydia."

Dave shook his head and exhaled loudly for dramatic effect. "Oh brother." Then an impish look appeared on his face. "Hey, Regan, doesn't your pal Kirby drive a white van? A Honda, isn't it?"

In her mind, Regan could see the Paisleys emerging from just such a van. She could also see Dave's small smile had grown into a big taunting grin.

"And Kirby Paisley really is tall, and dark, and not a bad looking guy, isn't he?

"Don't beat yourself up, Regan. You did get some new information for us. We didn't push very hard to interview the kids at the shelter; now we'll want to do a follow-up with them. And I should let you know something I didn't tell you before. You know how much I like to tease you — well, I left out that we weren't only looking at Paisley.

"We were looking at the minister, too. We've been looking at a lot of people. The Vic seemed to have a connection with pretty much everyone in the area, what with her doing odd jobs, babysitting, living at the shelter and all." He snorted, "Ironically, about the only ones who weren't connected to her were the Whitlaws, that is unless you count being buried in their backyard as a connection. They didn't even know her.

"Anyway, I kind of let you think we were only interested in your pal because it was so much fun to do," he laughed. "It really got you going. But Regan, I also left out that the minister wasn't any more willing to part with his DNA than your old buddy Kirby was; only he didn't cite privacy as the reason. He said it was somehow inconsistent with his religious beliefs. I don't know how you figure that one.

"And yes, I'll give you your other point, too. Sixteen-year-old girls can have some pretty strange ideas of what gorgeous means, especially Goth girls who like to look like death themselves."

"I've got a new property to post to the multiple listing service. Lunch in forty-five?" Tom asked as they returned to an empty office following their Tuesday morning tour of company listings.

"That sounds about right. I've got some paperwork that should take about that long."

"Your place or mine?" he quizzed with his hand on his office door.

"Come get me when you're ready," she said as she continued down the hall to her office.

Regan's paperwork was a final check of documents for an escrow that was closing Thursday morning. Everything was done. The escrow company was just waiting for the loan to fund so they could disperse money and send the deed to the Recorder's office for stamping. By noon on Thursday, Regan's clients would own a new home, and she and the seller's agent, the sellers, and the escrow company would all be collecting paychecks.

She was engrossed in sorting papers into tidy stacks according to their categories: listing contract, advertising, offer contract, disclosures, and conversation notes. She didn't notice her office door open, but she certainly heard it slam closed. She looked up into the face of the Reverend John Simon, looking as red and angry as he looked when she first saw him at Mithrell and Kirby's housewarming party more than seven weeks before.

"You stupid meddling devil," he spit out each adjective. "Do you have any idea what you've done?"

Regan didn't know who he was or why he seemed angry the first time she met him. She was at a disadvantage that day and had needed Rick Whitlaw to defend her. Today, she knew the man and thought it possible he was a murderer and the person responsible for the vandalism to Mithrell and Kirby's trees. She didn't need anyone's help answering him this time.

"Besides introducing Wiccans into your neighborhood?" Regan didn't raise her voice in response, but her contempt and seething anger matched his. "Wasn't that your complaint the first time we met?"

Tom appeared in the hallway outside her glass door, drawn by Reverend Simon's shouting. His hand was on the knob when Regan caught his eye and signaled him to wait with a slight raise of her hand and an almost imperceptible shake of her head. She didn't really feel threatened by the man confronting her. If he was a murderer, he preferred dark seclusion and unsuspecting girls for victims, not daylight, witnesses, and women prepared to fight back. Still it was reassuring to know all 6-feet-3-inches of Tom was ready to protect her if she needed help.

"Why don't you tell me what you think I've done; then I'll

tell you what I think you've done, and we'll see who the real devil in the room is," Regan challenged.

"You've hurt my kids is what you've done." He put his hands on her desk and leaned over so his face was close to hers. His voice wasn't as loud as it had been, but his face continued to contort with rage. "Some of them are runaways. They begin to trust me and my wife only when they start believing we aren't going to turn them in. We've been making good progress with most of the kids in our charge — at least we were 'til you sicced the Sheriff's Department on 'em. With Lydia getting murdered, those guys were all over us. You have no idea what it took for me to keep them away from my kids. Any trust we built up is gone, thanks to you. Now we have to start over."

His outburst ended, he seemed suddenly tired, overcome. His face returned to a more normal shade.

Regan's anger hadn't lessened at all. "Shouldn't you have been thinking about — your kids," she put as much sarcasm into the phrase as she could, "before you did what you did to Lydia?"

He opened his mouth, but didn't speak. It almost seemed to Regan that he collapsed as he dropped into one of the seats opposite her desk. His face reddened again "Yes, I should have," he said meekly. He lowered his eyes, seemingly no longer able to meet her gaze.

Regan had been prepared for a show of outrage. His words and demeanor caught her completely off guard.

Tom couldn't take standing in the hall any longer. He opened the door and burst into a completely silent room. "What's going on here?" he asked.

"Reverend Simon and I were having a talk about the nature of evil. Please join us," Regan said.

Tom sat next to Reverend Simon and swiveled his chair to face the minister. He rocked it back slightly. "Sounds fascinating. Don't let me interrupt you."

Regan decided to take full advantage of Reverend Simon's momentary vulnerability. "You were the father of her unborn child, weren't you?" she pressed.

The Reverend looked up quickly. The look of shock that appeared on his face seemed genuine. "What kind of man do you think I am?" His breath came in pants, gasps. "I could never ... as God is my witness ... of course I'm not the father. But I did do something horrible to her. She told me she was pregnant. When she needed my help the most, I told her I was disappointed in her and would never forgive her. And then I turned her out. If I hadn't done that, she might still be alive."

It was Regan's turn to be uncertain. "But Shiloh said you were always hugging Lydia and spent time alone with her," Regan protested.

"Lydia needed more attention than the other kids — more love. And she was so bright. I thought if I could get her to apply herself in school, there'd be no stopping her."

"Shiloh called Mithrell and Kirby witches. Did she learn that from you?"

"Probably," he said simply. "They are witches." He narrowed his eyes again, some of his anger returning. "But we can't ask her about where she came up with that label because she's run away. She left a note saying she felt responsible for getting her friends rousted, and that she was sorry for breaking the house rules about talking to strangers. Then she ran away. My wife and I are worried sick about what might happen to her.

"If anything bad *does* happen to her, I'll blame you for that, Mrs. McHenry." He said her name with total contempt.

Regan was truly shaken. The only question she could add was a feeble, "What about the oak trees at the Paisleys?"

"What about 'em?"

"Someone's been vandalizing them, carving pentagrams and the word 'murderer' on them."

"You think I had something to do with that?" He was on his feet again, his voice rising.

"You, or maybe some of the kids at the shelter," she replied.

"You are one sick, twisted woman," he said softly. He shook his head, squared his shoulders, and slammed the door on his way out.

Tom could see tears in his wife's eyes, not falling but glistening. "Sweetheart, I know how his accusations make you feel. Granted, that scene seemed genuine, but he's been trained to move a whole congregation every Sunday. Grain of salt, please. He could have just performed one spectacular act, figuring you'd run right to Deputy Sheriff Burke and tell him all about how innocent he must be."

🏠🏠🏠🏠🏠🏠🏠🏠🏠🏠🏠

Regan had learned to sleep at night regardless of how concerned she was about a complication in a real estate transaction. Her mind might take pieces of worries and mix them up to create fantastical dreams, with her concerns becoming bizarre story lines, but she still managed to sleep fairly well.

After Reverend Simon finished with her, she didn't sleep well at all. Every time she was about to free herself from the minister's scathing rhetoric enough that real sleep might come, her imagination took over and she would see Shiloh going down a dark secluded path.

The girl would hear something behind her — a broken twig or dislodged pebble, perhaps — then turn and see a tall dark man. Regan startled awake before he caught up with the girl. In that way she could keep Shiloh safe from harm — but she got no rest.

Between anxious awakenings that caused her heart to beat wildly, Regan tried to formulate a plan of action. Shiloh might have told some of the kids at the shelter where she planned to go. It would help if she could talk to some of them, but that option was no longer available. They'd be forewarned about her, probably even afraid of her, and that was assuming she could somehow speak to them without bringing Reverend Simon or his wife out in full attack mode.

She resolved to try the next best thing to direct contact, backing off one level to interview the families that Shiloh babysat for: the Forellis and the Whitlaws. She knew how to reach the Whitlaws. She needed an address and phone number for the Forellis.

She got out of bed to check the phone book in her office. If the Forellis weren't listed, she would use her computer and a realtor-friendly title company website to look up their property address. The online information would include when they purchased their house, the purchase price or at least how much it was worth at the time of their last refinance, how many rooms it had, and the square footage. She wasn't interested in that information, but it would also have their address and possibly their phone number.

Regan started with the phone book though, because it was easier. "Flores," "Forbes," "Fordeau," her fingers toured America's melting pot of names that suggested ancestors from Mexico, England, and France, before arriving in Italy. "Forelli." She was in luck. They were some of the few people who still allowed their full names to be published and who included their address. "Forelli, James and Amy, 3175 Alta Mar Vista, 555-1010." She made a note of their information and returned to bed — and, she hoped, to sleep.

Even though Regan had laid out her plan, she discovered she still couldn't relax enough for sleep to claim her. Every time she drifted toward a restful state, she again saw a young woman in danger. But now the face of the girl and the course the girl took were different. Now the girl was Lydia. And rather than looking over her shoulder in fear and hurrying away from the tall dark man, she smiled when she saw him and turned to run toward him, her arms outstretched.

Regan forced herself awake again before the girl reached the man. Her heart was beating harder than it had when she felt Shiloh's fear. She had to rouse herself before Lydia reached the man, before she would have to watch Lydia die, before Lydia would change from the happy smiling girl Regan saw in her imagination, to the cold and lifeless creature she saw in a shallow grave in the Whitlaws' backyard.

The clock next to her bed read 4:15. Regan gave up and got up again to go make a cup of tea. It might as well be strong and black, she decided: Irish Breakfast tea. She knew she wasn't going back to sleep.

Regan debated calling the Forelli's to ask if she could come by, rather than just arriving on their doorstep. She practiced various ways of introducing herself and requesting a chance to meet and ask some questions about Shiloh — she didn't even know the girl's last name. None of her trial introductions gave her a plausible reason for questioning them. She wasn't with the Sheriff's Department. She wasn't a private investigator. She wasn't even someone the girl's guardians, the Simons, would want asking questions about Shiloh. Regan decided to go unannounced and ring their doorbell. Better to just turn up and see what happened.

A tan young woman dressed in shorts and a tee shirt answered the door.

"How are you, Amy?" Regan asked.

"I'm … fine," the woman answered carefully. The hesitation in her voice revealed she was struggling to recall where or if she had ever met Regan.

A little boy, whom she guessed was somewhere between three and four years old, appeared behind his mother and put his arms around one of her legs. From his secure position, he smiled up at Regan.

"And you must be, let's see, Grimbly Didillebee? Is that your name?"

"No," he giggled, "that's silly."

"What is your name, then?" she asked.

He looked up at his mother, crossed one foot in front of the other and squirmed.

"It's OK. You can tell the lady your name," Amy said.

"I'm Christopher," he ducked his head as he said his name.

"Christopher, it's nice to meet you. My name is Regan." Then to his mother she added, "Regan McHenry."

Amy had an open countenance. Regan made a split-second decision: the best way to question her was to be absolutely straightforward. "I'm hoping you can help me. I'm trying to find Shiloh. She told me she babysat for you sometimes. She's run away, and I'm hoping she may have said something to you about having family or friends somewhere that she might go see. Anything you can remember might help me find her."

"I can't think of anything," Amy said. "I don't think she has any family. That's really all I know about her. We didn't really spend any time together, just polite 'hellos' when she got here, and a quick update about Christopher's schedule, that sort of thing. My husband always drove her home at night and paid her.

"Shiloh didn't even tell me about what happened to her family; her friend Lydia did. She used to sit for us sometimes, too, before …" Amy looked at her son, who had let go of her leg and was now crawling around on the floor, busily playing with a truck. He didn't seem to be paying attention to their conversation, but Amy stuck to euphemisms anyway. "Before she went away," she said.

"Sorry. I can't think of anything useful. Shiloh's a nice girl. I hope you find her."

"So do I. Thanks for trying to help." Regan turned and took a step from the front door. "Oh, just one other question," she said, turning back abruptly. "What color hair does your husband have?"

Amy looked puzzled. "I almost don't remember, he's had his head shaved for so long. But blond, I guess. Why?"

"Oh, it's funny how things jog your mind. Talking about babysitters reminded me that I used to babysit for a Jimmy Forelli when I was a kid," Regan lied. "I thought he might be your husband, but he had red hair, the kind that stays intensely red until it turns grey, so I guess not."

14

Regan's next stop was the Whitlaw house. She couldn't see it from where her car was parked in front of the Forelli's because of the slight bend in the road, but it had to be no more than six or seven houses away on the other side of the street. She decided to walk.

When the house came into view, she could see a small figure sitting on a low rock wall at the front of the property. The wall was new; it hadn't been there the day she talked to Joan about listing the house. That day. The Whitlaws had decided that selling their house now was out of the question, given the recent notoriety of the property. Joan must have put them back in fix-up mode.

As she got closer, she recognized the figure on the wall was Richard Whitlaw. His head was bowed down. He must be reading or concentrating on a hand-held electronic toy, she thought. As she got closer she saw he was holding neither a book nor a Game Boy; he was just sitting on the wall staring down.

Regan dropped down next to him. "What are you doing, Richard?" she asked.

"Nothing."

"Nothing, huh. Well, it's nice out here today. I guess it's a good day for doing nothing."

He shrugged. "I'd rather be at the beach."

"Everybody too busy to take you?" she sympathized.

"No. Dad took Raymond. Just not me. He wanted special time with him." Richard looked up into Regan's face. "He likes him better than he likes me."

She had grown up an only child and never had to deal with the awful possibility that her parents favored a sibling. She had two sons and was certain she couldn't pick a favorite, but she knew that wasn't the way it worked in all families. Sometimes one child became the family goat, the one who could never quite measure up to parental ideals. She didn't deny Richard his feelings with a patronizing, "I'm sure that's not true," comment.

"Mmm," was all she said. "Well, I'm glad you're here. I have some important questions to ask you and your mom. Can we go inside and do that?"

He was off the wall and rushing through the front door before she could take two steps. "Mom, Regan's here, she wants to talk to *both* of us about some important stuff. Mom?"

Joan emerged from somewhere at the back of the house. "Regan, I thought you knew we decided not to sell right now?"

"Yes, Rick told me. I agree the timing isn't good. I'm not here as your real estate agent. I wanted to ask you, and Richard," she emphasized his name, "a quick couple of questions about Shiloh. She told me she's a friend of yours,

Richard, who stays with you and Raymond sometimes when your mom and dad go out."

"Yes," he said, "she's really nice."

"I think so, too," Regan said. "Shiloh went away for a while and forgot to tell anyone where she was going. Some of her friends, like me, are kind of worried because we don't know where she went or when she'll be back. When she was here with you, did she ever tell you about any friends she might like to go see?"

"She said her best friend is Lydia," Richard offered after a moment's deliberation.

Regan saw Joan wince at the mention of the dead girl's name. "I'm afraid we can't offer much more than that," she said.

The front door opened and Raymond Whitlaw made one of his usual, boisterous running entrances. "Look, Mommy, a sand dollar without any broken pieces. I found it."

Rick followed close behind. "Regan. I didn't notice your car out front."

She noted there wasn't any warmth in his voice when he spoke to her. There never was. "I parked down the road a ways and walked. My car's in front of the Forelli's house."

"They thinking of selling?" he asked.

Joan answered for her. "Regan is asking people who knew Shiloh, if they know where she might be?"

"Shiloh?"

"You remember, the girl who baby ... the girl who is a special friend of the boys."

"Oh, of course, Shiloh."

"Regan says Shiloh's gone away without letting anyone

know where she went. She was wondering if she ever mentioned any friends she might visit to any of us."

Rick pondered, "No. I talked to her a little bit a few times when I took her home, but she never mentioned anyone. You know where you might ask about her though, my campaign office. She was taking a poly-sci class and asked me a lot of questions about my campaign, so I suggested she might check in there. I thought maybe she could earn some extra credit for her class and stuff a few envelops for me," he smiled broadly.

"I told Regan, Lydia is Shiloh's best friend," Richard tugged at his father's arm.

Rick's smile faded.

Raymond was standing on tiptoes at the kitchen sink, where he had turned on the faucet and was holding his sand dollar under the running water. He turned off the water, dropped to full feet, and turned toward the assembled group, "I don't want Shiloh to be a dead Indian like Lydia. I like Shiloh."

Out of the mouths of babes. That thought had crossed Regan's mind and probably had crossed Joan's and Rick's, too, but none of them dared say it out loud.

"I don't like Lydia," Raymond added, shaking water off his shell.

"That's because she wasn't really an indigenous person and you didn't get to help Professor Smithers dig in the backyard anymore, isn't that right?" Joan used current politically-correct language as she tried to apply a logical adult reason to her child's pronouncement.

"No. I don't like her 'cause she doesn't talk to me. She only talks to Daddy," he replied.

119

"I don't think so, sport. I never met Lydia," Rick said.

"Uh-huh," the boy insisted.

"No. I didn't know her," he asserted decisively.

"Uh-huh," Raymond squeaked.

Joan's cheeks flushed, "Gentlemen, please, let's not get into a peevish 'yes you did', 'no you didn't' argument."

Rick took Regan's elbow and began gently but firmly escorting her to the front door. "We don't have anything else to add, I'm afraid. I'll walk you toward your car.

"Sorry for my son's behavior," he said as soon as he closed the front door behind them.

Regan bristled. Rick Whitlaw had just broken several of the tenants of civil conduct which she held dear. First, he had decided the conversation had concluded without asking her if that was the case — that seemed to be the way he almost always ended with her, and she was getting very tired of it. This time he had even physically given her "the bum's rush," as her Irish grandmother would have called it.

More importantly, he had embarrassed his wife in front of her. That kind of behavior made her uncomfortable and must have made his wife so unnerved that she blushed. It wasn't the first time he had done that, either.

Now he was apologizing for his child's behavior without acknowledging his own faults. To her way of thinking, his actions were a clear sign of disrespect for his wife and sons, the very people he should be most careful to cherish and defend.

She never liked the man. Today's behavior compounded her dislike. She wouldn't have worked with him if he had been referred to her on his own, but she had immediately liked Joan and the kids so much, she made an exception. She was annoyed at herself for that, even more than she was at him. *Cardinal rule, Regan,* she reminded herself: *always go with your gut.*

In the next instant her gut took a major hit. Parked in the Whitlaws' driveway, obviously newly returned from a trip to the beach, was a large white vehicle. A van.

"Rick," she said, forcing casualness into her tone, "I thought you drove a Prius?" She deemed the evenness she managed to inject into her voice one of her better performances.

He hadn't felt embarrassed by his insensitive behavior, but being caught in flagrant ownership of what might be construed as a non-environmentally-responsible vehicle mortified him.

"Ah, well, yes," he stumbled. "This is really Joan's van. Sometimes she needs it for, well, soccer mom kinds of things. And sometimes when she goes off consulting, she has to carry a bunch of visual aids. Stuff like that. Sometimes we need to carry more gear than the Prius holds. As these things go, it does get good mileage. It's a Toyota Sienna rated at 23 miles per gallon. It usually just stays in the garage. We normally drive the Prius, but it's being serviced."

Regan was almost having too much fun enjoying Rick's self-inflicted discomfort to concentrate on anything except his feeble rationalization. Almost. But as he fumbled, she did take a fresh look at him. If one got past his smug self-centered rudeness, he was a nice looking man, a very nice looking man. One might even say he was tall, dark, and gorgeous.

121

Regan's final stop for the day was at the "Richard Whitlaw for State Assembly" headquarters. It was a small storefront in unincorporated Aptos on a section of frontage road between the Rio Del Mar and State Park Drive exits of the freeway. It wasn't a glamorous location, although it was visible from the freeway and plastered with large signs which were useful for increasing name recognition among passersby. Regan sold residential real estate: single-family homes, condos and townhouses, small multi-residential units like duplexes, and occasionally land. She knew almost nothing about commercial property and even less about commercial rentals, but guessing as best she could, she figured Rick's headquarters was affordable.

There was also bus service that ran by the property, helpful for student and older volunteers who might not have cars, and for other volunteers who wanted to drive less to lower their carbon footprint. Rick was not running on the Green Party ticket, but he did have his green environmental views and promises as a prominent plank of his personal platform. Even his signs were lettered in green, a subliminal reminder of his stance, she assumed.

A young man and a gray-haired woman were manning the phones when she went inside. Another young man greeted her from behind a desk that faced the door.

"Congratulations. You've made the right choice for State Assembly," he said affably. "How about a bumper sticker for your car?"

"I'm going to pass on that, but I will take a button and a brochure about the candidate's positions," she replied.

"I guess that means it's too soon to ask you to donate or to volunteer," he laughed. "Nate Adams." He held out both his hands: the right hand ready for a handshake and the left holding the materials she requested.

"You're good, Nate. Did Rick tell you how to greet visitors or are you self-taught?"

"Mostly picked it up on my own. My dad's in local politics in the valley where I grew up. I worked for him. And I have big plans for the future. Remember my name," he laughed again.

She shook his hand and took the button and brochure. "Regan McHenry." She put the pin on her lapel. "I'm going to read every word before I vote, just so you know.

"Do you go to UCSC or Cabrillo College?" she asked the young man.

"UCSC. Most of us who volunteer here do, although we do get volunteers from Cabrillo College and a few Grey Bears, too."

The older woman finished her call in time to hear Nate's comment, waved her hand with her wrist still on her desk and said, "He means me."

"Do you get any high-schoolers?"

"A couple."

"Anyone named Shiloh?"

"Yeah. Shiloh worked here for a while. She was doing a paper for a class. I was surprised, though, she came in a few times after her paper was finished, so she may have really cared about the election. But she stopped coming in, oh, probably by the middle of June. I guess a summer commitment is asking a lot of someone her age."

Regan had spent her drive to campaign headquarters replaying the argument between Rick Whitlaw and his son about whether or not Rick knew Lydia. She was still hoping to gather information that might lead to Shiloh's whereabouts, but she had devised another line of inquiry she wanted to pursue even more.

Regan segued smoothly to the question she really wanted to ask, "What about her friend, Lydia? Did she volunteer with the campaign?"

"I don't know any Lydias," Nate shook his head.

"I do," the older woman said. "She didn't ever volunteer here though, Nate. She just came in a couple of times to meet Shiloh. I don't think you were ever here when she came by, but Shiloh introduced her to me. She came in once by herself to see if the candidate was here, too."

"Was he?" Regan's heart raced as she waited for the woman to recall the event.

"I believe he was. That's right, he took her into his office," she pointed to a closed door off to her left. "I was sure he'd convince her to start volunteering after that private meeting, but I never saw her again.

"Of course, I blame Raymond for that. Raymond is the candidate's youngest. Rick used to bring him here sometimes. He was here one day when Lydia came to meet Shiloh. Raymond's a cutey but such a handful," she rolled her eyes.

"Shiloh got stuck watching him sometimes, when the candidate was here and she was volunteering. She didn't seem to mind. I think she babysat for the Whitlaws and already knew him, but her friend didn't take to him one bit. I remember her asking Shiloh how she could stand watching such a wild one as Raymond. My guess is Lydia figured out she'd get stuck minding Raymond, too, if she volunteered, so even after her talk with the candidate, she decided not to risk it," she chuckled.

"Now of course, with the election getting closer, this outfit is getting more serious about everything. No more kids allowed." She exhaled dramatically, "Thank goodness."

Regan thought her day had been an eventful one, but this time, before she called Dave and risked his ridicule, she wanted to tell Tom what she'd uncovered and see if he agreed there was a new prime suspect in Lydia's murder.

She had just turned right off Mission Street onto High Street at the Vintage Faith Church when her cell phone rang. She had never downloaded a favorite song, so it rang with the slightly jangling noise of a landline.

Regan didn't give out her cell phone number without a fight. It wasn't on her business card, and when clients asked for it, she always said it was better for them to leave a message on her work number, which she checked frequently.

There were several reasons for this. She lived in Bonny Doon, an area rumored to be a huge granite mountain that had moved over the eons from somewhere near Arizona as the tectonic plates along the eastern Pacific Rim slipped and groaned to their current positions. Supposedly Bonny Doon would leave California and slide up to Washington State, given another couple hundred million years. She wasn't sure about any of that, but she was sure cell phones didn't work well in Bonny Doon because of the granite underlayment, the hills, and possibly because the locals, "Dooners" as they called themselves, fought like crazy to keep cell towers from being built on their mountain. It was just good business practice to have clients reach her via a reliable landline. At least that's what she told them.

The real reasons she didn't like to give out her number were threefold. The first had to do with her fear of driving while under the influence of a cell phone. The second, a more important reason, had to do with invasion of privacy. Her privacy. The last client who wheedled her number out of her, called twenty-two times in one day, she kept a tally, with questions that didn't need answering or even a response.

The most important reason she didn't give out her number though, was because she didn't always trust herself to answer questions well off the top of her head. She learned in business that a well-reasoned answer beat a hurried response every time. She confirmed that lesson when her sons hit adolescence, and the answer to a "Ma, can I … ?" question had the potential to be life-changing.

Her reticence to share her cell number meant a ringing cell phone had to be Tom, one of her sons, or a good friend — the only people who currently had her number. A ringing cell phone meant she wanted to talk to the caller. She pulled into an open curbside space on High Street to see which of the special people in her life was on the line.

Tom greeted her with, "I'm at the bar at O'Mei, waiting for you. I'm in serious need of Gan Pung Chicken. Don't you hear Mushu Vegetarian calling your name?"

"Is *that* what I've been hearing? I'm glad to know it's not another problem with my car's transmission. I can be there in less than five minutes."

"I'll order a glass of Bonny Doon Pacific Rim Riesling for you."

Tom was seated at a table for two by the time Regan arrived. He was good to his word: her Riesling was waiting.

"How was your day?" she asked as she slid into the chair across from him.

"It was fine. Good. But you don't really want to hear about my day, do you? I watched you spot me and hurry to our table. I like it that you're happy to see me ..."

"Which I always am," she interjected.

"I believe you. But your smile was about more than delight to see my blue eyes. The canary feathers are still sticking out of your mouth, my dear little kitty. How was *your* day?"

"I think I know who killed Lydia."

"Besides Kirby or the minister?"

"Yes, besides Kirby or the minister."

The server arrived at that moment to take their order. Regan was near the point of spontaneous combustion by the time he finished.

The moment the server departed, she leaned forward and breathlessly whispered, "Rick Whitlaw."

"Why him?"

"He has the right look and he's the right age. I admit the minister was a stretch for ever meeting anyone's definition of tall, dark, and gorgeous, but Rick isn't. He really is an attractive man. I just didn't notice that until today because I always found him so annoying I never really paid attention to how he looked."

"Should I be jealous?"

"Stop it. I just told you he's annoying and a murderer. Shiloh told me Lydia snuck out at night to meet a man in a light colored van. It turns out Rick has a white Toyota Sienna, a van. He said it was Joan's, but he drives it, too. He took it to the beach today. The thing is, he's very sensitive about even having a vehicle like that. He said it mostly sits in the garage.

"People wouldn't associate him with a van. When they think of him, they think of an environmentally-conscious candidate who is truly a proponent of green living. They'd think Prius — and that's what he so publicly drives. If he took the van out at night, no one would ever think it was him, especially if he wore a hat or something."

"Or something," Tom teased.

"You're getting as bad as Dave," she feigned offense. "Here's the good part. Dave said all the neighbors seemed to know Lydia, all *except* the Whitlaws. Rick Whitlaw certainly says he never met her."

"Then why do you think he killed her, a girl he never met?" Tom asked matter-of-factly.

"Shiloh, Lydia's friend from the shelter, babysat for the Whitlaws. I went by today to ask the family if Shiloh ever mentioned where she might go if she left the shelter. You won't believe what their youngest son said."

Regan didn't give Tom time to even get out, "What?"

"He said he hoped Shiloh wouldn't end up like Lydia. He said he didn't want that to happen because he liked Shiloh. Then he said he didn't like Lydia. His mother offered an explanation for why that was, but he said he didn't like Lydia because she didn't talk to him. He said … and I'm quoting, 'she only talks to daddy.'

"Rick got into an argument with his son about that. He still insisted he didn't know Lydia."

"What makes you think he did? Couldn't his son have been mistaken? He's little, isn't he … four or five?"

"He's six, and he's one sharp little boy. I'd take his word over his father's any day. But I don't have to. I also stopped by Rick's campaign headquarters and talked to some of his supporters who volunteer there. One of them, an older woman, a completely lucid older woman," she added with a preemptive bob of her head, "remembered Lydia coming in one day and getting hustled off to Rick's office for a private meeting.

"He's been lying about not knowing Lydia. Why would he do that if he didn't have something to hide?"

"He's kind of overboard about looking just right for his campaign, isn't he?" Tom asked. "Didn't you tell me he was more concerned about negative publicity than finding a dead girl in his backyard? Maybe, since he wasn't involved in the girl's death, and didn't know anything about who killed her, he decided to simplify his life by just saying he didn't know her, period."

"That's lying to the authorities," Regan said.

"Yes, it is. But you have to think about it from his perspective. Lydia was only sixteen when she got pregnant. Jailbait. Suppose you were having trouble deciding which candidate was going to get your vote and you got a personal letter the day before the election saying something like 'my opponent was a *dear friend* of a sixteen-year old murder victim, whom authorities suspect was killed before she could name the father of her unborn child.'

"No real charges would have to be made — just a suggestion, an implied ..." Tom waggled his head and shrugged, "whatever. Yes, it's lying to the authorities, but it sure would be easy to rationalize, especially if he's one of those moral authorities who think it's OK for him to play by a different set of rules from everybody else."

"That would be him, all right." Regan suddenly thought of something else she deemed incriminating. "But ... you know," she said slowly in the midst of her latest realization, "I always thought it odd that Rick wanted to move so soon after buying his house. He said it was because of the possible difficulties he might have getting building permits after his backyard became an Ohlone burial site — well, that and some politically-correct twaddle about not wanting to offend any Native American voters. That story always seemed like nonsense to me.

"I bet Lydia told him she was pregnant, and he was already planning to murder her and bury her in his backyard by the time of the Paisley's housewarming party. Doesn't that make sense? He was familiar with the area since he lived there, and he knew he could arrange for privacy. Joan travels a lot. He could have planned the murder around one of her trips, and farmed-out his kids for an overnighter with some of their friends on the night he planned to do the deed.

"The lots are big in his neighborhood, so he probably could have been confident no one would happen on him while he killed and then buried Lydia."

"If he killed the girl, why would he bury her in a shallow grave in his own backyard? Wouldn't he want to dispose of her body somewhere else to distance himself from her murder?" Tom challenged.

"He probably felt his own property was a safe place to bury her. Remember, the UCSC anthropologist and his crew of students had literally just finished sifting every square inch of his property looking for Native American remains. He might have thought the authorities wouldn't look for another body on his property after that. And if he buried her nearby, he could control the burial site."

"If he wanted to oversee the body, then why sell the house?"

"He'd have to get Joan away from there eventually. If they didn't move, she would have started agitating for the second story addition they planned. He could have postponed the inevitable for a while by saying he was too busy campaigning to think about home improvements, but I know Joan. By next year, she would have been in full remodel mode.

"Besides, who would want to live with the body of a girl you murdered in such close proximity? Ick!" Regan shuddered. "I'd want to sell, even if it cost me some serious money, just to be away from the scene of my crime."

Tom shook his head, "Your reasoning is contradictory. If he was as calculating and callous as you make him out to be, and he wanted to control her burial site, he should have kept the house and built a deck or poured a patio over her before Joan could remodel."

Regan made a face, "Tom, what a ghoulish idea."

"It is," he raised his eyebrows, "but think about it. Would you take a chance turning a property over to someone else with a freshly buried body in the backyard? No, I don't think Rick Whitlaw would sell to get away from his crime — at least not so soon and without some additional camouflage. Too risky.

"Also, why would he bury her in his backyard and then bury her clothing on the Paisley's property?" Tom asked.

Regan sipped her wine as she considered Tom's question. She was only stumped for a moment. "New plan — I've got a better idea. Maybe he intended to bury her on Kirby and Mithrell's land — that way he could sell and get away from his crime without having to worry about her being found in his backyard — but maybe he had to change his plans because of the Paisley's holiday celebration in the woods.

"It would take a while to bury Lydia's body. He'd have to dig her grave, put her in it, cover her up, and then maybe scatter leaves and small branches over the grave so it wouldn't be obvious. He'd probably need some light so he could see what he was doing. He might have been afraid one of the people at Kirby and Mithrell's event would stumble across him doing all that, so he had to do the next best thing he could think of on short notice: he'd have to bury her at home."

"Then why bury her clothes at the Paisleys?"

Regan's response was a crisp, "To throw off the investigation. If the authorities found Lydia's clothing on the Paisley's parcel, they'd look for her body there, too, wouldn't they? They'd have three acres to search. It would take time and keep the focus away from him while Lydia decomposed, or he sold his house, or poured that patio over her, like you suggested."

Tom was dubious, "And those same celebrants wouldn't have noticed him burying her clothing because … ?"

"Because burying clothing could be done quickly and with little fuss. I don't think he took much time with her clothing since it was found right away."

"You're right, and that presents another question: if he was trying to keep Lydia's burial secret, why not bury her in her clothing? Why call attention to her death at all? Wasn't it already assumed by most people that she had moved away? She probably wouldn't have been missed."

"Maybe Rick didn't think about that." Regan inhaled sharply as she had another idea. She poured it out rapidly. "He could have been deliberately trying to point the investigation toward Kirby. That's probably why he cut that symbol into her chest, too. Maybe he intended to frame Kirby. What a monster!"

"I see gaping holes in your theories, sweetheart. You haven't convinced me he's the killer."

"What am I missing?"

"Let's begin with something simple: after Lydia's body was found, the sheriff's deputy in charge would have asked Rick Whitlaw where he was at the time of her murder. You could run it by Dave, but I think that's kind of a routine procedure. The deputy must have been satisfied with Whitlaw's answer since he didn't investigate him any further."

Regan was about to take another sip of her wine, but stopped with the glass half way to her mouth. "Oh — that's right," she said uncertainly.

"What? I just hit a nerve, didn't I?" Tom asked.

"You sure did. Rick might have the perfect alibi. I don't know how I could have forgotten. He said the family was going to be out of town in late June, which is when the Coroner thinks Lydia was killed. They were all in Atlanta for Joan's family's reunion. I even asked Joan about the trip, but it completely slipped my mind."

"There you go," Tom toasted her before taking a drink of his Sapporo.

Regan called Dave when they got home after dinner. Tom still thought she should tell him she caught Rick in a lie, and she wanted to ask how certain the authorities were about when Lydia died. But she didn't start her conversation with Dave by announcing she knew the true identity of Lydia's murderer. Tom had cured her of that delusion. She wasn't in the mood to give Dave any more ammunition about her jumping to the wrong conclusions.

Dave listened to her recitation of her day's investigation. She thought she might have heard a mild expletive from his end of the phone line when she told him about the volunteer remembering Rick and Lydia's private meeting, but she wasn't sure, and he usually didn't swear.

"I'll pass that tidbit along. Thanks, Regan. You notice I haven't once made a snide remark about how wild your mood swings and murder theories have become? I bet you're pretty proud of me for that?"

"I'm sure you're proud enough of that for both of us," she quipped. She wasn't about to let him deliver a zinger in the form of a backhanded compliment without calling him on it.

"I have a question for you," she said.

"Quid-pro-quo time?"

"Sort of."

"Shoot."

"How did the Coroner determine when Lydia died?"

"He didn't precisely. It's pretty amazing how much info can be picked up off a body, but it's still not like crime scene investigation shows on TV, especially if a Vic's been undergrounded for a while. The Coroner came up with a range of days for time of death. Deputy Sheriff Burke was the one who picked the likely day."

"How did the Deputy Sheriff do that?"

"Same way you tried to play detective today: asked a lot of people a lot of questions."

"But you," this time it was Regan who put Dave in the midst of the investigation, "came up with a specific date. How could the date be so precise?"

"Nice try, Regan, but you can't make the Vic get herself killed when your latest suspect didn't have an alibi. She was seen in downtown Santa Cruz by a neighbor who knew her pretty well on the afternoon of June twenty-first. It was assumed she was buried and probably killed at night, or the murder and burial might have been noticed by someone. Under cover of darkness and all that. That let Deputy Sheriff Burke establish the earliest she could have been killed was the night of the twenty-first. You with me so far?" he asked.

"I'm keeping up very well, thank you," Regan replied.

"Good for you. Next, a neighbor reported seeing a man in a cape go into the Whitlaws' yard on the twenty-first."

"Ah, the handy mysterious man in the cape," Regan said.

"Don't be sarcastic, Regan. It makes you look defensive. No one saw Lydia after the twenty-first. You still follow?"

"Yes. But that logic still doesn't make it completely certain she was killed on the twenty-first, does it?"

"Nothing in life is a hundred percent, Regan. But the Coroner puts T.O.D., that's time of death for you novices, no later than the twenty-third, and no one saw her after the twenty-first. So the twenty-first looks about right. Bet your guy was away that day, wasn't he? Far away?"

"Atlanta."

"Far enough. It's not like he could have killed the Vic after his evening stroll but before his morning jog. Not from Atlanta. Anybody see him in Atlanta, Regan?"

"Just a whole family reunion's worth of witnesses."

Dave chuckled, "And her theory crashes and burns. You know who I still like the best?"

"Who?"

"The preacher. Both the Wiccan's wife and the preacher's wife say their hubbies were with them all night on the twenty-first. Some of the guys say they would take the word of a preacher's wife over a pagan's word, but I believe your little gal, what's her name? It's unusual and I keep forgetting it."

"Mithrell."

"Mithrell," he said with a melodious lilt in his voice. "She has very believable eyes. You might even say they're bewitching," Dave bellowed.

Regan wasn't amused, but then Dave often found his witticisms more amusing than she did.

"Are you serious about Reverend Simon or was that all part of the setup for your little joke?"

"No, I meant it. Deputy Sheriff Burke says there's something about him — that he's a man with a guilty conscience."

"Reverend Simon says he feels bad about making Lydia leave the shelter when he found out she was pregnant."

"Yeah, that's what he says. And your buddy says he and Lydia liked to sneak out for ice cream sodas."

"Cones," Regan corrected.

"OK, cones. Those two must have had a contest to see who could come up with the schmaltziest story. If you want to play detective, why don't you analyze their stories and figure out what each of them isn't telling us. In the meantime, I'm gonna humor you. I'll pass along your discovery about Rick Whitlaw, even though I think it isn't really new information."

"How can you be so dismissive? He lied to the Sheriff," Regan protested.

"He wants to be in politics, right?"

"Yes. He's held some local offices and now he's running for State Assembly."

"Then that makes him a politician, right? So we already know he tells lies," Dave laughed.

16

Regan had an early morning on Tuesday. She was showing property to a very serious-minded young man, Scott Fogerty. He was a recent transfer to the area who had been referred to her by a client. She'd found a small jewel for him, or at least a house in Capitola's Jewel Box, an area so-named because the streets bore gem names like Emerald, Topaz, Jade, Garnet, Ruby, and Opal.

The owners of the house on Garnet were divorcing, but both were living in the house, sleeping in separate bedrooms until it sold. Regan had spoken to the husband the day before and arranged the showing. When she knocked on the front door he answered promptly and greeted Scott and her with a smile and a friendly manner.

"Come on in and have a look around. I'll be watching TV, but you won't be disturbing me if you have any questions because I won't be watching anything in particular; I'll just be trying to stay out of your way," he said genially.

All the doors except one were open and they viewed the small home quickly. They hadn't found the bathroom during their brief tour and assumed it was behind the one closed door.

"Is someone in there?" Regan interrupted the TV watcher and asked before opening the door. "I thought I heard water running."

"No, no, that's just the washing machine. It's a laundry and bath combination. I'm here all alone, except for you two, that is," he said through a big friendly grin.

Regan opened the door full width and motioned for Scott to go in first. He took one step forward and stopped abruptly. Regan peered over his shoulder at a full frontal view of a recently showered woman, her arm still raised from opening the shower curtain.

Regan could hear the helpful husband's riotous laughter behind her — no wonder they were divorcing, she thought.

The woman flinched, and seemed about to try a mortified too-late cover-up move, until she realized her grinning soon-to-be-ex had set her up and was thoroughly enjoying her embarrassment. She instantly regained her composure and then some.

"Take a good look, mister," she said to Scott. "These boobs are back on the market." She stepped out of the shower and turned around slowly and deliberately as she reached for a towel. "Rear view's not bad either," she said, looking over her shoulder seductively, "and everything you see is in like-new condition; he never did use any of it for more than a minute at a time."

Regan and her client didn't say anything to one another until they were back in her car. "Scott, I missed the washer and dryer," she laughed mischievously. "Did you happen to notice them?"

"No, ma'am. I didn't notice much about the house either, but I sure liked the special amenities." He smiled silently all the way back to her office, but decided he didn't want to buy the house.

As soon as Scott left, Regan checked her messages. There was one from Mithrell. "Happy news, Regan. We don't need to sell our house after all."

She immediately picked up the phone and returned Mithrell's call, curious to know what had happened to cause her change of outlook.

Mithrell had a simple explanation: "We know who's been vandalizing the trees. We aren't worried about our safety any longer."

"That's great news. Who is it?"

"Names aren't important. What matters is we don't feel the person is a threat to us, and the vandalism has stopped. And that deputy sheriff seems to have backed off on his pursuit of Kirby, as well. That's your doing, isn't it?"

"I did talk to my friend, Dave," Regan said, "about some things Deputy Sheriff Burke might have overlooked initially. They may have decided to redirect their focus for a while. I'd like to think that's what happened.

"In any case, I'm glad to hear you're feeling safer. I do wish you'd tell me who vandalized your trees though, Mithrell. There may be a clue to the murderer in the vandal's identity. Shouldn't you tell the authorities who the person is?"

"I'd rather the person who desecrated the trees tell the authorities why they did so. I'm certain that would be of more value than my accusations. I also believe living with their actions is difficult enough for them right now. The reason they felt they needed to take those actions must be causing them almost more pain than they can bear. I couldn't add to that burden.

"When they are ready to come forward and take responsibility for what they've done, they may need more support than I can give. The trees were sacred, after all." Her voice sounded incredibly sad as she said the word sacred. "Can I count on you to be there to support both of us?"

"*You* can certainly count on me, Mithrell. I'll help you in any way I can. I can't make any promises about the vandal, though," she said testily. "I think frightening your family is inexcusable. And that's not even considering what that person did to your property," she fumed, "to your trees."

"Please, Regan, hold off on judging until you understand."

Regan agreed to try and the conversation ended. Was there such a thing as sainthood among witches, she wondered? If there was, Mithrell should surely be up for it.

Regan, however, had an Irish temper, and regardless of how hard she tried not to be judgmental, she was angry with the person responsible for despoiling Mithrell and Kirby's sacred trees. She seethed every time she thought of a person in the woods carving the word murderer and a pentagram into their bark, and she grew even angrier when she thought of the fear Mithrell had endured because of the vandal.

Even though Mithrell had been careful not to mention names, Regan had her own prime suspect. The target of her enmity was the Reverend Simon.

She could envision Shiloh catching him returning from an

outing with a sap-laden knife. Or possibly one of the boys at the shelter guiltily confessed to her that he was the perpetrator, but only because of a direct order from the minister. Her scenes were imagined and very fanciful, but reality might be close to one of them. Maybe Shiloh ran away because she was disgusted by such behavior, especially from a man who seemed so virtuous.

For the briefest of moments, Regan held the horrible thought that the minister had harmed Shiloh, maybe used the knife he wielded on the trees on her, when she discovered his stealthy activities. She quickly banished that fear. Mithrell, who was one of the most astute observers of people she had ever met, was relieved when she discovered the vandal's identity. If Mithrell didn't feel endangered, then her own worries were likely unfounded.

Right now she was out of options. She was going to have to be patient and wait until the vandal came forward, as Mithrell promised he would, to own up to his deeds. But she hoped he would do it soon — she never counted patience as one of her strongest virtues.

"Ma?" It was mostly a whisper. "Ma?" A little louder, or maybe she was just closer to being awake. "Ma, it's me, Alex." Probably a dream. Regan pulled the covers higher to block out the early morning light, but she opened one eye as she did. Her youngest son was next to her side of the bed, not a dream but in the flesh, smiling down at her.

She could hear Tom's even breathing. She opened both eyes and blinked. "What are you — what time is it?"

"Shh," he put his finger over his mouth and motioned for her to follow him with his other hand. He disappeared from the bedroom.

Regan got up, tottered to her closet, slammed her feet into slippers, and grabbed her robe. She found Alex in the kitchen waiting for the water to sound in the kettle. He already had a cup set up with a teabag in it. Two empty Equal bags rested on the counter nearby, one more than she used.

"Can you take me to the airport, Ma? I have to catch a nine o'clock flight back."

"What time is it now?" a still half asleep Regan asked.

"There's plenty of time. It's not even seven yet."

"That's what I was afraid of."

"It's Wednesday. I bet you don't have any plans 'til at least noon."

"I didn't have plans to go to the airport, that's for sure. San Francisco or San Jose?"

"San Jose. Forty minutes, max. Less than an hour-and-a-half round trip for you."

"Wednesday morning. Rush hour traffic. Make it an hour plus, at least going."

"Then we have to leave really soon. I've got it all planned. Well, I thought I had it all planned. I'll tell you about it in the car." Alex had a smile on his face; his eyes danced.

Her tea water boiled and Alex poured it into her cup. She picked it up, teabag still in the cup. "OK. Give me ten."

"Thanks, Ma. I'll back your car out. Do you want me to drive?"

"Ten minutes and then I'll drive."

Regan took the shortest shower known to man, or woman for that matter, pulled on jeans that clung to her not quite dry legs, and a tee shirt that did the same to her back. She brushed her teeth and put on lipstick. She usually didn't wear much makeup, so looking at her reflection in the mirror with today's lack of it wasn't too shocking.

She intended to keep her hair dry in the shower; so much for good intentions. It wasn't bad on top, but the nearer it got to her shoulders, the wetter it was. Her hair got a cursory brush. Even though Regan never left home without earrings and felt undressed without them, she didn't bother with them today. Her ears were going to have to face the world naked this morning under limp, wet hair.

145

She downed her cooled tea in a swift motion, went out the sliding door and through the central courtyard, and headed to her car with a minute of her promised ten to spare. Her hand was almost on the driver-side handle when she thought of Tom. He'd wonder where she was. She decided to use that extra minute to leave a note for him, and went back in. A note was already sitting next to the coffee pot; Alex had written it for her.

She repeated the walk to her car which had been backed out of the garage, turned around, and aimed up the driveway by the now fast-asleep Alex.

Regan knew the way to the San Jose airport very well. She just had to remind herself she was driving to SJC, not SFO, a mistake she had made on a similarly early drive to return her older son, Ben, also asleep for the early morning drive, to college. She smiled at the memory. "None of us ever were morning people, were we?" she softly asked the sleeping Alex.

He woke up about three quarters of the way to the airport. "Sorry, Ma. I meant to stay awake and keep you company. And I was going to tell you why I'm here, wasn't I?"

"That, and why your plans suddenly left you in need of a ride to the airport."

"Oh, yeah," he laughed. "You remember the girl I brought home to dinner right before leaving on tour?"

"Lindsey?"

He smiled, "Lindsey." He said her name in a voice filled with awe, warmth, and wistfulness. "It's her birthday today. I decided to fly home to give her a birthday kiss."

"A birthday kiss? What a romantic son I raised. It's not

that I'm not delighted to see you three weeks before I thought I would, but why isn't she driving you to the airport after such a tender gesture? You look like you've lost weight, by the way, and the circles under your eyes are as big as I've ever seen them."

"I know, I *know,*" he held up his hands for emphasis. "I've had a long night, Ma, even for me.

"I thought ... well my plan was that Lindsey would be driving me to the airport. That's why I didn't let you know I'd be in town this morning; there wasn't going to be any time to get together.

"This whole trip was going to be a birthday surprise for her. I didn't even know for sure if I was going to be able to do it until a day or so ago, and since it was a surprise, I couldn't exactly check with her and ask her if she had any plans for today.

"It turns out she has a mid-term in the organic chemistry class she's taking at Cabrillo College this summer. Guess what time her test starts? Eight o'clock. The best she could do was to bring me to Bonny Doon this morning."

"I thought she went to UCSC?"

"She does. But she's taking organic chemistry at Cabrillo. That class is a bitch. Everybody takes it at Cabrillo if they can because it's easier at a community college than at UCSC."

"How is the band coping with one of their lead singers and their bass guitarist being gone?"

"I'm not gone. That's the beauty of my plan. We opened at last night's show, so we finished up by a little after nine. We packed up our gear really fast and blew town. For once our tour manager looked at a map before he booked us, and we

147

only had a short drive to tonight's gig. The guys dropped me at the airport on the way into town. I caught a redeye, and since I was flying west, I got to the San Jose airport almost before I left," he laughed.

"I jumped on a bus at the airport and came home. It dropped me downtown, only five blocks from where Lindsey lives. It was an easy walk to her place. I got there a few minutes before three a.m., no problem."

"Three a.m. I bet she was thrilled to see you," Regan chuckled.

"As a matter of fact, she was. I think she's the one, Ma. I really do." He sat in happy silence for a minute, a goofy grin on his face, thinking about his true love.

"Now, with your help," he gave her an exaggerated smile, "I'll get on a flight and be back in plenty of time for tonight's gig. Even with a five hour flight and losing three hours because of flying against time zones, I'll make it easily because we headline tonight and won't have to be on stage 'til late. I can sleep on the plane and I might even have time for a nap before we play."

"Well that certainly explains the circles under your eyes," Regan laughed.

"Lindsey is worth extra effort. Even the band supports me in that. It's just good luck we play Atlanta tonight. It's a Delta hub city. They fly to and from San Jose every few hours so I had lots of last minute flight options and could arrange everything."

Atlanta ... San Jose ... Regan's mind was whirring.

"Ma!" Alex yelled suddenly, "the exit! We're gonna miss it!" his voice went up an octave.

Regan barely had time for the briefest of glances in the rear view mirror before she swerved onto the off-ramp to the airport.

"They were in Atlanta," she explained excitedly to Alex. "That's how he did it."

"What are you talking about, Ma?"

"I'm talking about Rick Whitlaw being in two places at once."

Tom was putting his golf clubs into his trunk when Regan got back from the airport.

"Any coffee left?" she asked. "I could really use some."

"I saved you a cup."

He closed the trunk and caught up with her in the kitchen where she was doctoring the found coffee with massive amounts of sugar and milk.

"That note you left was the darndest thing. It was signed with your name, but it sure wasn't your handwriting, was it?"

"Alex wrote the note."

"Alex? Our wandering minstrel Alex?"

"In person."

"But he's in Waco or Charleston or Upper-Who-Knows-Where, isn't he?"

"Right now he's airborne, heading for Atlanta, but he was here this morning, having flown all night to come home and wish his girlfriend a happy birthday."

Tom shook his head, "Doesn't that boy understand the standards he's setting for the rest of us males?" he laughed.

"He says she's the one."

"Ahh," he drawled. "The One."

"The interesting thing is, he may have destroyed Rick Whitlaw's perfect alibi."

"Alex unexpectedly home, The One seen, the perfect alibi destroyed. This sounds like a pretty eventful morning. No wonder you need coffee. You want to fill me in?"

"OK. Rick Whitlaw — the tall, dark, and gorgeous white van owner who lied about knowing Lydia, the murder victim buried in his backyard — he of the perfect alibi — you with me so far?"

"So far. I've had my coffee, you know."

"Well, he was never a viable suspect because he wasn't in town the week before and the week after Lydia's murder. He was driving to, at, or driving back from a family reunion in Atlanta. Of course, the fact that Deputy Sheriff Burke had no reason to assume he knew Lydia helped, too."

"But now we know that last part's not true, thanks to my sweet super-sleuth," he alliterated and rolled his hand as if introducing her on stage.

"That's right. Now we know Rick tells lies. But he still had a great alibi for the time of Lydia's murder.

"Alex said he was able to make his trip with last minute plans and a multitude of flight choices because Atlanta is an airline hub," Regan continued. "When I asked him how the band was getting along without him, he said they weren't. He hopped on a redeye, and because of time zone changes, he got here just two hours later — our time — after leaving Atlanta. He said he'd be back before they performed tonight. I think that explains how Rick could have been in two places at once."

"OK. Now, coffee or no, you did just lose me."

"I remember Joan saying Rick took a day off from her family reunion to attend a seminar, something about organizing political campaigns. The seminar was in Atlanta and was just for one day, but suppose Rick slipped out the night before, after everyone at the reunion went to bed, flew home, killed and buried Lydia, and flew back to Atlanta? He could have made it back in time for it to seem like he had just been away for the day."

"Wouldn't Joan or some of her family have missed him in the morning before the seminar?" Tom asked.

"He could have left a note like I did, or rather Alex did, for you this morning. He could have said he left before Joan or anyone else was up. She would have just assumed he had a very early morning, wouldn't she?"

"I suppose it's possible," Tom hesitated.

"But?"

"An awful lot of details would have to come together with incredible precision for that to have worked. Let's say he could have booked a flight at the last minute, and let's say he could leave and return at acceptable times. If Alex made that work, Whitlaw could have. But how did he pay for it? If a bill arrived on a credit card, Joan might notice that. How could he explain it? If he used cash, well, he would have to pay and book in-person at the airport. And I think Homeland Security would get a little nervous about that. He wouldn't want to call that much attention to himself, so the cash option seems almost impossible."

"Maybe he has his own account, a separate one that Joan doesn't see or maybe even know about, that he could use,"

Regan suggested. "That would let him book online so there wouldn't be anything last minute about it."

"True. Let's give him that, too. Next point," Tom was in true logic mode. "Could he have been certain he could slip away at night without being discovered? Joan might have noticed he wasn't in bed. Could he count on her being such a sound sleeper she wouldn't miss him? I'd notice if you weren't in bed during the night. Wouldn't you miss me?" he asked coyly.

"Maybe Joan is a really sound sleeper," she shrugged, although she didn't like that part of her assumption.

"Even getting to the airport could have posed some real problems," Tom said. "If he got a taxi, he'd have to worry about meeting it. Some drivers beep to let their fare know they've arrived. He'd have to be afraid of drawing a horn-beeper."

"No, he wouldn't," Regan countered. "They drove cross country in their Prius. They don't fly because of trying to minimize their carbon footprint. Rick would have had a car, a silent car, I might add. Those things take some getting used to because they don't make a sound when you turn them on. It wouldn't have been a problem if the car was missing all day because everyone would know he had driven it to the seminar. No taxi needed, beeper problem eliminated."

Tom acquiesced and moved on to another obstacle. "To me, a family reunion means lots of people moving outside their normal environment. All it would take was one person out for a late night walk, sneaking a cigarette, up with a crying child. Anything. How would he explain driving away in the middle of the night if someone happened to see him?

Seems awfully risky to me.

"The really big problems for me start once he lands. He'd have a strict timeline once he got to San Jose. What about getting from the airport to his home? He'd need a rental car, wouldn't he? That would mean more time-unpredictability. I don't care how rental car company ads go, you always wind up waiting in line, coming or going."

Regan took an orange from the fruit basket and started peeling it. "Alex said he took a bus from the airport to Santa Cruz. Rick could have done the same thing," she suggested.

"Getting to Santa Cruz in the middle of the night is one thing. Getting to La Selva Beach is quite another. There wouldn't have been bus service there in the middle of the night."

"He could have planned ahead and left the van parked somewhere in Santa Cruz where he could reach it. No," Regan changed her mind. "I bet he had Lydia meet him at the airport." She stopped peeling the orange and caught her breath, "Oh, Tom ... he could have told her he was leaving Joan and running away with her that night." Regan was horrified to think of the cruelty she imagined Rick could have perpetrated.

Tom paused and shook his head, thinking about how Rick might indeed have gotten Lydia to help him murder her. "Phew," he frowned. His head shake grew from an appreciation of irony to an expression of disagreement.

"He's still got problems. No, it doesn't work. How would he know how long it would take to dispose of Lydia? If something went wrong and Alex missed a return flight, the band would have gone on without him; they could have covered if they had to. If something went wrong and Rick didn't get back to Atlanta on time, he could have been stuck with a recently buried girl on his very guilty hands. I just don't see it, sweetheart. He would have been gambling on a lot of things working precisely. Does he seem like that much of a risk taker to you?"

"No, that doesn't seem like him at all," Regan had to admit. "His life is about control and order. But, if a sixteen-year-old girl just informed him she was pregnant with his child and was going to go public, he might have decided he had to take the chance."

Tom considered for a full minute. "There certainly is that. Desperation can be quite a motivator."

Tom's opinion seemed to have done a 180. He supplied a final bit of logic for the gamble Rick might have taken. "Maybe he figured if he missed his booked flight, he could still catch a later one.

"When are you going to call Dave?" he asked.

"If I'm wrong again, this will be my third attempt at coming up with Lydia's murderer, and my third failure. Dave will have a field day with me."

"Remember, supplying suspects and destroying alibis isn't what you do for a living. You're just trying to help. How could he fault you for getting things wrong?"

"We're talking Dave here. He wouldn't be able to resist," she laughed. "Rather than calling him and breathlessly presenting my latest supposition, maybe I should sit on it for a day and consider all the problems with my theory that you just raised. When Dave brings up each of the problems you posed, and I'm sure he will, having ready answers should help my case.

"Besides, there's no need for me to rush. It's not like we're dealing with someone stalking young women at random. Rick Whitlaw won't strike again. If his alibi still seems broken to me tomorrow morning, I can call Dave then."

"You could do that," Tom said, "but I'm going to bet you don't make it past ten-thirty this morning without calling him."

Tom won the bet.

Even after thinking about it overnight, Regan still believed Rick's alibi was suspect. She was glad she had called Dave the day before to suggest he look into flight times from Atlanta to San Jose and also check to see if Rick's seminar had been held on June 22nd.

Unfortunately Dave hadn't answered when she called him and she had to do her prompting by way of a message on his machine. Leaving messages wasn't one of her strong points; she hadn't presented her premise as elegantly as she would have liked. But she had been very careful of her tone; her message had been serious and without a trace of teasing.

She had a busy morning coming, but there would be time to call Dave later in the day and ask if he had relayed her hypothesis to Deputy Sheriff Burke. She had showered and dressed and was five minutes from heading out the door when her phone rang.

"Regan, I told you I might need some support when our tree vandal was ready to confess. It looks like today is the day. How soon can you get to our house?" Mithrell asked.

"Give me an hour, no, better make it an hour and a half;

I'll need to do some rearranging."

The tree vandal had picked a bad day to bare his soul. It was Thursday, Broker Tour Day in a declining market.

In normal markets, realtors battled for listings. Most seminars aimed at the industry promised to teach how to get ten new listings a month. But in this sagging market, listings were easy to get. In a depressed market, agents didn't always want to take listings; an unsold property could become an albatross very easily.

Having unsold listings was expensive and time consuming. Eager-to-have-it-sold owners were always convinced if their realtor just threw more money at their property, if they just advertised more frequently, ran bigger ads, and paid extra for front page placement, their house would receive multiple offers.

In a market like this, it just didn't work like that. The truth was, it rarely worked like that.

Realtors often complied with their seller's wishes because advertising usually helped grow their business. Unattached buyers might respond to an ad and the listing agent could capture them. It was called double-ending. Agents loved it because, if they represented both the buyer and the seller, they didn't have to give half their commission to a buyer's agent.

It was completely legal, and most agents considered it completely ethical. As long as the listing agent was good at wearing more than one hat, they could represent a buyer as aggressively as any other agent could. That was the theory anyway.

Realtors also placed big flashy ads to attract the attention of other potential sellers. "Look at this ad, honey," a prospective seller-husband would say to his wife. "This agent is on the front page. That must mean he is very successful. I think our house deserves an ad like this. Let's give him a call."

In normal markets, ads sometimes did sell houses and made realtors money. In markets like this, they were just cash drains.

What really got homes sold in any market was agent showings, and one of the best ways to get showings was to entice colleagues to see listings during broker tour. In this distressed market, however, there were many more homes for sale than agents had time to see.

Regan had spent the past several days organizing a gigantic poker run — a time honored way to draw agents to preview properties. Agents went to participating houses and collected one envelope with a playing card at each property. The more houses they visited, the more cards they collected, and the better their chances were of assembling the winning poker hand.

When enough listing agents participated, their small contributions of cash added up to a sizable pot of prize-money, attracting many agents to tour their listings. It was inexpensive advertising, but it was effective advertising.

Now Regan was going to miss the event she had created. She called agents in the office until she found one willing to fill in for her. Freed up, she headed to Mithrell and Kirby's house to witness a confession.

Regan's car was the only one at the Paisleys' house when

she arrived. She rang the doorbell and turned her back to the door to look down their long driveway while she waited for the door to be answered. She expected at any moment that a white van would approach, driving slowly, guiltily, if a vehicle could convey shame and remorse, but nothing turned up the drive before Kirby opened the door.

"Kirby?"

"I'm working from home today, trying to, anyway. Come in. I'm going to aim you toward the library and get back to my desk. You remember where it is, don't you? Mithrell is waiting for you there."

"I remember. I'll find my way, Kirby. You get back to work."

The library door was closed. Even though she knew she was expected, she didn't open it. She knocked instead — just in case — a habit learned from years as a realtor. Mithrell opened the door at once.

"Oh, Regan, thank you for coming. I was just positioning tissue boxes."

Mithrell was theatrical and loved to present herself amid a swirl of color. Today she was in full regalia. She wore an almost floor-length flowing purple garment, cinched around her ample middle with strands of shiny satin ribbons representing every color of the rainbow. Her fingers were adorned with rings, mostly turquoise and moonstones, and some fingers boasted more than one ring. She wore a heavy silver and moonstone necklace that descended almost to her satin ribbons.

But for all her colorful presentation, her voice was somber, totally lacking the melodious tone and drollness that Regan associated with her.

"This is a day I'd like to skip, but it has to be faced. Since you know everyone involved, I thought you would be a good choice to hear confessions. I'm counting on you to give a good account to your friend, the policeman."

"Confessions, Mithrell?"

"Yes, confessions," she sighed. "Everyone caught up in this had seemingly good reasons for what they did, I'm sure, but what a mess we've all created. You'll see."

The doorbell rang before Regan had a chance to ask Mithrell to explain what she meant.

"Regan, could you excuse me for a minute?"

She nodded yes and sat down on a seat facing the library entrance as the vibrantly-hued Mithrell swirled out of the library to answer the front door.

Regan leaned sideways as far as the chair would permit and craned her neck, ready for her first glimpse of the desecrater at the front door. What she got was a good view of the Whitlaw boys bursting into the entry, full of their usual rowdy energy.

"Where's Arthur? Can we barbeque hot dogs for dinner, Missus Paisley? Can we stay up all night? This is gonna be so fun, isn't it?" Raymond Whitlaw asked in rapid fire mode.

"Arthur's in his room. Yes, we'll see, and yes it is." Mithrell's answers seemed to make sense to him.

"Arthur! We're here for our overnight!" he hollered as he tore up the stairs. Richard Whitlaw bounded up the stairs with only slightly less gusto than his brother.

Joan Whitlaw came in timidly and put a small suitcase down by the stair newel post. She looked awful.

"Thank you, Mithrell. I don't know what we'd do without you and Kirby."

"Come in and have some herbal tea. I've brewed some chamomile; it's very soothing," Mithrell said as she ushered her second guest toward the library.

Joan did as she was told without complaint, protest, or real awareness.

"Regan's here, too."

That announcement seemed to momentarily alarm Joan, but she quickly moved past her flicker of discomfort and smiled faintly at Regan.

Mithrell ushered Joan to a seat in the library and gently pressed her down into it before turning to a small table that was set with three teacups and a pot of tea.

Joan didn't say anything to Regan, and within seconds she seemed oblivious of her. She chewed her lips nervously, looked at her hands, and played with her wedding ring while Mithrell was filling the cups.

Mithrell handed the first cup of tea to Regan and moved to do the same with Joan. Joan looked up slightly and took the cup. It rattled in her hand.

"I'm the one who destroyed your trees," she blurted out, "I'm so sorry."

"Yes, I know you are," Mithrell said as she sat down with her teacup in hand. "And I know you'd like to tell me why," she added gently.

Joan sighed, "Where to start?" she asked no one in particular. "Several years ago, before Richard was born, Rick had an affair. He's always had a political career in mind, has always been involved politically. He met the girl while he was working for a candidate. She was young, just eighteen, but she pursued him so aggressively," Joan shook her head. "It was a brief, impulsive fling, he said, and I believed him. We worked things out and stayed married."

Joan looked at Regan, then back to Mithrell. "Everything was fine, our marriage was working, and we had the boys." She stopped speaking and sighed. "And then Lydia came along. She turned up with Shiloh at Rick's campaign headquarters. I happened to be there that day and saw how she looked at Rick when Shiloh introduced her to him. She was a predator just like the first girl was.

"We talked about her. Rick said he had learned his lesson and would never even be tempted by her. I think he meant it, and I believed him … but I kept watching her … watching her maneuver. And I watched him. He may have told himself he had learned, but he was fascinated by her … like a moth to flame. I might have killed her myself if I thought I could get away with it."

Regan watched hatred sweep across Joan's pleasant face, and knew she meant what she said.

"I didn't know what happened at the time, but I did notice a change in Rick before we left on vacation. He was tense and jumpy — distracted. Finally he told me his campaign was out of money and asked if he could infuse it with some family funds, maybe just as a loan, but probably as an investment in his future.

"I always considered his goals to be our goals. We both believe he will make great contributions after he's elected, and that he will eventually move to a higher elected office where he can have an even greater impact. I didn't have any problem with him using our savings and told him so. He said it was going to take a thirty thousand dollar investment. He seemed so uncomfortable with the amount, even though I wasn't ... well ... something just felt odd about it.

"Before we left for the family reunion, the thirty thousand dollars came out of our savings account and, I assumed, went into his election committee coffers.

"His mood didn't seem to improve on the drive, but I thought that was just because he was trapped in a car driving over two thousand miles with two restless kids, just to get to a family reunion that wasn't even for his family.

"There was a seminar in Atlanta during our stay that he was really looking forward to attending. I encouraged him to focus on that day and try to make the best of everything else. After about a day with my family, he announced he was going to leave for his seminar the night before it was scheduled. He said it was because it was being held all the way across Atlanta, and he didn't want to battle morning commuter traffic in a city he didn't know. I figured he wanted some more away-time from all the confusion at the reunion — that would be like him — so I didn't think anything of it."

Kirby came in and sat down quietly on the other side of the room. Regan noticed his entrance, but she didn't think Joan did.

"... spur of the moment, I decided it might be nice to meet Rick after his seminar and have dinner alone, you know, some time just for the two of us. It was going to be really easy for me to get away. The family had a big pizza and video night planned. Watching the kids was going to be easy for someone else to do, and I wouldn't be missing a big event night.

"I tried his cell all day. He didn't pick up. I finally decided he'd probably been polite and turned his phone off during sessions, and even though it wasn't like him to not check messages every once in a while, I thought maybe he was too busy, or that he got too involved over lunch with some conferees ..." Joan's voice trailed off.

"Well, finally I decided to have him paged, because if we were going to get together, I'd have to figure out how to meet him. I didn't want him to start back to the reunion while I was heading in the other direction."

"Yes, we understand," Mithrell said.

"They told me at the seminar they couldn't page him because he wasn't there. He was registered — but he never checked in," she said in a voice barely louder than a whisper.

"When he got back to the reunion, he apologized for not returning my calls ... and told me the seminar was terrific." Joan's lips quivered and she blinked repeatedly as she tried to hold back tears.

"The money from our savings never turned up in his campaign receipts either. I checked. When I confronted him, he started to cry. He admitted he had skipped the seminar and flown back to California to meet Lydia and give her thirty-thousand dollars.

"He said she was extorting him. She told him she was pregnant and that she would announce he was the father. He swore it wasn't true, but he said he decided to pay her off because, by the time the scandal broke and he fought back, his election would be impossibly compromised.

"You understand how it would be, don't you?" Joan

pleaded. "Even if that girl eventually retracted her claim or if he proved he wasn't the father, some people would always assume he had indecent relations with an underage girl. His career would have been destroyed.

"When Lydia's body was found, I ... I didn't know what to do. Rick swore he didn't have anything to do with her death. I didn't think my husband was capable of murder ... and yet." She closed her eyes and began to sob softly.

It took her a minute or more before she could go on. Finally Joan said, "We heard she had a pentagram cut into her chest and that there was talk of satanic rituals and horrible human sacrifice.

"Oh, Mithrell, I remember how disturbed you were when the Sheriff was questioning Kirby. I'm so sorry," Joan sobbed again. "But you told me there were many witnesses who would swear he was with them the night Lydia was killed. When they didn't arrest Kirby, I assumed it was because of that — that he had a good alibi.

"But Rick didn't. Her body was found in our backyard. I thought the Sheriff would investigate us as well. I thought if the authorities looked too closely at Rick, they might discover he was actually here the night the girl died. If they ever found out about him flying back home to meet her they would never believe he hadn't killed her. I didn't think Kirby was at risk. You have to believe me. I thought if I carved 'murderer' on your trees, it might keep the authorities focused on him and away from looking more closely at Rick.

"Now, it doesn't matter. The Sheriff and a deputy came to our house early this morning. They said Lydia was pregnant when she was killed. They said they knew about Rick taking money out of our account, and they knew about his roundtrip flight from Atlanta to San Jose on June twenty-first. They accused him of being the father of her baby. They asked him if he planned to kill her all along ... or if he just got so angry at her that things got out of hand. They said all that with the children in the house ... the boys might have overheard. And then they took him away for more questioning."

"Joan, do you think your husband killed Lydia?" Mithrell asked in a gentle tone.

"I don't know what I think. He gave her money. He was here the night she was killed. He lied to me." She stared into Mithrell's eyes. "He lied to me ... again. I don't know what to think."

"I have to come forward," Kirby said, "it can't be avoided any longer." He put his hands on his thighs, pushed his back into his armchair, and exhaled deeply. "Don't you think so, Mithrell?"

Regan was startled by Kirby's pronouncement. She had been so engrossed in Joan's story, she had almost forgotten he was in the room. Joan, who didn't realize he was there, jumped almost completely out of her seat.

"I don't see any other option," Mithrell answered.

"Kirby, you didn't ..." Regan was dumbfounded.

"Of course not," he answered sharply. "But I did make a couple of very bad decisions, and I convinced a number of quite honest people to abandon their ethics and lie for me, so I'm not completely innocent here, am I?"

"Do you know where they are questioning Rick? I'll drive you there. It's time I tell the truth to the Sheriff. Hopefully we can get Rick released before anything makes it to the news.

167

Joan, can you forgive me for not speaking up before?"

"I don't understand," Joan looked confused.

"Rick didn't do anything to Lydia. In fact, I'm going to supply an alibi for him. Damn, I wish I didn't have to do this."

He walked over to the women. "Come on, Joan. Let's go tell the Sheriff that Lydia was with me long after your husband was flying back to Atlanta," he said, holding his hand out to the dazed woman. "I'll explain on the way."

20

Mithrell fell apart the minute Kirby and Joan left. She shook and cried and threw her teacup across the library into a stack of books. "It was my fault Kirby didn't tell the Sheriff about Lydia," she said. Then she reached toward Regan, arms open wide, and barreled against her.

Regan was a tall woman wearing two inch heels. Mithrell was a short woman in flat shoes. Mithrell's head wound up resting against Regan's breasts. She rocked the little woman back and forth like one might do with a distraught child until Mithrell regained some composure.

"I knew I would need a tissue," Mithrell said finally, plopping into a seat next to a table holding a tissue box. "What a miserable way to live. Imagine having children with a man you think might be unfaithful again at any moment and might even be capable of murder. That woman carries such a daily burden — our travails seem very small in comparison. And we have one another and a community for support. She's all alone, poor thing.

"If I hadn't been such a coward, if I had allowed Kirby to tell Deputy Sheriff Burke the whole truth from the beginning,

169

she might not have had to live with such suspicions. Our sacred trees might still be with us, and we all might have been spared so much guilt."

"What did Kirby lie about?" Regan asked.

"He didn't lie. As I told you, we don't lie. I just insisted he leave out a part of what happened." She dropped her tissue and reached for a new one. "Oh, listen to me," she sobbed again, putting the whole box in her lap, "I sound just like one of those ... one of ... I sound just like those people who think it's not lying if you don't get asked exactly the right question. Of course you can lie by omission," she wailed.

"Deputy Sheriff Burke asked Kirby if he was with Lydia on the twenty-first. He wasn't, not in the sense that the question was asked. But we all saw her that night. She was alive when we last saw her. We didn't think we could add anything, any useful information, about what happened to her; but when the Sheriff's deputy said she had a pentagram cut into her body, we understood the danger to us at once. I decided it was safer not to get involved, and encouraged Kirby to leave out the part of the night when Lydia joined our coven."

Regan thought she didn't betray her astonishment at what Mithrell just said, but Mithrell was the most perceptive person she had ever met. It was as if she saw past Regan's face and read her thoughts.

"That's exactly what I mean, Regan. You know us and, I believe, like us, and yet — what are you thinking about us right now? I didn't mean Lydia converted to Wicca or became a member of our coven; she just appeared in our woods and then joined us during our ritual. Disrupted our

170

ritual is a better way of saying it. But if all those things I saw in your eyes crossed your mind, what sort of suppositions would Deputy Sheriff Burke make if we told him Lydia was with us the night she was murdered?"

Regan could feel heat in her cheeks, "I didn't think … I … I'm sorry, Mithrell."

"I understand. But now you must understand why I thought we shouldn't let the deputy know … everything. Some people still quote the Bible at us: 'You shall not suffer a witch to live.' I was afraid."

"What did happen in your woods that night? What is Kirby going to tell Deputy Sheriff Burke? Maybe there's a clue in what happened," Regan said. "Mithrell, I understand why you left out things, I really do, but I think it's always better to tell the whole truth," she added.

Mithrell smiled at her. Her expression was filled with sadness and knowledge she might rather not have. "I used to believe that, too. You must have a young soul, Regan. We believe in reincarnation; did you know that? This isn't my first time on earth. My soul is very old. I've witnessed a great deal of pain."

"Please tell me what happened that night," Regan asked. "Don't leave anything out."

Mithrell nodded. "It was after midnight and we were having our Litha, midsummer service. Lydia came into the woods running, laughing, and cavorting like a little girl. She demanded everyone stop what they were doing and wish her a very Happy Birthday. She had a bag with her which she opened. 'Come look what I got for my birthday,' she insisted. Kirby and Ellen, a member of our coven, asked her to please be quiet as we were involved in our rituals, but she kept insisting we all come look."

"From your description of her behavior, it sounds like she may have been high on something. Do you think she was?" Regan asked.

"It's possible, but I think she was just giddy with excitement," Mithrell said. "She had disrupted us so much, we decided our ritual was ruined, and that the only way to make her be quiet was to do what she wanted. Several members of our coven took a cursory look at what she had in her bag, but it was hard to make out by torch light, which was the light we were using. When we told her that, she reached into the bag and pulled out a handful of money."

"A handful? Could she have had thirty thousand dollars in the bag?"

"It was impossible to tell the denominations of the bills, but I would guess she certainly could have had that much money in it, yes.

"After everyone obliged her, she calmed down. That's one of the reasons I don't think she was on anything. She seemed able to be calm and reasonable once she had some attention.

"Next she asked what time it was. When we told her, she seemed disappointed. She said she thought it was later, and she had longer to wait for her teacher to come than she expected.

"Then she asked if she could join our circle. We had to say she couldn't. She didn't know the rituals, but we did tell her she could remain if she would promise not to disrupt us again. She agreed and stayed."

"Without any more outbursts?"

"That's right. After the ceremony was over, she asked what time it was again. She said she'd better go to their meeting place and wait for him, her lover, to come."

"Did she call him her lover?" Regan interrupted.

"No. I confess that's what I called him. She was always very careful to refer to him as her teacher, nothing more. I assumed they were lovers because she was pregnant and because, according to Lydia, they planned to be married. She said she had a note from her mother giving her permission to marry him even though she was underage. She laughed about that.

"By then she had dressed again."

Regan interrupted a second time, "Dressed again?"

"That's right. Our coven worships in the nude. We couldn't very well have her remain without disrobing, too. That would have been awkward," Mithrell added matter-of-factly.

"The last thing she said was that the money was her dowry, just like in times of old, and that her soon-to-be husband was going to be so surprised when she gave it to him."

"So, when she left, she was on her way to meet her teacher?" Regan asked.

"I think that's a correct assumption," Mithrell said.

"When she left, do you remember which way she went? It could be important. Think about it for a minute and try to remember," Regan said, her mind racing. If Mithrell said Lydia walked to the back of the woods, it would put her on a path to the Whitlaws. If she headed to the right of the house, that would be the easiest way to Reverend Simon's. "Which direction did she take out of the woods?"

"I don't have to think about it at all. I remember quite clearly. She went to the driveway and got into a white van and drove away."

"A white van? What kind of van, Mithrell?"

"I believe it was a Volkswagen van."

🏠🏠🏠🏠🏠🏠🏠🏠🏠🏠🏠🏠

There wasn't a news story on either of the local TV stations at 5:00 or at 11:00. A careful reading of the next day's *Sentinel* and *The Mid-County Post* produced nothing about an arrest of Rick Whitlaw. There wasn't anything in any of the media about Kirby Paisley, either.

Regan thought about calling Joan or Mithrell, but decided against making either call. Both families needed some time to themselves. She called Dave instead.

He greeted her with a jovial, "Hey, Regan, what took you so long to call? I know you heard Deputy Sheriff Burke entertained some guests recently. You must be squirming with curiosity about the details."

"Not at all. I'm already almost fully informed. I was just checking to see when I could expect a thank you call for all the valuable information I uncovered, you know, about Rick Whitlaw's knowing Lydia and being able to get back from Atlanta the night she was killed. You're going to say you were just about to pick up the phone, aren't you?"

"Nope. That sounds like a realtor line to me," he laughed. "Fully informed and not curious — you expect me to buy that? You want to know what happened when Deputy Sheriff Burke had his little chat with the candidate, don't you?"

"All right. You caught me. Maybe I'm just a bit curious to know how closely my hypothesis fits with what really happened." She wished that statement hadn't sounded so much like a confession, because she expected Dave would pick up on it and use it for another round of teasing, but he didn't.

"Darned close from what I hear. Your junior detective badge is in the mail. Seems your politico says he booked a room at a hotel in Atlanta for the night of the twenty-first, took a ride to the airport for a late evening flight, got to SJC about eleven, met the Vic, handed her a carry-on full of cash, did the reverse trip, and got back to his hotel in time for a late lunch.

"His cover was a seminar on the twenty-second. Pretty clever. He planned to hit the afternoon session of the seminar to cement his alibi, but the dope was so exhausted," Dave switched to a falsetto to interject a quote from Rick Whitlaw: "'Oh, so much emotional stress, I couldn't catch a wink of sleep airborne,' that he went to his hotel room for a sec, fell asleep, and missed the whole thing," Dave snorted. "None of that really mattered as it turned out. Once he put himself in San Jose on the night of the twenty-first, he was toast.

"What I want to know," Dave continued, "is how he got on a plane without any TSA screeners asking him what he was planning to do with all that cash. You'd think they'd notice thirty grand tucked into his carry-on along with his clean underwear. The candidate said he originally planned to leave the money in a baggage locker at SJC so he'd only have to worry about having a key with him — made a special trip over the hill to leave the money and everything — but TSA took out all the lockers after 9/11; they didn't want terrorists using them to stash time-delayed bombs."

Dave chuckled, "Poor baby says he was a wreck worrying about carrying all that cash, but the screeners didn't notice it. Makes you wonder how well they're doing their jobs, doesn't it?"

"Tom and I have a friend who did six roundtrips to Munich from Houston, who had to replace six pairs of nail clippers and a very threatening Texas-sized belt buckle," Regan said. "Those items got picked up during screening."

"So you think the candidate just got lucky, huh?"

"Maybe. Of course, our friend also had a Swiss army knife in his carry-on bag on every leg of every trip he took, that the screeners always missed."

"Amazing. Anyway, the politician said he never left San Jose, that the girl met him there, and was alive and grateful when she left him. Deputy Sheriff Burke figured that was garbage. He thought the guy met her at the airport, took her back to his house, killed her there to keep her quiet about the baby she was carrying, and buried her in his backyard, figuring he'd sell the house and move on. The flight the guy took back departed San Jose at three a.m., so it would have been real tight, but the deputy thought it could have been done.

"We figured he had the girl drive the family van to San Jose, and he drove her back to La Selva in it. The one little glitch in Deputy Sheriff Burke's scenario was how the guy got back to San Jose from La Selva. He didn't rent a car. We checked. And he didn't catch a cab. We checked that, too. The van seems to have been waiting in the garage when the family got home. But according to one of the deputies who was sitting in on the questioning, none of the deputies were too worried about the details.

"Mr. Candidate was about to need a change of clothes, he was sweating so hard. They figured he'd crack in another few minutes and confess, and they could stop looking for transportation means. Then out of the blue, in walks Mrs. Candidate with your Wiccan buddy, who says the girl was in La Selva with him and all his friends, from right after midnight 'til at least two-thirty, and that she showed them a bag of cash she said Whitlaw gave her.

"Man! The deputy says you've never *seen* so many grownups blubbering like little girls. The wife is crying to her husband about how sorry she is for suspecting him and how she deserves to go to prison for vandalizing the Paisley's trees. The candidate is slobbering to her about how he should have told her what was going on. Your pal Kirby is all misty about how he should have told the Sheriff the truth about seeing the Vic the night she was killed, and he's saying he doesn't want Mrs. Candidate prosecuted because if he had come forward, she wouldn't have damaged his trees and she wouldn't have thought her hubby was a murderer. Blah, blah, blah. You get the idea, right?"

"Uh-huh."

"I'm betting even Deputy Sheriff Burke was about to start crying, what with his tidy little case getting blown to bits. But, Regan, if you ever tell a soul I said that," he laughed, "I'll see you get a speeding ticket every time you leave home."

"Is Deputy Sheriff Burke back to suspecting Kirby?"

"Thing is, we never liked Kirby for the Perp that much. He always had all those witnesses saying he was with them when we figure the girl was killed. Sure, the thought crossed our minds they could all be in on the murder together, but we checked 'em out. You've got a lot of respected community members there. I wouldn't want to try and convince a jury they all colluded.

"No, what made him so interesting was that he had been seen alone with the Vic and acting kind of peculiar by some neighbors. Then, when he wouldn't give us any DNA and had such a fondness for lawyers, he looked guilty. But, when he came in with his revised story, he changed his mind about the DNA, too. We got samples from him and from your candidate, incidentally. Those things take a few days to run, but I bet neither is a match. In the meantime, we cut them both loose. No charges."

"Which is why there weren't any news stories," Regan surmised.

"Right. Mr. Candidate's name is unsullied, although after his performance, I doubt he's gonna be endorsed by the Sheriff's Department."

"Has what happened returned Reverend Simon to prime suspect status?"

"You'd think so. But when a deputy sheriff stopped by to see him the next morning to ask how he felt about making the DNA two-some a three-some — darndest thing, he said OK."

"I wonder why he changed his mind?"

"Don't know. Don't care. Hey, Regan, anyway, thanks for

the tip about Rick Whitlaw lying to the Deputy Sheriff and maybe being able to leave Atlanta for a day unnoticed. Of course, none of that matters now, but you can be such a pain when you don't feel appreciated, I thought I'd better say thanks and head that off."

"Dave, that's so sweet of you," she mocked in a saccharin-filled voice. "Of course you didn't really need my help. I'm sure you and the detectives would have discovered the lie and the trip on your own ... eventually. And you're right that it's all meaningless anyway, as it turns out, but since you're in such a magnanimous mood, can I run one more thing past you?"

"Shoot."

"Do you think there's any chance that where Lydia was buried, the pentagram, her clothes in the Paisley's backyard, even her pregnancy, is all a huge coincidence? Could she have been murdered by a random killer ... or by someone she showed her bag of money to, who decided to kill her and take it?"

Dave let out an exaggerated sigh, "Just when I thought you were starting to get the hang of this, you go and ask such a dumb question," he teased. "No, this wasn't a random killing, not likely a robbery either. No way. We're still looking for somebody she knew, somebody she knew well enough to make a baby with."

"But who's left?" Regan asked.

"That's the question, isn't it? Turns out it's harder to be a real detective than it is to be a real-a-ter," he said, deliberately mispronouncing her profession. "But don't worry, we pros will figure it out and get the guy."

"I'm sure you will. I've been spending so much time playing detective, my clients are going to start complaining. Ball's in your court." Regan was silent for a few seconds. "Just one favor, though," she hesitated. "Could you keep me up on how your investigation is progressing?"

Dave roared with laughter, "You're incorrigible."

"No, just tenacious, like any other real-a-ter."

21

Regan's Saturday workday started with a phone call from Gary Hammit of Aztec Realty. "I've got an offer for you on your listing on Caffey Way."

"Gary, that's great," she was genuinely enthusiastic. "How do you want to handle the presentation?"

"I'd like to present it to your clients in your office later today. How about two-thirty?"

Regan called her clients and asked if the meeting time worked for them. Given the state of the market, they said they would be happy to rearrange their lives in order to make the appointment.

"Gary Hammit is the agent with the offer, you said? He showed the house this morning. That's good, isn't it?" her client asked. "That means they really like the house, doesn't it … if they made an offer so soon? Besides, you know what they say: third one's the charm."

"Could be, but let's not get ahead of ourselves. Let's see what the offer looks like and take it from there."

Regan tried not to get too optimistic about the coming proposal. Her client might be credulous — she wasn't. There was nothing magical about a third offer. If anything, it had been her experience that the first offer was usually the best one a seller got, and the first offer on Caffey hadn't been good. It was contingent on the buyer selling his house, a difficult thing to do in the current market, before he could buy her client's house. The sellers declined the offer.

The second offer was worse than the first. It was from an investor and was what realtors call a low-ball bid. The investor said it was his best offer, take it or leave it. The sellers left it.

After those experiences, the most Regan would allow herself today was cautious optimism. Very cautious optimism.

Even if the offer was acceptable, moving this particular house to a successful sale would be a bit like maneuvering a helium balloon on a long string through a field of cactus on a windy day. Each move was going to require great care.

The house on Caffey Way had a lot going for it. The three bedrooms were all large. The baths were good sized, too. It had some desirable elements like nice wainscoting and moldings, pretty views, and good privacy. It also had a guest unit which, if the owner kept a low profile, might provide rental income, especially since the house was close to UCSC with its plethora of ever desperate-for-housing students.

But it had its share of problems, as well. The termite company Regan hired for the pre-sale inspection delicately described the extensive decks which wrapped around three sides of the house as "ready for upgrading." Translated from realtor jargon to regular English, that meant venture onto the decks only if your life insurance policy is current.

The roof was in great shape; some of the plumbing was not. There was evidence of leaking behind at least one shower wall. That might be a fairly simple fix, but it might also mean the dreaded M-word: mold. No one could know for sure until the walls were opened. Many buyers would say "No thanks" when they heard about the plumbing.

Then there was the issue of permits. The house had been completed and the garage and guest house started before the Loma Prieta Earthquake in 1989. Finaled permits were on file for everything done up to the date of the earthquake; nothing was on file for work done after that. Lack of documented and finaled permits didn't necessarily mean that the garage and guesthouse were completed without them; it just meant the County of Santa Cruz didn't know for sure, one way or the other. What a lack of finaled permits meant for a new owner was anybody's guess.

Realtors usually considered the likely buyer-profile for a given house and wrote ads aimed at those buyers. Regan had laughed with Tom about the target buyer for Caffey Way. She had even made up an imaginary ad with the headline: *Perfect home for chronic gambler with an open mind.*

Getting into contract was likely to be only the first in a series of painstaking steps leading to a sale. She didn't know Gary Hammit and she hoped he would be up to his end of the job.

Gary was prompt and greeted Regan and her clients with an affable smile and a warm handshake. He gave Regan a complete copy of the offer, the proper and courteous way to treat the seller's agent, and began explaining it to the sellers by 2:35.

While Gary talked, Regan took a quick look at the high points on her copy of the contract. The offered price was good, the close of escrow date acceptable, the paragraph that would have indicated the buyer needed to sell another house was crossed out. Excellent. The buyer had a good down payment and a loan commitment from a lender whom she knew and trusted. Perfect so far. She flipped beyond the last standard page and discovered four additional pages of hand-written addenda. Uh-oh.

Gary Hammit completed his presentation with his warm smile never wavering. "That's about it. You folks ready to sign on the dotted line?" He held a pen out toward her clients.

Regan covered the pen with her hand, "Thank you for the offer, Gary," she returned his smile. "We'll need a little time to discuss it. We'll get back to you."

🏠🏠🏠🏠🏠🏠🏠🏠🏠🏠🏠

Regan walked into Tom's office just as he was finishing a phone call. "Help," she pleaded. "I've been working on this contract for a couple of hours now, trying to understand what it says, but it's too much for me."

"I know I'm the broker here and therefore highly trained and brilliant," he laughed, "but you've been looking at contracts a lot longer than I have. If you don't know what you're reading, we're all in big trouble." He took the papers from her and sat in silence, reading.

After thirty seconds or so, he shook his head, and began reading out loud: "Whereas the buyer of the first part tenders an offer to the seller of the aforementioned property in the sum of eight-hundred and fifty thousand dollars less the ascribed repairs mandated by all parties concerned including but not limited to the buyers and their representatives appointed, assigned and/or hired prior to and concurrently with the ..."

"What is this nonsense?" he bellowed.

"It's all like that — all four pages of it. I'm afraid that hidden somewhere in the midst of all that pseudo-legalese is a clever bit of language obligating my clients to pay for ... well ... that's just it ... I don't know what it's asking them to pay for — or to do, for that matter."

"Have you called the agent who wrote it for an explanation?" Tom asked.

"I tried, but he doesn't answer his cell. That's the only number on his card, and it's where he told me to reach him." She handed Gary Hammit's business card to Tom. "His card sounds 'golfy' to me. Do you know him? Have you played golf with him?"

"*The Foursome at Aztec Realty*. Yes, the foursome sounds like a golfing term, but it's not. He's just part of a four-person team ... clever way to get people to remember him, though. I don't know him, but I do know Brian Parsons — he is a golfing buddy of mine — the card lists him as a team-member, too. He may know how to roust his partner."

Tom found Brian's phone number, dialed it, and handed the phone to Regan as soon as it started to ring.

"Hi, Brian, this is Regan McHenry, Tom Kiley's wife," she said when Brian answered. "I'm trying to reach your partner, Gary, but he doesn't seem to be answering his cell.

Do you have any other ideas how to reach him?" she asked.

"Why?" she repeated what Brian said for Tom's benefit. "He presented an offer on a listing of mine today, and ..." She stopped. The other agent had interrupted her with a lot more to say than she could relay to Tom.

Finally, Regan started to laugh.

Tom mouthed, "What?"

"OK. Yes ... I'll let my clients know ... Sure, you can fax it," she said, and gave him the office fax number. "Thanks, Brian."

"What did my friend have to say? That was clearly about more than how to contact your stray agent."

"He says ... well ... I can sum it up with: Gary's a nice guy, but he's a doofus when it comes to contracts. Each member of the Foursome has a specialty. One member is the listing agent; a second handles client contact, inspections, and escrows; the third is the buyer specialist who shows properties; and the fourth member handles writing and negotiating contracts. Guess which one Gary is."

"I'd guess he's not the contract writing specialist."

"You'd be right. Brian says he doesn't think Gary ever wrote a contract in his life. The team member who usually does was out sick today, and Gary must have decided he could handle it.

"All that effort to try and figure out what was being said, when it really *was* just gibberish. And all the time I thought he was being so clever and cunning," Regan giggled, "when really, he just didn't know what he was doing."

"Funny how that works, isn't it?" Tom said. "Sometimes our minds read more into what they're being told than they need to. Sometimes the simplest explanation is the right one. What was Napoleon's line? 'Never ascribe to malice that which is adequately explained by incompetence?'"

Regan put her fingers on her chin, "Hmm," she said pensively.

"Perceptive viewpoint, isn't it?"

"Napoleon? Yes it is ... but what you said before that — about the simplest explanation being the right one — I'm going to have to think about it, but you may have just hit on something very important."

By Monday morning Regan knew the question she wanted to ask. It was a simple query, really. Dave would probably label it and her whole line of reasoning simplistic, so she wasn't going to tell him about it unless the answer she got looked promising. He didn't need any more ammunition for his teasing.

Regan spent the rest of the weekend, at least when her mind wasn't occupied with the new Caffey offer, thinking about what Tom had said.

He had an interesting point about the simplest explanation often being the right one. Regan got the physical description of the man Lydia was seeing from Shiloh, and the idea about his age from Shiloh and Alex, who said Lydia referred to him as old. But for everything else, she had relied on Mithrell's description of him.

Mithrell said Lydia called him her teacher, her instructor in the mysteries of life. When she first heard that phrase, Regan read it like Mithrell presented it: that he was someone who advised her on a spiritual level — a guru or spiritual adviser. She also thought the phrase might have a sexual subtext. If she interpreted the phrase in that way, Deputy Sheriff Burke probably did as well, since he would have heard Mithrell's terminology during their interview.

But the more she thought about it, the more the phrase had a Mithrell ring to it. Mithrell admitted Lydia never said she was going to meet her lover; that noun was chosen by Mithrell to describe the man Lydia was looking forward to surprising on the night she was murdered. Maybe the spiritual-advisor-take on the phrase was another of Mithrell's inventions.

According to her, although Lydia was just a girl, she wasn't an innocent. If Regan remembered correctly, Mithrell pronounced Lydia an old soul, even a troubled old soul. Regan certainly thought Mithrell very perceptive and agreed Lydia wasn't innocent and had suffered a troubled childhood. She let Mithrell define Lydia and accepted her definition of Lydia's teacher as someone with mystical weight, a philosopher, as it were, someone an old soul would recognize and be attracted to.

Suppose that was a mistake? According to Mithrell's account, Lydia had come running and jumping into the woods like a little girl, demanding the Wiccans stop their ceremony to look at her money. That was childish behavior. But Deputy Sheriff Burke hadn't heard that part of Mithrell's story; she left that part out during his questioning.

Regan recalled her son said Lydia turned up at the band's show to let Matt know he had missed his chance and to taunt him with a description of the man she was seeing. That was something a hurt girl might do, not the behavior of a secure young woman. That exhibition wasn't consistent with the

189

behavior of a mature old soul.

Deputy Sheriff Burke hadn't had the opportunity to interview Shiloh about Lydia, first because Reverend Simon wouldn't permit it, and then because she had run away. That meant he only had Mithrell's initial impression for his working theory. He hadn't heard Alex's details first-hand like she had, either.

Suppose she filtered out Mithrell's notions, possibly encouraged by a child who, as Shiloh said, liked to be mysterious, and took the simplest explanation of who the father of her child might be from Lydia's own words, from the girl herself? That would make him, as Lydia herself said, her teacher. And Shiloh said, although Lydia never told her who she was sneaking out to see, she thought she met him through work or in school. That bit of speculation certainly didn't confirm he was a teacher, but it did nothing to eliminate the possibility, either.

Could it be that simple? Was the man who murdered Lydia her teacher? Had Lydia, like so many other sixteen-year-old school girls, developed a crush on her teacher? Could her teacher have taken advantage of her youth and pain and had a sexual relationship with her? That was the question Regan wanted to ask.

She planned to have a nice lunch with her friend Sally Dewalt, who worked at Cabrillo College in the records department, and ask her for the names of Lydia's teachers. Then she would see if any of them were tall, dark, and gorgeous. If she found one who fit the description, she'd let Dave know.

She smiled to herself as she looked up Sally's work

number and punched it into her cell phone. Dave wouldn't be able to tease her if her logic worked, now would he?

"Sally Dewalt, records."

"Hi Sally, it's Regan. Can I buy you lunch today?"

"This is going to be a first for me. I'm sure I've never turned down a meal, free or otherwise before, but I can't go to lunch today. It's almost the start of fall semester. I'm swamped. Rats!"

"Then I'll grab a couple of sandwiches from Eric's Deli and bring them to your office. What do you want?" she asked.

"Um, a Pilgrim's Progress, and could I ask for a fudge brownie, too?"

"You could, but it'll cost you a two-minute favor," Regan laughed.

"Anything, as long as it's only two minutes. Oh, Regan, don't get any coffee. We have good brew here. Its fair-trade, shade grown, all that stuff. We get it from Peet's in Capitola. It's better than anything you can get from Eric's Deli."

"All right. Pilgrim's Progress and a brownie coming up. No coffee. When and where?"

"Twelve-thirty? Second floor of the Admissions and Records building, room two-nineteen."

"See you then."

🏠🏠🏠🏠🏠🏠🏠🏠🏠🏠🏠

Sally dunked the last bite of her brownie into her coffee and popped it into her mouth. All that remained of her sandwich was the wrapper. "I've bolted my food and now I'm going to make you leave with just a quick thank you. My computer is glaring at me and screaming, you slacker. I've got to get back to work. Sorry."

"Not so fast," Regan joshed, "You owe me a favor first. For the brownie. Remember?"

"Oh, that's right. I forgot. Two minutes, that was the deal, wasn't it?"

"It was. It shouldn't take you more than that to look up the classes Lydia Feeney took and give me the names of the teachers she had for each of them."

Sally frowned as she entered Lydia's name on her computer. "I wonder if I should even be doing this. Why do you want to know who her teachers were?"

"I'd tell you, but explaining it might take longer than two minutes. I'm not planning on doing anything illegal with their names, if that helps ease your mind."

The screen with Lydia's history came up. It had a small identifying photo of her in the upper left corner, probably the same one that would have been on her student ID card. Sally squinted at the computer image and pressed print. "Lydia Feeney. Wasn't she the girl who was murdered a few weeks ago?"

"The same." Regan took the newly printed page from Sally's printer. "Thanks for this," she gave the paper a little shake. "Now you should get back to work," she grinned as she headed for the door.

"Regan, wait. This is interesting. You can't leave me like this. Now I have questions," Sally wailed.

"It's going to take a while to explain. I'll call you later." She waved goodbye and closed the door.

Regan ran down the steps from Sally's office building to the quad below, sat on a bench, and took her laptop out of her briefcase. She had already downloaded the full faculty roster for Cabrillo College before coming to lunch with Sally. She looked at the page her friend printed and found the list of classes.

According to Sally's printout, Lydia had completed six classes, all of which were identified as eligible for transfer to UCSC. She had an 'A' recorded for each of them. Alex was right: at fifteen and sixteen Lydia had been aceing classes at Cabrillo. What a waste.

She noted the teacher's name for each class in the final column on the paper. English 1A, Baer, she began. She moved down the roster on her computer screen. Baer, Bridget. Nope. She moved on. Econ 1A, Frietas. She repeated the process. Freitas, Deanna. Another woman, another no. Next was French 1A and 1B, Carstall. Lydia had taken both classes from the same teacher, Robyn Carstall.

Robyn was an ambiguous name, but further reading about the professor indicated this Robyn graduated from Mills College, an all women's institution. No again.

Intro to Human Biology, Edmonds. She looked up the name. Edmonds, Robert. Nothing ambiguous about Robert, but reading his blurb indicated he had been a teacher at Cabrillo since 1963. Even if he began teaching at twenty-two or twenty-three, right after completing his MS in Biology, he would be well into his sixties. He might still be tall, dark, and gorgeous to some women, but to a girl of sixteen he wouldn't just be old, he'd probably be an old grandfatherly geezer. Male, but not likely, she noted.

193

The last possibility was Environmental Science, Barge. Regan looked up the name. Barge, Roland. His blurb said he had been teaching at Cabrillo since 1990. Bingo.

🏠🏠🏠🏠🏠🏠🏠🏠🏠🏠🏠

Regan opened her cell phone. The message icon was blinking. It was a succinct message from Dave, "No matches." He might tease her, but he was keeping her informed as she had asked. The DNA taken from Lydia's fetus wasn't a match for Kirby, Rick, or Reverend Simon.

She hit speed dial to Arlene Smith, her favorite escrow officer. Arlene greeted her with an eager voice. "Regan, do you have an escrow for me? Please have an escrow for me. The market is so slow, they're talking layoffs again."

"I didn't mean to get your hopes up, sorry. My listing on Caffey Way is working, maybe I can talk the buyer's agent into using you if we get into contract, but you know local tradition says it is his call," Regan suggested.

"Who's the other agent?"

"Brian Parsons."

"Brian," Arlene said gleefully, "my old pal, Brian. I think I'll give him a call and remind him what good friends we are and how I saved his bacon on that escrow on Sylvaner Circle," she laughed. "But first, what can I do for you?"

"I'm feeling very lazy. Could you look up a property for me?"

"Sure. What's the address?"

"It's the address I need." Regan hoped Professor Barge

was a homeowner as she said, "The owner's name is Barge, B·A·R·G·E, first name Roland."

"Got it. He owns four-nineteen Moore Street. I don't have a phone number for him though."

"That's OK, I don't need one. How does he hold title?"

"As a single man."

Regan frowned. That was a bit of a glitch in her reasoning; she expected a married man. "Not joint tenancy or tenants in common with anyone?"

"Not even an unmarried man, so we know he's not divorced, just a never-been-married single guy."

"Thanks, Arlene. Good luck with Brian."

Moore Street. That was handy; she was going to go right by Moore Street on her way home. Regan decided to swing by the address and see if a white van happened to be parked in the driveway. It was unlikely, but it couldn't hurt to look.

Single man ... Regan had expected him to be married and trying to hide an affair from his wife. It wouldn't have been the first time murder had been committed to keep that kind of secret.

Maybe Roland Barge had a long term girlfriend and had lied to Lydia about his marital status. He could have done that to keep Lydia from demanding instant matrimony or threatening exposure when she realized she was pregnant. Sure, that could be what happened. A teacher who was having an affair with one of his students wouldn't hesitate to mislead her in that way.

Of course, it didn't really matter that Roland Barge was unmarried — Lydia was underage. That fact alone could have meant serious trouble for him, especially if he was her professor.

A tall dark-haired man dressed in baggy shorts and a sweatshirt with its sleeves pushed up was outside of 419 Moore, washing a red sports car in the driveway. She parked in front of the house. She debated using a good real estate cover story for why she wanted to talk to him, but decided against it. She wanted to see his reaction to a direct question about the dead girl. If he had a guilty conscience, maybe his demeanor would betray him.

"Professor Barge?" she asked as soon as she was within earshot of the man.

"In the flesh," he smiled as he turned to face her. "I'm sorry," he frowned slightly, "you have me at a disadvantage. I don't remember your name."

Wow, she thought, no problem fitting him into the gorgeous category. She held out her hand, "Regan McHenry."

He looked first to the bucket he held in one hand and then to the sponge he held in the other.

Regan nodded slightly and dropped her hand.

"Regan McHenry. Were you in one of my classes at Cabrillo or at UCSC? Sometimes I get so confused with teaching at both places, I don't know where I am, let alone the names of all my former students." He hesitated awkwardly and Regan could almost feel his embarrassment. "You aren't one of my current students, are you?" he asked sheepishly.

"I'm not a student of yours, or a former student, but I wonder if I could ask you a couple of questions about someone who was — Lydia Feeney."

"Oh, poor little thing," he shook his head. "It's just terrible what happened to her. You do know, don't you? Oh, of course you do, or you wouldn't be asking me about her, would you?" he answered his own question. "How silly of me."

Her saying Lydia's name hadn't provoked the kind of reaction she hoped to get from Roland Barge, but it did elicit quite a response. He put down the bucket and tossed the sponge into it. He didn't seem to notice the soapy water the sponge splashed against his bare legs.

"I was just so upset when I heard. Lydia was one of my brightest students. She had such intelligence, such curiosity, and all in such a young woman. I felt she had a brilliant future. I know some of her other teachers were put off by her Goth look, but I knew that was just a phase."

He rambled on, nonstop. "She was planning to transfer to UCSC when she had enough credits, and she was trying to decide on a major. She liked science, at least my class," he beamed, "so of course I wanted to encourage her in my field of environmental studies. She couldn't take classes for credit yet at UCSC, not until she could officially transfer, but I'm an adjunct professor there and suggested she audit my class and maybe some others, just to get a feel for which field she might like to pursue."

His garage door creaked and began to open. A blue Honda pulled into the driveway and carefully rolled past the red sports car and into the garage. In a couple of moments a young blond man emerged from the garage with a bag of groceries.

Roland motioned for him to come over to where they were talking. He leaned over slightly and gave the young man a little peck on his cheek, "Regan McHenry," he began the introductions, "I'd like you to meet my life partner, Terrance Howard."

She wondered if there was such a word as "unbingo."

"As I was saying, she did sit in on my class and one or two others, as well. Of course I was *sure* she'd find my class more interesting than any of the others," he chortled.

"She said my class at Cabrillo was her favorite, so I was absolutely certain she'd decide on environmental studies. But I was mistaken. I lost her. Lost her to ... oh ... what was it ... something that started with an 'A,'" he rolled his eyes, "astronomy, archeology or anthropology, I always get those two confused, agronomy ... something like that."

🏠🏠🏠🏠🏠🏠🏠🏠🏠🏠🏠

Regan drove past the main entrance to UCSC, up Empire Grade Road past the west entrance to UCSC, and out into the country toward home, thankful the whole way that she hadn't shared her insight about Lydia's mystery teacher with Dave. There was a limit to how much fun she was willing to provide him, when it came at her expense.

Dave was right. What did she think she was doing trying to solve a murder? It had been different last year when the victim was a friend of hers, and the authorities hadn't believed her death was anything more than an accident. She had to try then. The situation was very different this time.

She couldn't even rationalize her involvement by saying she was trying to help her clients. The Sheriff had backed off of Kirby as a murder suspect, and the vandalism of the Paisley's property had been resolved. Even Rick was in the clear, and no word of his brief detention had leaked to affect his campaign.

Still, there was one loose end to take care of before she got back to her day job full-time. She needed to make amends with Reverend Simon.

Realtors were expected to develop a thick skin. For all the public relations advertising the National Association of Realtors broadcast, as a group, realtors still ranked in the bottom quarter of most-admired professions, and people were rarely shy about reminding them of that. It was part of the job to know, on any given day, that a lot of people resented the commissions realtors earned, felt their job was easy, and might even believe, deep down, they didn't care about their clients or tell the truth about the houses they sold.

She had definitely developed a thicker skin since becoming a realtor, and she could handle those disparagements because she knew they generally weren't true; certainly they weren't true in her case. Still, she tried to make sure the wide-spread bitterness toward her profession had nothing to do with her personally. She set high standards ethically and professionally. She took responsibility and tried to correct mistakes when she made them. And she apologized when she messed up.

She had been wrong about Reverend Simon; she had accused him of vile things verbally and in her thoughts. In Santa Cruz, many people would say she had to apologize for the sake of her Karma.

She just knew she had to apologize because it was the

right thing to do.

After the way their last face-to-face ended, Regan expected she would have to mollify and plead to get Reverend Simon to see her. That wasn't what happened. He was courteous when she called, and he said he had a free hour at three that afternoon.

Regan parked at his church and followed his directions to his office. He said she should walk to the back of the sanctuary, open the door at the right, and come in. At 3:00 p.m. she was apprehensively knocking on his office door with a cold hand and a mouth full of cotton, in a way wishing he had refused to see her.

A calm voice called through the door, "Come in, Mrs. McHenry, I've been waiting for you."

She opened the door expecting to make eye contact with the minister, but his eyes were downcast, reading a single sheet of paper. "Please sit down," he said without looking up, "I'm almost finished." He indicated a straight-back chair on the opposite side of his desk, the same arrangement she had offered him at her office, their roles now reversed, and with him clearly in control this time.

There were two doors at the back of his work place; one that was slightly ajar revealed a bathroom. The other, open wide, led into a large room with several sofas, TV, ping pong, at least one computer station, possibly others — she couldn't see all of the room — and a hallway with a number of doors off of it. A teenage girl was curled up on one of the sofas, reading. Regan decided that section must be the shared space of the youth shelter where Lydia had lived.

His office held not only his desk but also a single bed, neatly made and covered with quilts, a small TV, and a tall secretary with four drawers at the bottom and a three row bookshelf on top. It was good she hadn't seen his office before, when she believed the worst about the man. She would have seen a perfect spot for an assignation with a sixteen-year-old. Today she saw only an office set up to double as an overnight private suite for an adult shelter supervisor when it wasn't in use as an office.

Within moments he added the page he'd been reading to the top of a small stack of pages on his desk. He looked up in greeting; his look wasn't stern, but it was hardly filled with warmth.

Reverend Simon got up, put his hand on the knob of the shelter door, and said, "Excuse us, please, Amy," to the reading girl. He closed the door and returned to his seat. He leaned back in his chair with his hands folded across his midsection. "Yes," he said to Regan.

"I've come to apologize."

Another, "Yes."

"I accused you of being ... of doing horrible things."

"I remember."

"I was wrong about you, and I'm sorry."

"Sorry for what you thought about me or sorry that you were wrong?" The slightest smile appeared at the edges of his mouth.

"The former," she said, "and honestly, given how uncomfortable I am right now, maybe some of the latter."

His laugh was immediate; he was satisfied with her response. "An honest woman." He rocked back in his chair. "And if I match your honesty, I started us off badly at the Paisleys' party, as I recall."

"You were abrupt."

"Mmm." His lips disappeared as he pressed them together. "I was looking at the world in a very negative way that day. Rick Whitlaw had recently told me we had pagans in our neighborhood. That started it. And then Lydia, God rest her soul, told me about ..." he hesitated, "her pregnancy. I was so afraid she'd be a bad influence on the other kids — no — I'm not being completely honest, and I do think that's what we're both trying to be here. I was concerned about the other children, certainly; but it was my disappointment in her, coupled with my guilt for not protecting her, that made me turn her out. It was a very un-Christian thing to do.

"Then I heard Mithrell and Kirby had taken her in and were helping her, doing what I should have done. Pagans behaving better than a Christian pastor." He shook his head. "My pride was damaged and my understanding of my faith was challenged. I went to that party, having worked myself up into quite a state, ready to make a scene and drag Lydia out of there. I ran into you first.

"After Rick pointed out that pulling Lydia out of there

wouldn't have been appropriate, I came back here, tried to calm down, and prayed for guidance. I got quite a bit more than I expected, as it turned out.

"Rick I already understood. He's a figurer. He figured he had the green votes and the liberal votes in his district. He figured if he appeared concerned about the presence of Wiccans he might make points with me, and I might deliver some Christian Conservative votes for him. There are a few, you know. The district he wants to represent doesn't just include your Santa Cruz types, it picks up voters in the farming valleys and into Monterey — different kinds of folks," he smiled.

"I had a hard time with how to think about Kirby and Mithrell, though. I believe the Bible is the word of God. It tells me pretty clearly how I should feel about them. But here were these pagans being good people, behaving like Jesus said we should. I took my confusion out on you. I'm sorry for that."

"It seems like you're doing more apologizing than I am," Regan said.

"You know, you're right. And later, I did have good reason to be angry with you, as I recall. You accused me of having an improper relationship with Lydia, vandalizing the Paisley's trees, and maybe making Shiloh run away, didn't you?"

"I'm not sure I accused you of the Shiloh part, but I thought it, even if I didn't say it to you. I do apologize for all those accusations. They were completely wrong," Regan said.

"Apology accepted. Let it go."

"But I can't, Reverend Simon. I can't let go of my part in

making Shiloh run away. You said she left because she felt guilty about getting the Sheriff down on the kids at the shelter. I was the adult in the room. I manipulated her, got what I thought was incriminating information about you from her, and passed that misguided information along, certain it would get to Deputy Sheriff Burke.

"I owe her an apology for that, but I can't tell her I'm sorry because she's gone." Regan felt the stinging precursor of tears, the same herald she felt in her office when Reverend Simon suggested she had caused Shiloh to run away. She blinked rapidly and looked down, hoping to forestall them. "I'm worried about her."

"Maybe I can help you there," he said gently, "but you've got to stop bringing my kids into this mess. Shiloh's on her way back. I wired her bus fare yesterday."

"She's OK?" Regan asked eagerly.

"She's fine. She hitchhiked to some distant cousin's house in Washington State, thinking she could stay with them. They're in no position to keep her. They convinced her to call me.

"You know she didn't run away just because she felt guilty for talking to you. She ran away because I was sitting on her so hard. I was afraid someone would get a hold of her like they did with Lydia. I'm being given a second chance with her. I'm determined with God's help to do a better job than I did with Lydia."

"They're very different girls," Regan said. "Don't expect the same problems from Shiloh that you had with Lydia."

He snorted. "That's exactly what Mithrell told me. She said Shiloh's not going to be seduced by attention from an older man, because she isn't looking for a father figure.

"My wife and I have always run the shelter with a kind of tough-love philosophy: lots of rules and staying on the straight and narrow, or you're out. We've imposed discipline and structure for the kids. From now on, we're going to put a little more emphasis on the love part. That means I can't just set out rules and demand obedience. I'm going to work more on guiding by example, maybe being a little more like the Paisleys.

"Oh, I'll probably still watch Shiloh carefully around boys like any other dad would do," he smiled, "but I'm going to let her have some freedom, too. I'll let her babysit and not worry about the fathers of the kids she watches. I won't let myself get resentful if she listens to the prattle of one of her teachers more than she does to me."

Regan leaned forward in her chair. Reverend Simon's words had just stirred an idea in her mind. "Did Lydia have a favorite teacher, a man who influenced her?"

"She sure seemed to. I'd been trying to get her to look more respectable, not like a devil worshipper with all her black everything. The more I pushed, the more she resisted. Then one day, she said her teacher told her he thought she'd look better in light colors and with her hair the color it really was. It took less than a week for her to change her style.

"She talked about her teacher constantly." He put his hands on his cheeks and bobbed his head left and right, imitating Lydia. "'Professor says, teacher says, he's so brilliant.' I told you I believe what the Bible says. Her professor kept talking about early man and the evolution of man. That's not how I believe we came to be. We got into it a few times, Lydia and me. I didn't think he was a good influence on her, and I didn't like it that he seemed to have so much control over her. I told her I wanted her out of his class.

"She obeyed. She said she wasn't taking the class anymore, but she acted differently toward me after that. She didn't talk to me in the same way; she seemed to close up. She stopped telling me about her dreams for her future."

"I'm confused." Regan was back to thinking of the soon-to-be septuagenarian who taught Lydia biology, and wondering if the girl could possibly have thought she was in love with him. "Lydia got an 'A' in her biology class, so she mustn't have dropped out. We are talking about her biology teacher, aren't we?"

"No. We're not talking about any of her regular teachers at Cabrillo. She was sitting in on some other classes, trying to decide what field of study she might want to pursue for a major, and I believe she was doing the same thing at UCSC. The teacher she talked about so much was an anthropology professor. But I don't know if he taught at Cabrillo College or at UCSC."

Regan's day job was going to have to wait a little longer for her full attention.

24

Regan's second search of teachers at Cabrillo College, this time in the Anthropology Department, produced results similar to her first search.

Most teachers were women and could be eliminated immediately. She quickly reduced her suspect list to three male names. The Anthropology Department had better blurbs about its professors than the other divisions did. Each professor had a headshot and full bio on their website. The first name she clicked produced a pleasant looking man with a shock of white hair and blue eyes. So much for the dark part of Lydia's description.

The second teacher was a bald Professor Emeritus as old as Lydia's biology teacher. The last professor on her list was due back for fall classes, having spent the past eight months on sabbatical digging in north central China. There was no way he could have fathered Lydia's child.

But Regan wasn't ready to give up her idea. If Lydia didn't have an anthropology professor at Cabrillo who was tall, dark, and gorgeous, maybe she did at UCSC. Alex had mentioned that Lydia was auditing classes at UCSC, and

Professor Barge said she audited his environmental studies class at UCSC. Regan started another web search.

She might have been on the right track all along. Right reasoning, wrong learning institution. With a couple of clicks she had "UCSC faculty, Anthropology Department."

There were three male teachers Lydia might have taken anthropology from at Cabrillo. All had been easy to eliminate as possible suspects because of their age, hair color or lack of hair, and locality. The Anthropology Department at UCSC had eighteen professors and more than half were male. From their photos, all of them had darkish hair except for one who was totally bald. It was always possible the photos were taken years before and not updated, but all of the teachers appeared to be somewhere between mid-thirties to mid-fifties.

They were all possibles, and she didn't have a Sally Dewalt to help narrow her search field. Or did she? Smiling out from his bio was a face she recognized, Jerry Smithers, "the anthro guy." The Sheriff had called him to look at the first set of remains the Whitlaw boys unearthed. Wasn't he practically like a quasi-member of the Sheriff's Department? She guessed he might be willing to help her.

She had talked to him another time, too, at Mithrell and Kirby's party. He had seemed like a friendly enough sort. It was worth a try.

Regan punched in the phone number listed on his introduction page. Seconds later, the friendly voice she remembered said, "Jerry Smithers."

"Hi, Jerry, this is Regan McHenry. I'm not sure if you remember me. I was at the Whitlaws' house when the Coroner called you about the Ohlone remains found there, and we ran into one another again at the Paisleys' housewarming party."

"Oh, yeah, yeah, yeah. The real estate lady. Man, you're good."

"I'm, sorry, I don't ..."

"I've been thinking about calling you," he talked over her pause. "OK, I confess I would have called you, but I couldn't remember your last name. I was going to call Mithrell and ask her for your phone number, but, what can I say, I'm disorganized and slow. Maybe lazy, too. So I hadn't quite gotten around to it. But you called me. Wow, we must have some kind of psychic connection," he laughed.

"Why were you going to call me?"

"I don't know if you remember, but I told you I was just about to make the exalted leap from assistant professor to associate professor. Well, I made it. I'm now Dr. Jerald Smithers, Associate Professor of Anthropology. Cool, huh? It hasn't gone to my head at all — you can still call me Jerry." His laugh increased in volume.

"One of the perks that come with my new title is more bucks. Still not enough, but maybe enough to swing a house in this pricey area. A small house. Maybe a fixer. Probably out in the San Lorenzo Valley where prices are lower. Dr. Jerald Smithers, Associate Professor of Anthropology *and* homeowner. Got a nice ring to it, don't you think?"

"It definitely does." It was her turn to laugh. "Is another of your titles owner of a shiny new black SUV, as well?"

"You remembered I said I was going to give myself one as a fortieth birthday present? Man, you are good. Yep. That's another of my titles, all right. My old ride was in such bad shape. I thought about giving it a decent burial, but I gave it to one of my grad students instead. That's practically the same thing. He thinks he's brilliant; maybe he can figure out how to get the passenger door to close in less than three tries."

"I'll be happy to work with you on finding a house." Regan was enthusiastic — Jerry was fun. "Have you spoken to a lender yet?"

"No, but I know my credit score is really good. I looked myself up on one of those credit places."

"That's great, but you still need to talk to a lender. I'll email you the names and phone numbers of some trustworthy mortgage brokers, if you like."

"Sounds good."

"Now I have a little confession to make."

"Anything juicy? I like those confessions best," he said.

"Sorry, no. I called to ask you for a favor."

"No psychic connection?" he tried to sound despondent.

"I'm afraid not. I'm trying to track down who Lydia Feeney took classes from."

"Who? Why?"

"You may have seen stories in the news. After you finished digging in the Whitlaws' backyard, a murdered girl was found buried there."

"Wow," he drew the word out. "I must have missed that. I'm not big on the local news, unless it's UCSC politics. Between keeping up with that and academic journals, I don't notice much else," he said.

"The Sheriff was investigating Kirby Paisley, a minister who runs a shelter where the girl lived, even Rick Whitlaw briefly, as suspects."

"Whew. I've got to pay more attention to my surroundings. So why are you involved in this? Why do you want to know about this Lydia Feeney person?"

"Several reasons. It turns out my son knew her. She'd been to my house when she was younger. I knew her because of that.

"It was pretty rough on the men who were suspects. Rick and Kirby were clients. You've met them. Kirby's a gentle soul and both wives involved, Mithrell and Joan — I really like them. It was hard to see them go through having their husbands suspected."

"Are you saying they're no longer suspects? Incidentally, I notice you didn't say anything nice about Rick Whitlaw, just now."

Regan let Jerry's comment about Rick Whitlaw pass. "Kirby, Rick, and Reverend Simon, the minister, have all pretty much been ruled out. The murdered girl, Lydia, was pregnant. The deputy sheriff in charge of the investigation thinks the person who killed her was the baby's father. All three suspects submitted a DNA sample and were ruled out because their DNA didn't match the fetus."

"So who's the deputy sheriff looking at now?"

"That's another reason why I'm involved. The authorities are out of suspects right now, although they haven't absolutely dismissed Kirby as a possible murderer. I don't want them stirring things up with him again, just because they haven't got any better ideas.

"But I also don't want them forgetting about Lydia. The main reason I'm involved in all this is I saw her in her grave.

That's not something I can easily put out of my mind. I want the person who killed her found and punished.

"Mithrell said Lydia told her — don't ask, their connection is a long story — she was in love with her teacher. Mithrell added some other adjectives that made the teacher sound more like a guru, a spiritual adviser, or something like that.

"I started wondering if maybe Lydia just meant her teacher, period. That's what I'm hoping you can help me with."

"Have you told anyone else your theory, I mean did you try telling the Sheriff what you think?" he asked.

"Not yet. I've got this good friend, Dave, who's a sort of cop — second long story. We ... well ... we tease each other every chance we get. I thought I was going to find the murderer and drop the name on him. I was going to be right about the name this time, not make the kind of mistake I made about Rick Whitlaw — third long story, *really* long story," she laughed. "So I checked out the teachers Lydia had at Cabrillo College where she had been taking classes. Let's just say it's good I didn't tell anyone my theory because ..."

"Fourth long story?" he chuckled.

"Very good, Associate Professor Smithers."

"Go on, Nancy. What's your current theory?"

"Nancy?"

"Yeah. Amateur sleuth like *Nancy Drew*."

"At least you didn't call me Miss Marple. My friend Dave would have enjoyed playing with the old lady age-reference and called me that. My current theory, which I'm still not sharing with anyone but you is: maybe I got the teacher part right, just not the school.

"My son thought Lydia was auditing some classes at UCSC. I also talked to Roland Barge. Do you know him? He teaches at Cabrillo and he's also an adjunct professor at UCSC in Environmental Sciences."

"Nope, no faces flash before me. He doesn't sound familiar," Jerry said.

"Well, he also thought Lydia was auditing some classes at UCSC. And Reverend Simon, who runs the shelter where Lydia was living, said she was influenced by an anthropology professor."

"I ruled out anthropology teachers at Cabrillo. Now I'm interested in knowing if she audited or sat in on any classes in your department, and if she did, who her teacher was."

"You really are the detective, aren't you? No one from the Sheriff's Department has asked me for help and I'm pretty tight with them, or at least with the Coroner. You're a clever gal, putting all this together," he complimented.

"I can ask around, but it's a little bit complicated. I can start by checking class records, but if she just audited a class, there may not be a paper trail because she may not have registered for the class. If she just sat in on a lecture a time or two, it gets even harder to figure out which classes she might have taken. You sure she wasn't enrolled?"

"Absolutely sure. She was only sixteen and hadn't graduated from high school. She had a 4.0 at Cabrillo but not enough units to be ready to transfer."

"Sixteen?" He issued a long burst of air she could hear over the phone. "Oh, I see the problem. I need to ask about single guys too then, don't I? This isn't only about married men fooling around on their wives, is it?"

"You really are very good, very perceptive," Regan said admiringly. "I'm so glad I called you."

"Tell me her last name again. Spell it, please."

"Feeney. F·E·E·N·E·Y."

"I just thought of another wrinkle," Jerry said. "Some classes have guest lecturers and some have TAs, teaching assistants, so that kind of ups the number of possible men the girl could have been involved with, if your theory is right."

"If you could ask around I'd really appreciate it. I have a printout of classes Lydia took at Cabrillo. It has a photo of her on it. I'll scan it and email it to you. It might jog peoples' memories if you can show them a face."

"Sounds good."

"Mithrell and another person who knew Lydia said she described her boyfriend as tall, dark, and gorgeous."

"Great. I can skip all the short blond ugly guys, then," he joked.

"Yes, you can. There is one other thing that might help. Mithrell said Lydia was driving a white van the night the police think she was killed. She told Mithrell she was going to meet her boyfriend and she didn't have a car. Another person said Lydia's boyfriend might have driven a light colored van or SUV, so maybe the van was his."

"OK. I'll keep my eyes open and see if I can spot any swarthy but good-looking anthropology teacher-types driving a white van. I always liked *The Hardy Boys* when I was a kid. This might be pretty interesting, Nancy Drew," he said with clear enthusiasm.

"I always liked *The Hardy Boys* when I was a kid, too,

much better than *Nancy Drew*. They got into trouble sometimes, but when they did, it usually wasn't their fault. She, on the other hand, always seemed clueless when she was about to walk into danger.

"And then it always seemed like she wound up in some secluded place, tied up and waiting for the bad guy to come back and have his way with her. She'd just sit there hoping for rescue, which always came in time, fortunately, but not because of any proactive behavior on her part. That Nancy Drew was too passive a girl detective for my liking. I thought she was pretty dumb, even for an amateur sleuth."

Jerry didn't call her the next day or the day after that. By the third day, Regan was checking email hourly and her patience was exhausted. Two days ago, right after their phone call, she had emailed him contact information for several lenders, as well as the student ID photo of Lydia. She had a legitimate reason to follow up with him about his home purchase. If he hadn't been her surrogate investigator, she would have already followed up with him as his realtor. But for some reason, she was reluctant to push him about the teacher names.

Regan finally decided this whole exercise in waiting was silly. She picked up the phone and called his office number. "Jerry Smithers," he answered.

"Jerry, Hi. It's Regan McHenry."

"That must mean you're calling me about real estate, otherwise I would have expected you to say you were that girl detective ..."

"Nancy Drew? Can we stop splitting my personality? Please?"

"OK, Regan it is, then. Which do you want to talk about

first, sleuthing or buying my first house?"

"You caught me," she replied. "Sleuthing."

He laughed, "I thought so. Here's what I've got so far. I was right about not being able to look up records; however, I am a very popular and well connected man. I flirted with several women — of course, I'd be doing that anyway, so no big imposition there — and found out Lydia Feeney may have audited an anthropology class taught by Sam Jorgen. I'm in the process of tracking down some students who were in the class to see if they ever noticed her, and if they did, if they ever saw any meaningful looks between the two of them.

"The other possibility is Harry Richardson. He's a guest lecturer who did a series of lectures in Madeline Harris' class, and he drives a van, although it's light blue, not white. How sure was Mithrell the girl was driving a white van?"

"She seemed very definite about it."

"You mentioned someone else saw the van, right? Who was that? Did they say it was white, too?"

Regan decided to do as Reverend Simon asked and respect his kids' privacy. "The other witness wasn't sure it was white, only that it was a light color," she said with deliberate vagueness.

"Hmm. Should I rule out Harry Richardson?"

"If you don't mind asking questions about him as well, I wouldn't do that just yet."

"No problem. Do you think we should have a secret code, something like suspect 'S' for Sam Jorgen and suspect 'H' for Harry Richardson, in case the villain taps our phones? Too much?" he laughed.

"What have I unleashed on the unsuspecting City on the

Hill that is UCSC?" she asked merrily. "We better move on to house hunting and quiet you down. Did you have a chance to call any of the mortgage brokers I recommended?"

"I did. I called Julie Hanford. She sounds really pretty. I told her all about myself. I think she likes me. She says she can't wait to meet me."

"Julie's lovely and very capable, but if you really want pretty, you should see her granddaughters."

Jerry groaned.

"I'll give her a call and see what she says about the price range she's determined for you. Then I'll email you some listings that work. You can pick out three or four you'd like to see and we can start from there."

"We have a plan," he said gaily. "Oh, Regan, just curious, what does your police friend think about your theory?"

"I don't know. I still haven't told him about it yet. I'm still reluctant to look foolish if this all turns out to be a wild goose chase."

🏠🏠🏠🏠🏠🏠🏠🏠🏠🏠🏠

Regan's next call was to Julie Hanford. She'd been a mortgage broker for more than thirty years and was co-owner of her company. Julie could size-up a client with a few questions, check their credit rating, and tell Regan the upper limit of the mortgage they could afford. There were never any surprises when Julie prequalified a client. Regan liked that; surprises were rarely good things in real estate transactions.

"Regan, thanks for the referral. Your Jerry Smithers is

quite a character," Julie said with a little giggle in her voice, "and he just may be able to buy something. He's not golden, but he's close. I think I can make him work."

To realtors and lenders, anyone with a credit score over 760 was golden. It was a magic number that unlocked the best and easiest loans available.

"He's paid off his student loans and has faithfully paid his credit card balances every month, but he's never had any other credit. It's almost impossible to get stellar credit scores without some long term debt like a mortgage or a car loan, but I have one loan I think will work very well for him."

"How long would he have to be paying on his car before it would affect his credit score positively?" Regan asked.

"It doesn't take long, just three or four months to make a difference."

"Hasn't he been paying on his SUV almost that long?"

"He bought it in late June, but he paid cash, so that's not going to help his credit score," Julie said. "It's too bad he didn't finance the car and leave that money in the bank for the down payment on the house. His credit scores mean he's going to need twenty percent down, so cash on hand really limits him. He probably could have qualified for another fifty thousand in purchase price if his credit scores had hit 760. Then he could have paid off the SUV after we got the higher scores. It's kind of goofy, but that's the way the system works. Oh, well. We do our best with what we have.

"His max purchase price is three-fifty — maybe I can squeeze three-eighty. I'll likely be able to get him that extra thirty-thousand once we verify he has his promotion."

"I thought he already made associate professor?"

"He has on paper. He can call himself that, but he hasn't actually received a raise and won't until his first paycheck in the new school year."

"What about parental help?" Regan asked. "A lot of first time buyers have to ask mom and dad for help, don't they?"

"We talked about that, but he said he's the oldest of a big family. His parents still have one in college and are tapped out after helping him and his three other siblings get through school. No assistance there; he's going to have to be a self-made man."

"It's sounding like he was right about the San Lorenzo Valley. Maybe I'll suggest a foreclosed property in Watsonville, too," Regan said.

"Don't waste your time. I already made that suggestion. He's committed to North County."

"OK. Thanks, Julie."

🏠🏠🏠🏠🏠🏠🏠🏠🏠🏠🏠

There were eight properties available in Jerry's price range. None of them would ever be mistaken for a mansion. They were all in the San Lorenzo Valley, and not in its most desirable areas. Jerry eliminated the best looking house, a property on Hoot Owl Way, because it looked like it was barely clinging to the side of a hill, and because he said he didn't think anyone could take him seriously if he told them he lived on Hoot Owl Way.

They decided not to go see the A-frame even though it looked like it was in good shape. Jerry didn't think he liked

221

the idea of an A-frame, and Regan told him candidly they were hard sells, something he would have to consider, since someday he would be selling it to move up to a better home.

Regan suggested they eliminate the large house with end-of-the-road privacy because the directions for getting there required finding a remote street, taking four turns onto ever more challenging roads, and finally driving a half-mile down who knew what, to get to a house described as "full of potential."

"That was discouraging," Jerry complained as they got back into Regan's car and left the next-to-the-last house he wanted to see. "Is it a requirement that all the houses in my price range have large snarling dogs in their backyards?"

"That's not fair, Jerry. The last house didn't have a large snarling dog," Regan laughed.

"It does if you go by volume. Four small yipping dogs equal one large snarling dog. I've got a friend who teaches at UC Davis. He just bought a twenty-five hundred square foot house for less than I'm going to have to pay for a hovel."

"Location, location, location," Regan replied, "the realtor's mantra. If you were looking in the Sacramento area where your friend is, or in an inland community like, say, Tracy, where so many subdivisions were built before the real estate boom turned bust and foreclosures overwhelmed the market, you could afford an almost-new home with three or four bedrooms, three baths, and a two-car garage, and still have money left over for furniture.

"But if you lived in either of those places, you couldn't drop by the beach after classes and be a newly selected

Associate Professor of Anthropology in the University of California system, now could you?"

"Good point. Not that I'm a surfer dude," Jerry drawled, "or anything like that, but doesn't it also get to be about one-hundred and sixty-four degrees in the summer in those places? You're right. I appreciate where I am. I'll do whatever I need to do to stay here," he said emphatically.

"It's too bad I blew it on my SUV. Paying cash seemed like a good idea at the time, but Julie explained how I didn't help myself doing that."

Regan sympathized, "It does seem counterintuitive to buy on credit and have debt in order to up your credit scores. You'd think whoever determines those scores would give you points for saving enough money to buy outright. I'm impressed by the way. You must be a frugal guy."

"No need to be impressed. 'Freddie Frugal' is hardly my nickname," he chuckled.

"Then how did you come up with so much cash?" she asked. "Did they give you a signing bonus with your new title?"

"Look — there in the sky," he pointed out through the corner of her windshield, "a porcine migration. No, my dad floated me a no-interest loan based on my future great expectations."

That story didn't jive with what Jerry had told his mortgage broker. Regan wasn't surprised. It was curious how often clients who put their trust in a mortgage broker and told them the most intimate details of their lives, weren't always completely truthful about their finances. Jerry's deception had no affect on his credit score. Still, for whatever reason, he didn't tell Julie the real story about how he funded his SUV.

She supposed that was one reason realtors liked to have loan commitments when offers were presented. There was a real difference between being prequalified for a loan, a snapshot process that was based on the buyer's say-so, and having a true loan commitment where everything the borrower claimed was lender-verified.

Regan stopped her car in front of the final house on their list for the day. As soon as they opened the car doors, they heard snarls and wild barking coming from a chain link enclosure at the right of the property.

Jerry threw her a snide look but didn't say anything. The listing agent opened the front door as they approached, shook hands with each of them, and invited them in as he explained, "Don't worry about the dogs. I put them in their dog run. They're really very nice guys, just big and a little defensive of their house, is all. Come in and have a look around."

Regan now understood why the showing instructions said "contact agent before showing." The house was surprisingly nice looking on the inside, but the pungent odor of old dog was unmistakable. It was a quick tour.

Jerry was unusually quiet as Regan maneuvered her car back to the road and began the trip from Boulder Creek, where they had been looking at houses, down Highway 9 toward Santa Cruz. He still hadn't said anything by the time they got to Ben Lomond, several miles closer to Santa Cruz.

"Please don't get discouraged," Regan offered. "There are other houses out there."

"Hmm? Sorry, I was lost in my own thoughts."

"Which were?"

"Not about buying a house. I was thinking about the murder ... about Lydia."

Regan noticed the change in the way Jerry referred to the victim. She was no longer "the girl" or "Lydia Feeney." She had become Lydia. It was getting personal for him. It was for her, of course, but she had known Lydia. She began to feel a little guilty. Maybe she shouldn't have involved him in her quest for the mysterious teacher. Maybe it was asking too much of him.

Regan knew firsthand how hard law enforcement personnel worked to keep a professional distance between their private lives and the brutality that their line of work sometimes put in front of them. They had to. If they weren't able to do that, they could crack. Far too many law enforcement officers suffered from broken marriages, depression, and even suicide.

Regan came from a family which was dotted with Irish cops. She watched the job overwhelm her cousin Kevin, a nice guy she thought of as an older brother. Regan had a still-vivid memory of him, by then a tough and seasoned cop, crying as he told her about finding the body of a four-year-old girl who had been brutally murdered. The tiny victim was the same age as his daughter.

Finding the child, letting her murder get inside his head and his heart changed him, and changed the way he looked at his neighbors and at humankind. It probably wasn't the first horror he'd witnessed doing his job, but it was the one that broke him.

He drank too much after that and his marriage fell apart. Most people who knew him blamed his drinking for ending the marriage. Regan blamed whoever killed the little four-year-old for killing his marriage, too. Alcohol was just the way he tried to cope when he couldn't take the pain anymore, when he stopped liking people and stopped trying to help them, when he started counting the days until he could take an early retirement.

"I've been trying to figure out which of the two men I told you about had the capacity to kill Lydia," Jerry said. "It's possible either one of them could have known her and had a motive to kill her if, like you said, either one of them got her pregnant. They'd go to jail, wouldn't they, since she was underage?"

"They might," Regan replied.

"Even if they didn't, getting an under-aged girl pregnant …" he puckered his lips and exhaled loudly, "that could get a man registered as a sex offender. It could end a promising career teaching, that's for sure. So I really do see how either might have been motivated to kill her under the right circumstances. But I've taken a hard second look at both of them," he paused, unusually pensive for a moment. "Neither one seems like a killer. Wouldn't you think it would be obvious if someone was capable of murder?"

"If it was easy, law enforcement agents wouldn't have to conduct investigations. They could just spend all their time looking at suspects until they recognized the bad guy. In my business, I spend a lot of time paying attention to cues: body language, speech patterns, and that sort of thing. I'm pretty good at reading people, but spotting a murderer — no," Regan said. "I don't think you can tell just by looking."

"I've been following up, asking questions of students, that

sort of thing, but I'm doing it very quietly, very carefully. I'm trying not to let the people I'm questioning know that's what's happening.

"I'm really afraid of making a mistake," he confessed. "You said how traumatic being accused was for the men the Sheriff suspected. The academic world is a microcosm of the bigger world, only more secretive and more competitive. It's also isolated and inward looking. It's like you take a community and squeeze everyone in it together tightly — so tightly no one can breathe without everyone else feeling it.

"At UCSC we watch one another … study one another. There's a tremendous amount of infighting and jockeying for research money because it can bring promotions and prestige. Everyone is trying to build bigger, better reputations than their colleagues have. And then there's always competition from the wunderkind, the bright new light trying to outshine you. Rumor campaigns can do a tremendous amount of damage. I don't want to cause problems for innocent people."

"I understand."

"Are you sure there isn't anything else you can tell me? Did the person who saw the van, not Mithrell, the other person who said the boyfriend's van was a light color, get a look at the driver? Can you think of anything else that would help aim me?"

"The other witness didn't see the boyfriend. Unfortunately all we have to work with is the 'tall, dark, and gorgeous' phrase, and that leaves an awful lot of room for interpretation. I'd define tall as six feet or more, but then I'm tall myself. Lydia was tiny; it's possible everyone seemed tall to her. I figure the gorgeous part is even more subjective," Regan shrugged.

Regan was quiet for a moment. "Sorry. I can't come up with much else. My son said Lydia taunted one of his friends, a boy she had been throwing herself at for years, that he had missed his chance, that she was involved with some old guy. It's hard to know who a sixteen-year-old might consider old, but from the bio photos of your department, it looks like almost every one of your male colleagues has dark hair and might meet Lydia's definition of old."

"See, that's just why I'm afraid of making a mistake. That general a description, without any real witness, does fit a lot of men. It even fits me," Jerry smirked, "especially the gorgeous part."

"I still haven't told my theory to Dave, that's my cop friend's name. Maybe it's time I do. Maybe we should let the professionals take over. They have a lot more resources than we do for finding the truth. If they thought my idea had merit, they could ask every dark haired male anthropology professor, guest lecturer, and teaching assistant for a DNA sample," Regan said. "They could even ask you, especially since you're so gorgeous," she teased.

"Why don't you give me a few more days before you do that? Someday I'd like to be known as Jerry Smithers, Associate Professor of Anthropology, homeowner, and Hardy Boy Extraordinaire."

His tone momentarily contained his usual full-of-fun animation, but his tenor quickly returned to a more serious note. "Mostly I'd hate it if some of the people I've questioned figured out what I've been doing and thought I set them up as suspects. I know I wouldn't wear the label snitch or even the lesser title of feather-ruffler very well, especially not when it was time for a peer review. I have to be very careful with my reputation, especially if I hope to ever make full professor and be in a position to buy a real house. Right?"

"Absolutely," Regan agreed. "OK, my lips are zipped, at least for a couple more days."

26

By the next morning Regan felt like a dummy. She had been so involved in trying to think outside the box of Mithrell's creation, she didn't look at something else that now seemed obvious.

Mithrell had been clear that Lydia hadn't told her who the father of her child was. Lydia had been so secretive about his identity she hadn't even shared his name with her best friend, Shiloh. Lydia may have enjoyed having a special secret, but Regan doubted that was the only reason she kept his identity so private. She suspected the boyfriend had demanded Lydia keep their relationship secret. He might have suggested a privately shared love affair was more romantic, but realistically, no adult man could have a sixteen-year-old introducing him as her boyfriend.

And Lydia had been careful to oblige him.

Still, he had started out as her teacher before he became her lover, and he was probably a captivating professor whom Lydia held in high regard.

When Lydia told Reverend Simon about her professor's interesting lectures on evolution, he reacted negatively.

Reverend Simon himself said he ordered her to stop attending what he considered to be subversive classes. His reaction must have startled her, because according to Shiloh, he had encouraged her educational endeavors until then.

Given his new displeasure with her education, might Lydia have looked elsewhere for a confidant? Wouldn't the girl have looked for a non-judgmental adult she could confide in to replace Reverend Simon?

Mithrell had been a genuine friend to Lydia. Wouldn't it have been reasonable that exceptionally bright Lydia, finally mentally stimulated by learning at UCSC, would have sought her out for encouragement and approval? Mithrell wouldn't have taken offense at someone talking about evolution. She would have simply listened to Lydia's passion for her professor and his subject matter and let the girl openly share all she wanted.

As Lydia's relationship with her professor became more that just educational, she might have begun speaking about her professor, who was now also her lover, in an enigmatic way. That would have been especially true if he had cautioned her that the romantic part of their relationship needed to be clandestine. If he told her they needed to wait to go public until she was older, or not his student, or until he could get a divorce, or whatever it was that Lydia said made their relationship complicated, she would have begun guarding her references to him even with her best friend, Shiloh, and with her adult friend and confidant, Mithrell.

But still, she may have talked about him openly and enthusiastically as her fascinating professor. If Lydia sometimes gushed about what she was learning from her professor, and other times altered the way she spoke about him when she thought of him as her boyfriend, Mithrell might well have thought Lydia was talking about two different men. Mithrell's mystical mindset might have perceived the lover aspect of him as a separate man, Lydia's mysterious guru, her teacher in the mysteries of life.

Why hadn't she thought of that before? The answer she was looking for might have been hiding in plain sight all the time she'd been playing detective and involving Jerry in something that made him uncomfortable. What she needed to know might have been as simple a question as: "Mithrell, who was Lydia's favorite professor?"

Regan called Mithrell first thing in the morning. She got the family answering machine. The greeting had been changed from their standard message to a current one: "We are enjoying the last bit of summer vacation before Arthur goes back to school. Please leave a message for us if you are calling before August twenty-first. We aren't promising to return your call before we come home, but if your message is enticing enough, we may at least listen to it. Ciao."

The phone beeped an invitation to speak. Regan began, "Hi, all. It's Regan McHenry. Let's see, how can I make my question sexy? I can't, so here goes anyway. Did Lydia ever mention any classes she was taking at UCSC, any professors who impressed her, especially anthropology professors? I've got Jerry Smithers trying to help me find out who she took classes from, but it's difficult because she was only auditing, so there aren't any enrollment records. We haven't had much success so far. Maybe you'll remember something helpful.

"If you do, please call right away at 555-0428, or use my

cell, 555-2013. See how badly I want to reach you? I've given you my cell number and you know I don't give it out lightly. Thanks. Hope you're having a great vacation. Bye for now."

Regan took her phone with her and headed to the kitchen. The coffee was just finishing its perk cycle — Tom's handiwork. He had interrupted its brewing, poured a cup for himself, and taken it out to the back patio. She did the same.

Both her hands were full, but fortunately Tom had left the slider to the patio open. She walked out onto the warm bricks to be greeted by Tom's hand, first held up in a warning position, and then slowly moving to point out the hawk.

Tom had always enjoyed birding. She had not until a red shouldered hawk had taken to perching on one of their trees, a small redwood that had its top snapped off during a violent wind storm. The hawk had discovered it and decided it made a perfect hunting roost.

The severed tree was no more than sixty feet from where they sat, and the broken tip where he perched put the predator at their eye level. He, they decided the hawk was a male because of his coloring, hadn't become tame, but he was used to them watching him. He could study them from his roost as well as they could monitor him. As long as they didn't threaten him with sudden moves, he tolerated their presence, confident he was the superior creature who could escape if they came too close.

They were free to talk in subdued tones in the raptor's presence, but he was more watchful if their voices were loud. They concentrated on keeping them low whenever he was perched.

Regan inhaled deeply. She missed the after-rain pine and redwood fragrances from earlier in the year; their final spring rain had been in April. But the remaining star jasmine blossoms on a nearby trellis left a faint perfume in the air.

"What's your day off look like?" Regan asked.

"I may be forced to get in a game of golf. George Weston just called. One of their regulars is sick. They need a fourth. I didn't want to let them down, so I reluctantly agreed to play. Of course, I told him I'd want to check with you first before I made any promises. Tee time is one-fifteen unless you have some plans for the day that include me."

"I don't have any real plans at all. If the weather stays this perfect I may not move all day. One-fifteen you said? You should be back for dinner, right?"

"Definitively."

"Good. I think I might need some caring sympathy by then."

"Why is that? Did the Caffey escrow crash?"

"No. So far, so good. We'll see if the buyers can hang on to a loan long enough to actually buy the house. No, that's not it. I'm thinking of calling Dave later. He may roast me alive by the time you get home.

"After the whole Rick Whitlaw debacle, Dave made it very clear he would appreciate it if I stopped poking around the Lydia Feeney murder investigation and left things to the pros."

"But of course you haven't, have you?" Tom chuckled.

Regan raised her eyebrows and shrugged like a guilty eight-year-old. "Not exactly. I've got a new theory about Lydia's murderer that I wanted to check out, so I've been kind of working on it."

"Why didn't you just tell Dave your idea and let him follow up on it with the Sheriff?"

"Because there was, I guess still is, a good possibility I'm wrong again. I didn't want him having fun at my expense if my current theory is another bust."

"You haven't told me what your idea is or what you've been up to." His voice filled first with curiosity and then a touch of concern. "You're not putting yourself in any danger, are you?"

"Not unless you consider Googling dark-haired scholars dangerous. Mithrell said Lydia described her boyfriend as tall, dark, and gorgeous and said he was her teacher in the mysteries of life. Remember? I told you that?"

"I remember the tall, dark, and gorgeous phrase, not the rest."

"I started wondering if Mithrell read too much into the 'mysteries of life' part of what Lydia said. Mithrell might. She's kind of magical herself, so I thought she might have interpreted or even embellished Lydia's words describing her teacher to make him someone more exotic or spiritual than he really was. Maybe all Lydia meant was he was her teacher, as in ordinary go-to-lectures teacher."

"That sounds logical and not like something Dave would make fun of you for proposing."

"Not until he looked up her teachers at Cabrillo College like I did, eliminated the women and the men well over seventy like I did, and began investigating a really attractive man who would no doubt introduce Dave to his boyfriend like he introduced me to him."

"Oops. I see what you mean," Tom laughed. "He would be teasing you about that by now, wouldn't he?"

"Oh yes. Besides, if Dave got Deputy Sheriff Burke to follow my hypothesis into those dead ends, he might have decided my idea was completely wrong and stopped investigating in that direction.

"That would have been a real shame because I think my idea is right. I just got the wrong place in mind to look for teachers.

"It turns out Lydia was auditing classes at UCSC. The Deputy Sheriff probably would have missed that. I would have if I hadn't remembered Alex telling me that's what she was doing, or if I hadn't continued talking to Professor Barge after he introduced me to his life partner.

"I have an ally in the form of Jerry Smithers, the UCSC anthropologist the Coroner uses when he needs to verify a burial is ancient, trying to figure out which professors Lydia might have come in contact with if she was sitting in on some classes."

"Do you have any suspects in mind for Dave?"

"I think Jerry might have uncovered a couple of likelys, but he's reluctant to pursue his inquiry any further. I don't know how he can anyway. I told him I'd give him another couple of days to try, but I really don't see any point in waiting to talk to Dave.

"I just know when I explain my theory, he's going to start in with me, especially when I tell him a dozen or more men fit Lydia's description and suggest he should convince Deputy Sheriff Burke to get a DNA sample from each of them to match against Lydia's fetus. As Jerry pointed out, according to my criteria, even he looked suspect," she laughed.

"Your theory sounds pretty reasonable to me. I'm going to venture a guess Dave won't criticize you for anything except not calling him sooner. Why don't you give him a call right now while I'm here for moral support," he grinned. "If I'm wrong I'll take you to dinner tonight — anywhere you want to go. Fair enough?"

"Fair enough," she nodded.

Regan began to punch in Dave's phone number. Her phone issued a shrill beep with each number she entered. The hawk jerked his head to one side, watching her intently.

"Dave Everett," his answering machine picked up.

"Dave, its Regan. I've been doing a little investigating about Lydia Feeney's contacts. I know what you're thinking, but don't go there. You're going to be impressed when I tell you what Jerry Smithers, the Coroner's anthropology expert, and I have discovered," she said, mentioning Jerry's name to give herself some authority by association.

"Lydia was auditing classes at UCSC. We think she was sitting in on an anthropology class and that her teacher was the one who got her pregnant. Call me."

The hawk let out a high pitched "key-aah" and soared from his watching roost.

"Do you think I scared him with the phone call?" Regan asked.

"Hard to say. You might have, or he might have spotted some prey he thought he should catch."

27

Regan's phone rang while she was eating a late lunch on the patio. She had her phone with her in case Mithrell or Dave returned her call. She glanced at the caller-ID as the phone rang a second time. Caller unknown. It wasn't either of them, and it wasn't someone she loved. *Ignore it,* she told herself as it rang a third time. *It's your day off. Let it go to your answering machine, that's why you have one.*

Even as she reminded herself of all the excellent reasons she had for paying no attention to her ringing phone and instead enjoying a day of solitude, she knew the battle was lost. Sometimes she was simply too curious a person for her own good.

She had decided to pickup by the time the phone sounded a fourth ring. She was resigned and prepared to press the talk button and say, "Kiley and Associates Real Estate, this is Regan," when a voice in her head whispered, *Don't do it. Screen the call first.* She smiled — the day-off gods must be intervening and telling her to fight for her day of rest by at least screening the call.

She headed for her office, willing herself not to rush. She

could hear the caller begin his message by the time she started down the hall.

"Hey, Regan, it's Jerry Smithers. You're not blowing me off just when I decided to buy the A-frame in Boulder Creek, are you?" She acquiesced and pressed the talk button on her handset. She owed him after all.

"No, I'm not snubbing you," she said.

"Regan, it's Jerry," he said again oozing enthusiasm. "I decided to drive by the A-frame on your list. I like it. Would you show it to me today?"

"I'm kind of booked today," Regan fibbed. "How about tomorrow?"

"I can't tomorrow. I can't for the rest of the week. If you meet me at UCSC, I'll drive. Come on, Regan, if I'm willing to take you out in my gas-guzzler and drive round-trip to Boulder Creek twice in one day, you know I'm serious," he laughed.

"OK. You wore me down." She didn't echo his enthusiasm, but as usual, she was amused by his manner. "The house is vacant as I recall. When do you want to go?"

She heard the sharp beep of her answering machine announcing the end of its recording time. She knew it was making the same piercing noise on Jerry's end, too. "Sorry about that."

He didn't seem to notice the beep. He continued, his enthusiasm not diminished in the least. "It is vacant. I looked in a window. How soon can you get here?"

She calculated time for a shower and added fifteen minutes to get from her house in Bonny Doon to either entrance of the University. "Where will you be on campus?"

"My office is at Porter College. I can see some vacant visitor parking spaces from my window. Shakespeare Santa Cruz is in full swing and we get the Performing Arts parking lot overflow. Things can get tight around here; I'll go out and lay down in one of them if you want me to, just to reserve a spot for you."

"I can make it in an hour. Stay upright until then."

"Great. I really appreciate this, Nancy Drew."

🏠🏠🏠🏠🏠🏠🏠🏠🏠🏠🏠

Regan was on time. Jerry was sitting on the curb with his feet stretched out into a visitor parking space, reading, when she pulled up. She laughed when she saw him. He was nuts in a very entertaining way. He jumped up and waved her into the spot and then stood on the curb with a big smile on his face.

"You really are serious about this, aren't you?" she asked.

"Oh yeah, deadly serious. My chariot awaits."

He directed her to a big shiny black Chevy Trailblazer parked nearby. As she walked past the vehicle to the passenger side, she noticed the license plate was an ordinary one. "I thought you were going to get vanity plates that said anthro guy or bone man."

"I was, but a number of other people must have had the same idea. Both those plates were taken. I'm trying to think of something else clever and related. Suggestions are welcome."

They left the university and began retracing the trip she

had just made by heading back up Empire Grade, the ridge road into the Santa Cruz Mountains and Bonny Doon. Jerry drove past the road that led to her house on the coastal side of Empire Grade. He continued on past the downhill turn to Felton, Felton-Empire Road, defined like an Irish thoroughfare by its destinations, Felton on one end and Empire Grade on the other.

She would have turned right at the intersection and dropped down into Felton to pick up Highway 9; it was a scenic ride and she knew it well. Instead of scenic, he opted for Alba Road, a steep brake-burner of a road most drivers avoided, at least in the downward direction which they were travelling. Alba Road would put them on Highway 9 in Ben Lomond, much closer to Boulder Creek and their objective, the A-frame house on Fireside Avenue.

"You're a brave man taking this road," she told him as he turned down Alba on what felt like the first drop of a roller-coaster ride.

"I like to take risks — they get me going. Besides, we're in my road warrior," he smiled.

They arrived at the house without incident and she used her lockbox key to give them access.

Within moments Jerry's enthusiasm disappeared. He gave the interior the most cursory of looks and sighed. "You know, now that I get a better view of the inside, I don't think I like it."

Regan suppressed a killing look as she considered how she had sacrificed her day off so he could see his quickly abandoned dream house.

"Let's go see the other house that's still on the list," he

suggested, "the one on Apple Tree Road."

"If you don't like this house, I doubt you'll like that one. Remember it's a fixer in a remote location and I don't think the road to it is very good."

"Great. I've hardly had my SUV off-road. If we see the last house, we will have looked at all the houses on your list. We can eliminate any loose ends. I like tying up loose ends, don't you? Then I can have a fresh start with nothing hanging that I might regret missing."

"I didn't bring directions for finding the house. I know it's a convoluted route."

"More fun," he grinned, "I opted for GPS." He entered Apple Tree on his GPS keypad and the first direction told him to return to Highway 9.

Regan threw up her hands in mock surrender. "You win," she laughed.

"I always do," Jerry said. "While I drive, you can give me an update on your murder investigation."

"Wasn't I supposed to be waiting for you to do more discrete questioning in the UCSC community?"

"I guess you were," he exhaled loudly. "I got squat. Have you had any talks with your friend Dave yet?"

"No, but that reminds me, I had an idea and put in a call to him this morning. Let me check messages, maybe he's returned my call by now."

Regan rooted through her purse and got out her cell phone. The mail icon indicated she had multiple messages waiting. "I'm popular today," she said as she put the phone to her ear for the first message.

There was no introduction, but she recognized Mithrell's

voice immediately. "Yes Regan, Lydia was auditing an anthropology class at UCSC. What an odd question. I'm certain Jerry Smithers would remember that, since she was taking it from him. She thought he was wonderful, so wonderful she kept pushing me to let his students dig on our property. She said she could vouch for them, but I refused to let them because I didn't feel comfortable around that man. His soul is missing a piece."

The panic came in the same instant as her understanding. Regan's memory, which always produced photo-like images, flashed first to Jerry at the Paisleys' housewarming party, waving a chicken leg in his hand, telling her how Mithrell had denied him digging privileges even though one of his students had vouched for him.

The second image she saw was much more ominous. She had been the first to leave the Whitlaws on the day the Ohlone burial was discovered. The Coroner, Dave, and Jerry were still inside. Her car was parked curbside in front of the house. She had stopped at the bottom of the driveway and waited for the deputy sheriff assigned to crowd control to help her past the yellow crime scene tape. As he held up the tape, she had ducked slightly and turned toward the house as she slipped under it. In her final glimpse of the house she saw the clearly marked white coroner's van, Dave's SUV parked next to it, the Whitlaws' Prius behind the Coroner's van, and behind Dave's SUV, an old white Volkswagen van.

Regan's messages continued. She listened to them between beats of her pounding heart. There was Tom's voice, warm and loving, "Do I owe you dinner? Let me know where you'd like to go. Let's go out even if I win the bet and Dave hasn't roasted you alive."

The next one was from Dave. "Regan, we've got to talk ASAP." He said it, not in her friend's voice, but in the terse official voice he reserved for when he was a cop on the job.

Finally, there was a second, this time more urgent message from Dave. "Regan, Jerry Smithers may well be the guy we've been looking for. Call back immediately."

No doubts were left in her mind. She was alone in a vehicle with a murderer. They were heading for a remote vacant house. She had walked into it ... Nancy Drew.

"What's wrong?" Jerry's question snapped her to attention amid a rush of adrenaline.

"Nothing," she smiled, hoping she said it believably. "Well, nothing I can do anything about. One of my escrows just crashed and burned," she lied, hoping to cover any of her reactions to the phone messages that Jerry might have noticed. "I'm upset of course. Nothing from Dave. That's disappointing, but sometimes he takes a day or more to get back to me if he's busy. I'm a low priority in the crime-solver's world," she forced a tiny laugh.

"My husband left me an offer of dinner out. Let me set it up." Regan hit speed dial to Tom. She would have preferred Dave's number, but if Jerry glanced at her phone he would see the name of the person she was calling on the display screen. She was afraid to risk it.

Her decision was a wise one. Jerry craned his neck subtly, but now that she was watching his moves, she could tell his new angle indeed let him read the name on her phone before she put it to her ear.

Tom picked up before the first ring finished.

"Regan, are you all right? The Sheriff thinks Jerry Smither's is the killer ..."

Regan interrupted him, "Hi, honey, it's me," she said lightly. "I'm going to take you up on that offer of dinner. I'm in Boulder Creek with Jerry Smithers looking at some houses."

"Regan, get away from him right now!" Tom demanded.

"I'm in the mood for something robust, so how about Scopazzi's?" she asked in a casual manner. "It seems so remote; we haven't been there in a long time. I don't have my car. We drove in Jerry's new black Chevy Trailblazer; I think he wanted to show it off." She smiled at Jerry. "I'll ask him if he can drop me off there after we see this last house on our tour."

She turned to Jerry, "You wouldn't mind, would you?"

"Ah, sure," he hesitated, "sure."

"He says he can."

"I understand. Tell me where you are," Tom's tone was urgent.

"No," she denied her panic and forced a small chuckle, "he's not that nice. It's going to be on our way back from 410 Apple Tree Road. That's where we're headed. That reminds me, we were at a house on Fireside and decided to see Apple Tree on the spur of the moment. It's vacant, so it was easy to do."

"You're in his SUV between Fireside and Apple Tree Road," Tom said. "Got it. Regan, I don't know how long it will take to get help to you. Get out of his car right now. Jump out if you have to, but get away from him."

"Please don't lecture me. I know how important you feel it

is that every agent log in who they're with and what they're going to see," she hoped her voice had just a touch of annoyance and apology in it, "but obviously I couldn't put that address into the log, because I didn't know we were going there."

She rolled her eyes at Jerry who was paying close attention now. She covered the phone's mouthpiece and whispered to him, "My husband's so particular." She waited again, as if giving Tom a chance to lecture her some more about the office log she just made up.

"Uh-huh, 410 Apple Tree Road. Thank you for understanding. OK. See you at the restaurant. I'm going to start drinking without you. I know it's going to be early for dinner, but come quickly if you don't want a drunken wife."

"Regan, get away from him, *now*," Tom implored as she hung up.

"That worked out well. I'm not going to have to cook tonight," she smiled a broad artificial smile, closed her cell, and pretended to return it to her purse, but she palmed it and slid it into her pocket instead.

"I didn't know you had to keep a record of who you're with when you show people houses," Jerry smiled as artificially as she had.

She took a deep breath. Was it possible he bought it? "Oh, yes," she lied believably. "Being a real estate agent can be a dangerous profession. It's office policy that we never go out with anyone we haven't met; and when we do show property, we have to sign in the name of who we're going out with and which properties we plan to see."

Regan looked directly at Jerry and spoke slowly, "It's kind

of like leaving a fingerprint. Now Tom knows where I am, and he knows I'm with you."

"Hmm," he sighed. "I had everything worked out, Nancy Drew, but you've just presented me with a bit of a dilemma."

He reached forward on the console under his window and pressed a button. Regan's door and all the other doors clicked a metallic sound. "Childproof locks," he said.

Jerry's GPS instructions pinged and a soft female voice told him, "Prepare to turn left in two hundred yards." He slowed, following his GPS instructions, and turned off busy Highway 9 onto Pleasant Road, the only access to a series of smaller roads used by the residents of the area. It was a well-paved road, still relatively well-traveled, but there were houses close along both sides that made the setting decidedly more residential than Highway 9.

"I had the perfect alibi, now I have to think about it. Maybe you can help me sort things out here." His voice lacked its usual lighthearted merriment.

"It seems right now I'm not really here with you. I have at least one witness who will swear I'm not. Right now I'm giving a makeup test to one of my students, a pretty little thing who wasn't feeling well the day of final exams. She expects me to make exceptions for her. She seems to think we're in love and going to be married. We have to wait a year or so though, 'til she's not my student any longer. I've already been called before a review board on something like that once, well technically twice, but who's counting?" he laughed.

"She's very loyal, but not that bright. She's really struggling to keep up. That's the real reason for the makeup test today. She took the first exam with her class, but failed. I thoughtfully, and lovingly I might add, suggested it might have been because she wasn't feeling well. 'You know how hard it is to concentrate when you're not well,' I suggested.

"If she doesn't pass today, she's going to fail my class. It would be easier for her to get a good mark if I could grade her paper, but it would look strange if I did hers and my TA graded all the others, right? There's no way I can grade her paper.

"But Professor Helpful here," he touched his chest as he referred to himself, "mentioned she'd probably do better if she had her class notes with her. I explained to her that I couldn't condone cheating, of course, but that I had a lot of work to finish, and asked if she would mind if I worked in my office while she took her test." He let out a little burst of air through his nose. "I couldn't compromise my ethics, could I? But you can see why she would swear I was in the room the whole time, if anyone asked her. She'd get a passing grade, maybe even an 'A', and I'd get an alibi. Win-win.

"But, like I said, she's not too bright. I think she's going to fail some other classes or drop out of school before too long. She's overly sensitive, poor thing. Her failing will be a big disappointment to her parents. Letting them down like that might make her so despondent that she runs away or even, who knows," he shrugged, "commits suicide."

He let out an exaggerated sigh. "That happened once before with a pretty young student of mine. And then there was Lydia, of course. I seem to be haunted by more than my share of tragedy." He sighed again and briefly took one hand off the steering wheel to put it over his heart.

"Your alibi's shot. I told Tom I was with you, you heard me." Regan sounded more assertive and confident than she felt. He had just confessed an implied past murder to her, hinted at a future one, and connected himself to Lydia. He couldn't let her go after that.

"Didn't I say we needed to think about some new ideas?"

"Turn left at the next intersection," Jerry's GPS instructed him in her silky feminine voice.

Soon they were on River Street. It was still a populated residential area, but the road was rougher than the previous street had been. Jerry drove more slowly. Regan decided it was time to heed Tom's advice. At the speed they were traveling, she might get pretty banged-up if she jumped, but she had to take the chance.

Regan readied herself to jump and tried her door. She pulled the handle repeatedly, but nothing happened.

Jerry smirked. "Regan, I told you: childproof locks. What? Do you think I'd lie to you? I'm not a liar. I've always been completely truthful with you," he added with a big friendly grin.

"This is hard for me. I really hate to abandon plans that are so elegantly devised. You see, not only do I have my student who will swear I was in class with her all afternoon, but my SUV is parked near there, too. Well, not really, because here we are in it, but it sure looks like it's parked at Porter College.

"Who would guess sweet little old English Professor Dorothy Beckett, who's attending an educational seminar in Vancouver right now, would drive an SUV just like mine? Dorothy doesn't have a garage and hates to park her pristine new vehicle in front of her house when she goes away. Her last vehicle got keyed when it was parked in her own driveway. She's got long tenure with the university and a lot of clout. She got permission to leave her new SUV by her office at Porter College when she's away for a day or so, especially when she's going to a university-promoted conference like she is right now.

"I switched our license plates late last night when I was sure no one would notice. Brilliant, right? So there's my 'bonguy1' plate still at Porter College on a new black Chevy Trailblazer. You'd be amazed how many smiles and comments that plate generates for me. I'm confident someone's noticing it right now and would have remembered seeing it, if any law enforcement official were to ask. Would have been sweet … right? But now you've told your husband you're in my SUV. We gotta' come up with another plan, don't we?

"Now I know what you're thinking, Regan." He mocked her voice with a slight whine: "'Jerry, you went to an awful lot of trouble, and you were never even going to be a suspect. I didn't tell my cop friend my theory; the deputy sheriff isn't going to put it all together because he hasn't had the conversations with the people I've had; and besides, the authorities wouldn't think one of their own, their very own anthro-guy, could be a murderer.' You're right, too. But I'm thorough, Regan, and like I said, I don't like loose ends."

Regan saw a young woman, carrying a little blond child, come out her front door and walk to a car parked at the top of her driveway. The woman opened the back car door and was about to put her toddler inside. Regan pounded on her window and screamed, "Help me! Help!" She waved frantically. The woman saw her and stopped her efforts. She said something to the child. The tot nuzzled his mother's neck, shyly held up a tiny hand, and made a little fluttery movement. The woman smiled and joined her child in waving.

Regan couldn't hear what the woman said. No doubt the woman hadn't heard her call for help either. But Regan was better at lip reading than the young mother was — besides, the woman's words were easy to understand. She said, "Bye-bye."

Regan cowered and braced for Jerry's reaction to her desperate attempt. She expected him to hit her or worse, but he scarcely seemed to notice what she had done. He was still rolling his scheme over in his mind.

"So, I'm in a classroom at UCSC and my SUV is in the parking lot. What do you think, Nancy Drew? You see how cool my original setup was? But I'm going to have to improvise now and make a couple of changes because of your attempt at cleverness."

The female voice of Jerry's GPS system spoke again, "Turn right onto Wild Brambles Road."

There were considerably fewer homes along this street. Several of the houses had old cars parked out front, left to rust or up on blocks in the process of being cannibalized for parts. This neighborhood was more rural and more wooded. Houses along the street weren't cared for as well as the houses they had passed.

The neighborhood wasn't considered dangerous, but it was a hodgepodge of renters and owners. Most people who lived here didn't know their neighbors. She was stereotyping certainly, but Regan thought people here would be unlikely to notice something out of the ordinary, and if they did, they wouldn't notify the authorities.

"You know what they say ... how does it go? Umm ... oh ... yeah, yeah, yeah, when one door closes, another one opens. That's it. You closed my carefully planned door with your call, but I think I'm seeing another one you opened." Delight crept back into Jerry's voice.

"I was going to have to take your keys and drop your car somewhere. I hadn't decided whether to roll it off a really steep part of Empire Grade or drop it in town, unlocked, with the driver side door open like you met up with a carjacker or someone like that.

"Now I'm thinking I don't have to dispose of your car at all, which is great because I wasn't really one-hundred percent satisfied with either of those options. I do have to change my plans for you today though. Right?" Jerry continued to consider out-loud; the meter of his sentences picked up speed.

"New plan — tell me what you think." He quizzed Regan as if they were co-conspirators. "First, I have to use your little key thingy to open the door at Apple Tree Road. I noticed your code was 2366 by the way, so if you're a little too stressed to remember it, don't worry about it.

"Feel free to correct me if I'm wrong, but I bet that thing leaves a trace somewhere that lets a computer know when and where you used it."

Another smile. "Next, I'll tell everyone I dropped you at Scopazzi's like you asked me to. Can't you hear the Sheriff?"

This time he deepened his voice: "'So, Professor Smithers, you say she was OK when you dropped her off?'

"That's right, Sheriff," he play-acted. "She said she was going to order a glass of chardonnay and wait for her husband.

"See how believable I could sound?" he said excitedly. "Notice I didn't say anything about being the last one to see you alive; that would have given me away. I could play it kind of like I did when you told me about Lydia. You had no idea I knew her, did you?" He raised his eyebrows in a questioning look.

He was right. She hadn't known. He had lied credibly and she had believed him.

"I thought not," he laughed when Regan didn't correct his impression. "I've discovered if you tell a story blatantly, you can get away with lots of things. It's the people who look guilty when they lie who get caught.

"I'm going to strangle you — sorry — you probably won't appreciate that part too much. That piece stays the same. We'll just attend to that little detail in the house instead of in the forest.

"My original plan was that today you'd go in the ground. I've got the place all ready for you in a nice little fairy ring of redwood trees. I guess you've figured out by now, I've been here before." He let out a little giggly-sound which chilled Regan more than anything he had said so far. "And I've done this before, too.

"But now I'm thinking, after what you told your husband, the cops may feel obligated to search the property, even though they'll probably believe you left the house on Apple

Tree alive and healthy. Yeah, they might want to be thorough, so they might search — might even bring in cadaver dogs, if for some reason I can't charm them into fully accepting the idea I left you happily headed into Scopazzi's."

He let out another of his little blood-chilling giggles and continued in his psychopathic sing-song meter. "I might even suggest they do that. I've watched those dogs work; it's a real nose-down operation — no pun intended," he chuckled. "The really amusing thing is the way what the dogs do affects what their handlers do. They all look down. Dogs and deputies, they'll all be focused on the ground, looking for a burial.

"So what would happen if I hid you in plain sight instead of burying you? A few of those big garbage bags I've got in the back should do the trick. I'll pop you in one of them, add a few layers more, maybe work a couple of redwood branches into my creation as camouflage, and hoist you way up into the trees for a while. It should be fairly easy. I've got plenty of rope in back to help me do it.

"Those doggies are going to smell your scent between where I parked and the house, but nowhere else. And with their conscientious noses sniffing dirt, plus your wrapping, I don't think they'll pick you up buried Zoroastrian-style. That should cement my story. Oh, oh, great idea," he added, almost breathlessly. "I'll take your purse and drop it out front of Scopazzi's, too. Oooh — and I could break off a fingernail or two of yours and drop them on the ground by your purse. It might look like you had a struggle with someone and got forced into a car." He turned to her with kind sarcasm, "Now I don't want you to worry. I'll wait 'til you're dead to take your fingernails … you won't even feel it."

Jerry's GPS lady indicated he was approaching Apple Tree Road. "Turn right in two hundred feet," she chirped emotionlessly. Regan spotted the road sign, such as it was. Even so, the turn might have been easily missed except the listing agent had put a red and white directional arrow under the street sign, pointing down the road.

They didn't go more than fifty feet after the turn before the paving ran out. There was one house on either side of the pavement and then Apple Tree Road became little more than a tree-lined and rutted gravel road, one that obviously wasn't often used.

"You're awfully quiet, Nancy Drew. Are you trying to find a flaw in my new plan? I appreciate that. I'm also glad you seem to understand how hard it is for me to change the setup mid-procedure like this. And you haven't said anything stupid like, 'You'll never get away with this,'" he added in another mocking imitation of her voice. "Good for you.

"I'm usually very detail-oriented. I like to plan ahead, like I did with Lydia, but I'm thinking the spontaneity with you will be fun ... a rush, kind of." He licked his lips with the very tip of his tongue.

"You've still got a very interesting future, by the way. Nothing will change there. Let me tell you about it now, since you won't get to enjoy it firsthand. After a respectful but brief amount of time ... say a week ... I'm going to buy this place. I'll have your husband write the contract, if you like. I know you realtors don't get paid for showing property; you have to make the sale to make any money, right?"

Regan didn't answer.

"The soil here is acidic because of the trees. I was

counting on your flesh going pretty quickly, but wrapped in plastic during the dog days of August will work well in that regard, too. Don't worry, either way I'm going to keep close tabs on you. I'll be moving you soon, and doing, if you will, a little post mortem plastic surgery on you.

"Some of your teeth will have to go. We can't have any dental work which could be used to identify you. Hmm — maybe you'll have to suffer a smashed face. Yeah, yeah. Your teeth don't have enough wear to match your age. I blame our modern diet for that — not enough grinding of course grains — better get rid of all your teeth. We have to remove any possibility you'll look like a modern burial because — and this is the really cool part — you're going to become Ohlone." He seemed filled with childlike glee. "You're going to become my very own backyard bones."

"How many women have you killed, Jerry?" Regan asked. She was surprised how calm she sounded; she certainly didn't feel calm.

"You'll be number four. But I want you to know you're the only one I'm going to take such uncommon steps with."

"You don't consider cutting a pentagram into Lydia as an uncommon step?"

"Nah, that took minimal effort. I'm a friendly guy. By the time Lydia told me she was pregnant, I'd had time to get to know the people in the neighborhood. I figured if she was found with that pentagram, it might make the Sheriff look at Kirby Paisley or even Reverend Simon — the wild evil warlock dedicating a victim to Satan, or the crazed betrayed minister murdering his ward for participating in devil worship. It was just kind of a game.

"I probably should have taken a little more care with her, as it turns out. I should have gone a little farther, opened her up and taken the fetus so there couldn't have been a question of DNA. It would even have played well with my ritual-murder theme. But I didn't bother. Like I said, I'm lazy.

"It's really too bad about Lydia. It's not like I have an affinity for jailbait, just my students. I want you to know that. When we started, she said she was nineteen and I believed her. Who knows, we might have had a future together if she hadn't gone and gotten herself pregnant. I liked her a lot. Then she turned up pregnant, underage, and determined to have the baby. She even had a note from her mom that it was OK for her to get married.

"Well, that might have worked for her, but it would have finished me as a professor. I tried to explain that we'd starve, but she didn't get it. She thought if we had some money, her family fantasy could still happen. She came up with this harebrained scheme to blackmail Rick Whitlaw. That idea scared the daylights out of me. He hadn't touched her. If she could blackmail him on appearances, what could she do to me if I ever fell out of her favor? She really left me no choice. Ah, well," he shrugged, "no point brooding about what might have been, right?

"Truth be told, I didn't expect Lydia to be found anytime soon. My crew was finished at the Whitlaws' dig and they had re-landscaped, so I didn't expect any more digging on the property. I overheard Whitlaw telling you they were going to move. I figured their backyard was going to be a secure dumping ground for quite a while.

"And, of course, that would have been the case if those

little brats hadn't dug her up. It still wouldn't have been a problem if you hadn't started playing detective so doggedly, talking to people the Sheriff wasn't talking to, and asking annoying questions that no one else was asking. Then you got that idea about all the UCSC anthropology professors supplying some DNA. Yikes! I would never have become a suspect if you hadn't started playing connect-the-dots.

"Don't get me wrong," he grinned, "you provided some real entertainment for me. It was apparent you hadn't put it all together yet, and it was kind of fun seeing how obvious I could be before you did. Turns out I could be very obvious. I guess you don't need to be that bright to sell real estate. Evidently you just need tenacity, and you seem to have that in spades.

"I was sure you'd eventually make me the missing link though, so you're going to be number four.

"But I'm getting distracted here and we're almost to the house. We, well you, don't have much time left, so I better tell you the rest of my plans for you. I do think you're smart enough to appreciate the irony in your future.

"The least interesting thing that could happen is that your body is never discovered. But let's say it is. If it happens in the next couple of decades, I'll be the one called, because remember, you're going to be doctored to look like indigenous remains, and I'm the Coroner's go-to-guy for anthropological finds.

"Of course I'll say you're Ohlone. Don't you love it? I might even write a paper about you. Who knows, maybe something with a catchy subtitle like 'Dr. Jerald Smithers, UCSC Professor — I'll be a full professor by then — holds the record for single Ohlone burials after one was discovered in the backyard of a house he used to own.'" He elbowed her, "Since I'll be a full professor by then, I'll own a nicer house by then, too. At the very least, I'd use you for some course work, just like the genuine discovery on the Whitlaws' property.

"Even if you aren't found during my career, there's always future potential for you. You may be discovered decades from now, well after I've retired. I'm going to leave a couple of artifacts with you for authenticity. The things I'll leave will make you look like an important member of your tribe. Who knows, maybe some up-and-coming young anthropology hotshot of the future will find you, write a paper like I was going to do, about how unusual you were to be buried solo, maybe even base his Ph.D. on you. You could become the Piltdown Man, sorry, woman, of the Santa Cruz Mountains." His laugh was uproarious.

"Oh, I hope I'm still here, you know, in my extreme old age, if that happens. After he, or she, I'm not gender biased, publishes, I could come forward and explain how I did everything." He could hardly get the words out amid his chortling. "What could they do to me if I was, say, ninety five? But the notoriety at that time in my life," his voice went up an octave, "what a hoot!"

He smiled merrily at her. "Looks like we've arrived. We better get on with this," he said as he stopped in front of a dilapidated house at the end of Apple Tree Road, turned off his SUV, and pocketed the keys. "Hand me your purse," he commanded.

Regan resisted her first instinct, which was to try to hit

him with it. She had to think quickly of action and likely reaction if she was going to have a chance of surviving this day. Hitting him with her purse would still leave her trapped in the Trailblazer with an angry Jerry between her and her way out. Hitting him would accomplish nothing useful. Her attack would have to begin differently.

She thought if she could get away from him long enough to get back into his SUV alone, she could lock the doors to keep him out, get the vehicle started, and drive away with him running after her ineffectually. She had hoped he would leave the keys in the SUV, but by taking his keys, he had already eliminated her first idea for escape. Since he had the keys, he could unlock the doors.

"Here you go," she said as she handed her purse to him without a fight. He grabbed her arm, opened the driver side door, and pulled her toward him across the front seat as he climbed out of the SUV. She struggled to clear the center console without getting hurt, but she couldn't avoid it altogether. If she lived, she'd have some nasty bruises on her thighs. Regan barely managed to get her footing as she was dragged out his door after him.

She had to make him let go of her. To do that, she had to startle him, shake him up. Regan needed to make him believe she was in charge of what was going to happen to both of them today.

"Here you are, a Ph.D., Associate Professor at UCSC, already moving up the ranks fast, capable of such clever, detailed planning," she said as he hauled her toward the front door of the house, "and yet you're so incredibly naïve and dumb."

Jerry dropped her purse at the door and twisted the fingers of his left hand through her hair. He let go of her arm and used his right hand to search through her purse for her lockbox key.

"Really," he said. "How do you figure that, Nancy Drew?"

Regan derided, "Right there, there's your clue. Nancy Drew — please," she put as much disdain in her voice as she could muster. "Nancy Drew was a child who stumbled into situations. I'm a woman who just set you up. I'm cleverer than you are. You just made a full confession to a woman wearing a wire with a direct feed back to the Sheriff. Uh-oh," she taunted.

He straightened up, let go of her hair, and spun her toward him, holding her tightly by both arms. His eyes narrowed. Regan met his gaze full-on and smiled slowly. "Fooled you by acting like I thought I was trapped, didn't I?"

"You're lying," he hissed.

She leaned in toward him until her body was almost against his, and tilted her head back slightly. She hoped it would seem as if she was positioning herself so whatever he said next would be picked up more clearly by her make-believe wire. His grip on her arms just above her elbows forced her hands low. She gripped his belt for balance, for insurance.

"Would I lie to you, Jerry?" she mocked as she brought her knee up sharply.

His cry and collapse were immediate. He let go of her and held his crotch as his knees buckled and he went down. The first part of her plan, such as it was, had worked. She was out of his SUV and free of his grasp, at least momentarily.

Regan bounded away from the house, passed the SUV, and started running down the driveway, grateful she had dressed for showing country property. Her jeans and flat shoes gave her mobility, and hopefully speed.

She didn't know how much damage her knee had done to Jerry; all she knew for sure was he had released her and she had at least a few moments head start to get away.

But once he recovered, his strides would be longer than hers. He might be able to quickly overcome her advantage. She knew she couldn't run along the road for long; she had to create another equalizer.

Regan had paid careful attention to Apple Tree Road on the way in, noting how it twisted and turned repeatedly. She was counting on those curves now for wooded cover, and hoped that by running in a straight line through the woods, rather than along the road, she would hit occupied houses before Jerry could overtake her.

She cut into the woods at the first bend in the road and blasted through the scrub on a direct heading to Wild Brambles Road.

She emerged from the woods at the next bend and ran on the gravel road for thirty feet before it turned again, and she returned to the woods on her straight line race. As she entered the woods a second time, she ventured a moment's glance behind her. It was just a momentary distraction, but enough of one that she didn't see a protruding branch in her path. It caught her face and tore her cheek. She felt a sharp sting. When she reflexively put her hand to her cheek, it showed fresh red blood. She determined not to give in to that backward-looking impulse again.

Regan repeated her running pattern two more times before she heard the gravel road ahead of her being crunched by vehicle wheels. Overwhelming panic returned. Jerry wasn't trying to follow her — he was driving to cut her off.

She continued through the woods, but at a slower pace. She had been covering ground rapidly, filled with adrenaline and motivated by fear and the hope of escape. She was uncertain how far she had come or how close she was to houses that might hold help. The gravel warning had renewed her fear, but now she was also tiring and wasn't certain what the road ahead held for her. It might be help, or it might be Jerry.

Had he seen her as he passed, or had she been far enough into the woods that he couldn't see her and didn't know how far she had come? The cell phone she had slipped into her pocket was still there. She debated staying in the woods and calling for help.

If Regan's indecision hadn't slowed her pace, she would have run out onto the road again. Instead, she could see an opening ahead and a clearing that meant she was coming to another section of the road. She moved forward cautiously.

The hood of a dark vehicle which was stopped in the road came into view. Regan froze where she was, crouched down, and then slowly moved sideways until a tree blocked the line of vision between her and the vehicle. She tried to take deep breaths quietly; she was terrified Jerry would hear her panting.

Finally she moved slightly, carefully, until she could peek from behind the tree. She strained to see the driver-side of the SUV. Was Jerry in it, behind the wheel, waiting for her to

263

emerge?

She managed to maneuver closer so she could see more of the vehicle. The driver's door was open, but Jerry was nowhere in sight.

Regan dropped down behind the tree and turned so her back was against it. She frantically scanned her surroundings, afraid she would see a restored Jerry grinning down at her. Nothing. Perhaps he hadn't spotted her yet.

Regan fingered the cell phone that was still in her pocket, started to take it out, but decided not to. If she called, help would come eventually, but if she made any noise, even a whispered 9-1-1 call, Jerry might well find her and kill her before help could come.

Her heart raced … but only partly from running. A sudden wrenching sixth sense told her she was no longer alone in the woods. Regan spun around to confront her assailant. In that same instant, his hand covered her mouth.

"Gotcha. Regan, it's over," he whispered. "Shush."

He transferred the portable GPS tracker from his hand to his jacket pocket and un-holstered his service revolver.

"Does he have a weapon?" he asked in little more than a murmur.

Regan kept her voice as soft as his, "I don't think so. No," she answered. Then she threw her arms around Dave, who returned her embrace with a quick bear hug of his own.

"I want you to scream when I tell you to, like you just broke your leg or something. Then I want you to get into my SUV and close the door as quietly as you can. Here are my keys. Hit this button and lock yourself in. If I'm not back in five minutes, I want you to drive out of here. Understand?"

"But what ..."

"No arguments," he cut off her protest.

Regan nodded silently. "What are you going to do?" she whispered.

"I'm going to be a damsel in distress." He pointed at her, "Now."

Regan screamed like the terrified woman she had been just moments before, and ran for Dave's SUV. The chirping sound of the remote locking the doors around her was one of the sweetest sounds she had ever heard.

Dave tapped on the SUV window a few minutes later, motioning for her to unlock the doors. He climbed into the driver's seat, "He must have seen me and recognized the trap. I heard crashing through the underbrush off in the other direction. Let's get you out of here. We can let the Sheriff clean up."

"I forgot you had a midnight blue Chevy Tahoe," Regan offered a lopsided little smile. "Did I ever tell you what a beautiful SUV this is?"

Dave snickered. "You better call Tom and let him know you're OK. It's a safe bet he's pretty nuts by now. You won't believe what I had to do to make him stay put at your house."

Regan took out her cell and hit the speed dial to Tom.

He picked up on the first ring, "Regan?" She could hear his fear and emotion as he said her name.

"Dave's got me. I'm safe, I'm fine."

Dave leaned toward her phone. She pushed the speaker button when she realized he wanted to say something. "I'm going to run her by the 'doc in a box' in Scotts Valley. She's OK, but she's got a nasty cut on her cheek. I think she's going to need stitches."

"I'm on my way," Tom replied. "I'll meet you there."

"Hey, Tom? You might want to bring her a change of clothes ... shoes, too. She's kind of a mess."

Regan looked down at herself. Her clothing was tattered and filthy. There was blood on her right shoulder and down the right arm of her jacket. In the safety of Dave's SUV, she became aware of scrapes and scratches and started to ache all over. Her body convulsed in a violent shiver.

"It's really cold in here; could we turn on some heat," Regan asked.

"It's eighty-one degrees outside. You're not cold; what you're feeling is more like shock. After what you've been through today, that's what happens when you know you're safe," he smiled. "Next, amateurs usually start to cry."

She shook her head, "I'm not going to."

"Good." Dave hit a number on his cell. "Dispatch? The code 207, kidnapping in progress, is terminated. I'm taking the victim to Scotts Valley Urgent Care to have her checked out before I bring her in."

Regan could hear a siren approaching, then another.

Dave continued, "Suspect is in a black Chevy Trailblazer or on foot in the vicinity of 410 Apple Tree Road in Boulder Creek. Suspect is a Caucasian male, approximately six feet tall, dark hair and eyes, age ..."

"Forty," Regan said.

"Forty. Last seen wearing ..."

"Jeans, a dark blue long-sleeved shirt and brown hiking boots ..."

"You want to do this?" Dave teased. "Last seen wearing

jeans, a dark blue shirt, and hiking ..."

"Brown," Regan said. "His boots are brown."

"Brown hiking boots. Suspect is not believed to be armed, but is considered dangerous," Dave concluded.

They pulled off the road as much as possible to let a California Highway Patrol vehicle go by with its siren wailing. It was followed by a Sheriff's Department cruiser, its siren also blaring, and moments later by another cruiser. Regan turned to stare at them. "Why so many?" she asked.

"Kidnapping in progress trumps most other violations," Dave said gently. "Everyone wants a good outcome; they all want to help."

"What about murder? I figured out he killed Lydia, but not until it was too late. If you hadn't found me," she hesitated, "he told me I would be number four for him."

"Number four?" Dave asked.

She nodded wordlessly. Regan was quiet for a few moments, thinking. Dave let her have some time without comment. Finally she asked, "How did you know to come here and find me?"

"We got lucky today, Regan, beginning with the Paisleys. They wanted to get away for a little R and R. The Sheriff told them that was OK, but that your buddy Kirby needed to let us know his whereabouts if he left town."

"I thought he wasn't a suspect anymore because his DNA wasn't a match to the fetus," she said.

"The murder was still unsolved. I didn't like him for the Perp; Deputy Sheriff Burke wasn't as convinced. Paisley was still on his short list. Your pal Kirby's become a poster boy for cooperating with law enforcement, so he had Deputy

Burke's direct number with him and was checking in periodically. When you left your message for Mithrell, asking if she knew who Lydia was taking anthropology from at UCSC, and said Jerry Smithers was trying to find that out for you, it set her off. She told Kirby and he called Deputy Sheriff Burke. The Deputy thinks you're a nice lady and he knows we're pals, so he called me after he couldn't raise you at work or at home.

"Tom keeps his cell with him when he plays golf; you remember what happened before he started doing that, don't you?"

Regan remembered the close call she'd had earlier in the year and nodded.

"Good thing he does, because I couldn't get a hold of you. You guys know how to retrieve each other's phone messages — that's so warm and fuzzy and romantic," Dave said in a saccharine voice. "So he checked your messages for me."

Dave had started making fun of things again, Regan noticed. He hadn't done that since he found her. Things were getting back to normal. She really was OK. She really was safe.

"Where we got really lucky is you were slow today. You didn't answer Smither's call until after he started leaving a message, and you didn't erase what he said. We had Boulder Creek to go on, so I high-tailed it there and hoped for some direction.

"I'm proud of you, Regan. The way you told Tom where you were and who you were with was pretty smooth. Gutsy, too. He relayed your location to me; I patched it into my GPS to let me find Apple Tree Road, and then connected to police

269

GPS where they were working on tracking your cell phone location. That was another good move, keeping your phone alive and in your pocket. That let me pinpoint you to within a hundred feet."

Regan decided not to let Dave know the phone had been another bit of luck. She kept in on and in her pocket more like a security blanket than anything else. She didn't know the authorities had the ability to track her with any amount of precision, or that they would, for that matter.

"I don't want to scare you, you look pretty shaken up already, but — no — I do want to scare you, Regan." Dave's voice was a mixture of relief, concern, and exasperation. "You came really close to not getting out of this one. One more day of you not letting anyone in on your conclusions about Smithers and he would have killed you.

"He wouldn't have gotten away with it, but that wouldn't have mattered much to you if you were dead, now would it?" His vexation grew, "If your Wiccan friends hadn't picked up their messages today and taken immediate action ... or if you'd moved quicker and his message hadn't started on your answering machine ..."

"I get it, Dave," Regan interrupted. "I'd have been another dead body," she said softly, feeling another shiver.

"Do you get it, Regan? This can be a dangerous business. Leave it to the pros. No," he said, "I know you too well to think you'll do that. Better idea: if you have to play detective, keep me in the loop at all times."

"I don't intend for there to be a next time. I'm hanging up my magnifying glass and burning my copy of *Detecting for Dummies*."

"I sure hope so," Dave shook his head.

Regan looked at him mischievously out of the corner of her eye, "But if I should ever get involved in something again and I tell you my theories about a crime, do you promise not to tease me about them?"

"Me? Promise not to tease you? You want to take away one of my favorite pastimes? Regan, what kind of friend are you?" he grinned.

Epilogue

Jerry Smithers left several sets of tire tracks going into the woods as he tried to find another way out, but the redwoods stopped his escape. His four-wheel-drive was useless in the dense woodland. The dead end road, Jerry's trap for Regan, became his trap instead. He was cornered by Sheriff and CHP cruisers before he had driven three hundred feet from the house on Apple Tree Road.

He surrendered without a fuss, grumbling unconvincingly that he had no idea why he was being arrested. He was held on suspicion of kidnapping and murder and court-ordered to give a DNA sample.

Dave called the next week, just before the story hit the local news, to let Regan know the test results confirmed Jerry was the father of Lydia's baby. He also told her something that wasn't in the news: a hair had been found in his old Volkswagen van, the one he had given to a grad student, which was a match for Lydia.

Jerry finally admitted to dating her, but denied killing Lydia. He was arraigned on first degree murder charges in her death and waived his right to a speedy trial. It would probably be at least a year before he would come up for trial. In the meantime, the authorities were looking into disappearances and suicides among Jerry's female students. They had already discovered two cases which warranted further investigation. The authorities planned to delve farther back into his past, as well.

There was a memorial service for Lydia. It was a

traditional service. Alex wrote a song for her and the band played it at the service, which was conducted by Reverend Simon.

There were so many news stories preceding the service that, in death, Lydia became something of a temporary celebrity. So many people attended her memorial service, they spilled out the church doors. Shiloh said Lydia would have liked the song and the service, and she thought Lydia would have liked it that so many people cared about her.

Tom and Regan sat with Alex and his girlfriend at the service. Lindsey was a lovely young woman; it was apparent she and Alex were in love. If she was indeed "The One," Regan decided she would be pleased to have her as a daughter-in-law — but not just yet. Lindsey and Alex were the same ages she and Alex's father had been when they married — when they married, had two sons quickly, and divorced. Could she figure out a way to tell Alex not to rush, to spend a little more time growing up, without it seeming like she didn't like Lindsey? She planned to think about how to do that.

Mithrell and Kirby planted new oak trees to fill in the empty spaces along their driveway. They hoped the trees would be, if not large, at least established and growing well by next year, in time for their annual May Day party.

Rick Whitlaw was elected to State Assembly in a close race. Even though his platform was popular in his district, he had probably been right about negative publicity hurting him. Many people blamed the finding of a body on his property for the tightness of the race.

In his victory speech, he promised to work tirelessly for

273

his constituents and for the environment. Regan believed he would.

Rick and Joan finished the initial remodel of their house just after Thanksgiving. On December fifth, the day when Rick was in Sacramento taking his oath of office, their house caught fire and burned to the ground. Faulty wiring was blamed. The electrician who worked on their remodel had an excellent reputation and the fire wasn't his fault. The blaze started in a part of the house the Whitlaws didn't think needed rewiring. In hindsight, they regretted that decision.

The December day their house burned, the air temperature was unusually high and a gusty wind blew hot and dry off the land instead of inland from the ocean. The house burned so intensely, the fire spread to the trees in the backyard before it could be stopped. It destroyed all the trees in the garden near the house, including the peach tree.

Had the fire started during the dry time of late summer, when off-shore wind patterns were common, the fire would have spread into the woods and the whole area might have burned. But there had been a couple of good rains in late November, so fire danger was low and there was no damage to the surrounding homes or land. The Whitlaws were all in Sacramento with Rick, of course, so no one was hurt in the blaze.

The last time Regan had called to see how the family was doing, Joan sounded excited. She was interviewing building contractors and reviewing architectural plans. She and Rick were surprised how smoothly their rebuilding plans had gone with the County; the Native American burial on their property hadn't caused any permit hang-ups.

Joan said she was talking to landscape contractors as well. After the new house was built, they planned to have the landscaping professionally redone, too.

Joan told her that after all the news stories about the murder, gawkers began driving down their street and slowing as they passed their house. That behavior stopped after the fire. Joan said the fire couldn't be considered a happy event, but it marked the conclusion of a series of sad events. She said it like an afterthought, but Regan knew her well enough to know it meant much more than that.

New house. New landscaping. In time, there might not be many memories left of backyard bones. In time, Regan thought as she hung up. And for most people.

About the author

Nancy Lynn Jarvis has been a Santa Cruz, California, Realtor® for twenty years. She owns a real estate company with her husband, Craig.

After earning a BA in behavioral science from San Jose State University, she worked in the advertising department of the *San Jose Mercury News*. A move to Santa Cruz meant a new job as a librarian and later a stint as the business manager for Shakespeare Santa Cruz at UCSC.

Nancy's work history reflects her philosophy: people should try something radically different every few years. Writing is the latest of her adventures.

She invites you to take a peek into the real estate world through the stories that form the backdrop of her Regan McHenry mysteries. Details and ideas come from Nancy's own experiences.

If you're one of her clients or colleagues, read carefully — you may find characters in her books who seem familiar. You may know the people who inspired them — who knows, maybe you inspired a character.

Follow Regan McHenry Real Estate Mysteries on Facebook

or

Visit Nancy Lynn Jarvis' website
www.GoodReadMysteries.com

where you can:

Read the first chapter of the books in the Regan McHenry Mystery Series.

Review reader comments and email your own.

Ask Nancy questions about her books and the next book in the series.

Find out about upcoming events, book club discounts, and arrange for Nancy to talk to your book club or group.

Read or print Regan's recipe for the chocolate chip cookie dough that she and Tom always have ready in their freezer.

Books are available in large print and for your Kindle, iPad, and other e-readers.

Made in the USA
Columbia, SC
31 December 2019